"What's the m— — — — —ire you so much of a lady that you find discussing anything as base as money repugnant to you?"

"On my wedding night, yes! It makes me feel very cheap."

"I see. It is not indelicate for a lady to marry for money but it is indelicate for a gentleman to refer to it. What curst hypocrisy!" He stood up and glowered down at her. "Well, you'll get no hypocrisy from me. My reason for marrying you was to breed sons. So off to bed with you, my lady. I'm not a patient man."

Claudia rose from her chair. She turned and glared at him, her blue eyes disdainful, her head held proudly.

"Take care, madam wife," he warned her softly. "You will find it difficult to look down your proud nose at me when we are in bed together."

His words fell like chips of ice on her spine, causing her to shiver involuntarily. But she did not flee. Instead, she stepped toward him. She put her hands behind his head and pulled his face down to hers, her soft body resting briefly against his. Then she kissed him full on the lips.

He was too stunned to respond, but when she released him and stepped back, he said, "What the deuce did you do that for?"

"Because I am not very brave. I would be too frightened to get into bed at all if I thought a monster was coming to me. I had to reassure myself that, somewhere inside you, there is a man."

# THE BEST OF REGENCY ROMANCES

**AN IMPROPER COMPANION**                    (2691, $3.95)
**by Karla Hocker**
At the closing of Miss Venable's Seminary for Young
Ladies school, mistress Kate Elliott welcomed the invitation to be Liza Ashcroft's chaperone for the Season at
Bath. Little did she know that Miss Ashcroft's father, the
handsome widower Damien Ashcroft would also enter her
life. And not as a passive bystander or dutiful dad.

**WAGER ON LOVE**                           (2693, $2.95)
**by Prudence Martin**
Only a rogue like Nicholas Ruxart would choose a bride on
the basis of a careless wager. And only a rakehell like Nicholas would then fall in love with his betrothed's grey-eyed
sister! The cynical viscount had always thought one blushing miss would suit as well as another, but the unattainable
Jane Sommers soon proved him wrong.

**LOVE AND FOLLY**                          (2715, $3.95)
**by Sheila Simonson**
To the dismay of her more sensible twin Margaret, Lady
Jean proceeded to fall hopelessly in love with the silver-
tongued, seditious poet, Owen Davies—and catapult her
entire family into social ruin . . . Margaret was used to
gentlemen falling in love with vivacious Jean rather than
with her—even the handsome Johnny Dyott whom she se-
cretly adored. And when Jean's foolishness led her into the
arms of the notorious Owen Davies, Margaret knew she
could count on Dyott to avert scandal. What she didn't
know, however was that her sweet sensibility was exerting a
charm all its own.

*Available wherever paperbacks are sold, or order direct from the
Publisher. Send cover price plus 50¢ per copy for mailing and
handling to Zebra Books, Dept. 3151, 475 Park Avenue South,
New York, N.Y. 10016. Residents of New York, New Jersey and
Pennsylvania must include sales tax. DO NOT SEND CASH.*

# An Unquestionable Lady

### Rosina Pyatt

**ZEBRA BOOKS**
**KENSINGTON PUBLISHING CORP.**

ZEBRA BOOKS

are published by

Kensington Publishing Corp.
475 Park Avenue South
New York, NY 10016

First Zebra Books printing: October, 1990

Printed in the United States of America

# Chapter One

Miss Claudia Tallon paced back and forth across her bedchamber, from ill-fitting door to lattice window, ignoring the wind gusting through both with enough force to ruffle the dimity curtains and bedhangings.

On the orders of the new Lady Tallon there was no fire in the hearth to cheer her on this freezing January day in 1817. She ignored that, too. By now she was accustomed to the many spiteful means employed to show her that not only was she no longer mistress of Tallon Manor, she was of no account at all.

In fact, Claudia scarcely noticed the cold. She was so consumed by rage that she felt if she stopped pacing, she would surely explode. She was not one to pity herself, but it was all so unfair. She had done her best to hand over the management of her beloved home without rancor or regret, just as she had done her best to keep the peace in the miserable months that had followed.

She had even submitted with docility when she had been moved from the pretty south-facing bedchamber that had been hers all her life to this secondary guestroom at the back of the house. She had also borne with dignity all the slurs a jealous and vindictive tongue could heap on an unmarried and unwanted female of twenty-six.

None of this had been enough and, not half an hour ago, her self-control had finally cracked. This had been brought about by Lady Tallon decreeing that the priory ruins in the grounds of the ancient Essex manor must be pulled down because her obnoxious eldest son had bruised himself falling from one of the old walls.

Claudia had seen red. She had called Lady Tallon a vandal and fought fiercely for the preservation of her home as she knew and loved it, but to no effect. She had no status with which to win the battle. In truth, she had nothing. No money. No hope. No means of escape. Unless . . .

She stopped her restless pacing and swerved toward her desk, sitting down before it and taking from a drawer a newspaper over three weeks old. It was folded open at an advertisement she knew by heart, so many times had she puzzled over it. It both repelled and attracted her, and to make sure there was no mistake she read once more: *Gentleman offers Security and Social Position in return for Marriage with an Unquestionable Lady.*

There was something reassuring about the stressing of certain words with capital letters, as there was in the lawyer's name and City of London address following it. It appeared as respectable and above board as any such advertisement could be, but why would an affluent and well-positioned gentleman need to advertise for a wife?

Because he was old? Hideous? Infirm? Not really a gentleman at all? A tradesman, perhaps, wanting to marry above himself to increase his social standing? The questions were as endless as they were intriguing, but of one thing she was convinced. The advertisement hid far more than it revealed. Claudia did not lack

6

resolution, but it seemed to her that only a deranged or truly desperate lady would put herself at risk by answering it.

There was a tap on her door, and a maid came in without awaiting permission to enter, a liberty none of the old servants would have dreamed of taking. They had all been dismissed, of course, Lady Tallon being jealous of the respect they had for their former mistress.

The curtsy this new maid dropped was perfunctory, and she said without any of the customary courtesies or any attempt at refinement, "Lady Tallon says as how you must come down this minute to play spillikins with Master Henry."

"His nurse's job, surely?"

"Lady Tallon says as how Master Henry is in such a mood he can't tolerate his nurse nohow."

What Lady Tallon was saying in effect, as they both knew, was that Claudia must atone for her outburst. Concessions were not enough. She must grovel. Claudia, fatalistically aware she could eat no more humble pie, replied, "Pray tell Lady Tallon, with my compliments, that I am in such a mood I can't tolerate Master Henry—er—nohow."

The maid gasped but, finding herself being coolly scrutinized, withdrew without voicing any of the objections that sprang to her lips, a victim of the inbred authority that so rankled with Lady Tallon.

Claudia sighed. Appeasement was at an end. There could be only confrontation now. She was too proud to apply to other relatives or friends for help. The advertisement was the only straw she could clutch at. She was very sure it would break in her hand but, drawing her writing-tablets toward her and dipping her quill in the inkwell, she began to write to the lawyer whose

7

client was discerning enough to desire marriage with an unquestionable lady.

Tallon Manor was not more than fifty miles removed from London, and since Mr. Hector Tigwell replied to her letter by return of post, within five days Claudia was sitting in his office facing him across his desk. The introductions had been made, and the small silence that had fallen was due to each taking careful stock of the other.

For her part, Claudia saw as yet no reason to flee for her life or honor. Mr. Tigwell, middle-aged, distinguished by excellent manners and a neatness of person, did not look at all like a white slaver, and from the number of clerks laboring in the outer office, his practice was well established and respectable.

For his part, Hector Tigwell regarded Claudia with as much pleasure as he would have regarded the pot of gold at the end of a rainbow. In the weeks following the appearance of the advertisement he had interviewed all manner of governesses, companions and maids claiming to be more gently born than they were. The two or three genuine ladies who had applied had been of such advanced age or unattractive looks that he had not dared to recommend them to his client.

Miss Claudia Tallon, however, appearing late on the scene, might have been the very model for the Lady he had been ordered to find. There was fine breeding in her regular features, intelligence in her large and very blue eyes, humor in the curve of her lips, and her ivory complexion was flawless.

She was dressed on this cold day in a practical but beautifully cut blue mantle, lined with silk and trimmed with ermine. She had put back the hood to reveal hair of gleaming black. Everything about her, from her composure to her soft white hands, attested to Quality, Mr. Tigwell thought blissfully. He cleared his throat, and was about to ask as tactfully as possible what catastrophe had caused Miss Claudia Tallon of Tallon Manor to consider marriage with an unknown man, when she forestalled him by saying, "Before we go any further, will you assure me that your client is indeed a gentleman?"

With all his lawyer's skill Mr. Tigwell avoided a direct confirmation, replying instead, "He is of the first rank and extremely wealthy."

"There must be something peculiar about him," Claudia persisted. "Is he old? Maimed? Infirm?"

"He is none of those things. He had his reasons for contracting a marriage in this unusual manner, as assuredly as you have yours. They need not be nefarious because they are, for the moment, obscure."

"No, indeed, but—oh, this is very difficult! Must we box in the dark? It would help me a good deal to know his name."

"That I am not at liberty to reveal. This is a matter of great delicacy and it must be an object with all parties to avoid unseemly gossip. I shall tell my client about you. If he finds you suitable, I shall arrange a meeting. He will then introduce himself and detail his requirements in a wife. If you are both satisfied, the marriage can take place without anybody but the three of us knowing how it came about."

It made sense, and yet she was uneasy. More than ever she felt that some kind of deceit was being practiced on her. Now was the time to draw back, to go away—but to what? A home where she was unwanted. At least the unknown gentleman must genuinely *want* a wife to go to such unusual lengths to procure one. She had almost forgotten what it was like to feel wanted, and yet . . .

Sensing her doubt, Mr. Tigwell went on hastily, "I gather some change in your life has made the married state seem preferable to your single one? I read in the newspapers of the demise of your father, the eighth baronet, and that he was succeeded by a remote relation. A year ago, was it not?"

"Ten months. My second cousin, Edgar—I should say Sir Edgar now—did not get on with my father, so he was a stranger to me. He was on holiday with his family in Italy when my father died but he returned to take up residence six months ago."

"How awkward for you; but you still live at the manor. Presumably he quite rightly offered you shelter?"

There was a wry note in Claudia's voice as she replied, "Rightly, perhaps, but reluctantly. I have been mistress of the manor since my mother died ten years ago. That was resented, perhaps understandably. I am not used to being idle, and the servants quite naturally looked to me for instructions. I was also my father's hostess and we did a great deal of entertaining, in both London and the country. That, of course, is now at an end and I miss it. I am not useful anymore, but very much in the way. To be fair, I can appreciate why Sir Edgar and Lady Tallon will never really feel the manor is their own home while I remain there."

"Lady Tallon is of a jealous disposition?" Mr. Tigwell hazarded.

"It is more than that. She is unsure of herself." Claudia sought for tactful words to explain, found none and went on truthfully, "She is of the merchant class and uneasy in polite society. This makes her belligerent. She thrust herself upon our neighbors without waiting for them first to call on her. She was—repulsed. She blames me for this, saying I have turned my friends against her, but this isn't so. Her hostility toward me is so blatant that everybody has noticed, and dislikes her for it. She appears to think that only by making me inferior can she be superior. It is ridiculous, of course, but it makes the atmosphere at the manor difficult."

"I should think it makes it impossible. No wonder you are contemplating matrimony!"

"I have come to believe that anything would be better than going on as I am," she replied with a bluntness that showed the force of her feelings.

"You must have had many offers in the past?"

Claudia was expecting this, but for the first time a certain reserve entered her manner. She glanced at the emerald and diamond ring on her right hand as she replied, "I was betrothed to an army officer during my début Season. Thomas Grettling of the Dorset Grettlings. He was killed the following year at Corunna." She shrugged off Mr. Tigwell's murmur of sympathy, continuing, "It was eight years ago. Ancient history now. I was never able to return the regard of any other man and so I turned my back on romance. I was convinced that marriage was not for me, but now . . ."

". . . you can see its very obvious advantages. I think you are being very wise."

She disconcerted him by contradicting, "I think I am being extremely foolhardy but I have little choice. The pride which prevents me remaining at Tallon Manor also prevents me seeking refuge with other relations. A spinster is always something of a sore thumb unless a general dogsbody is needed, and that wouldn't suit me at all. Nor do I have any money to recommend me. My father was bankrupt. He couldn't settle after my mother died, and took up with the Prince of Wales's set, a privilege that ruined him."

There was no need to elaborate. The Prince's extravagant lifestyle was a national scandal. "Whist at a pound a point, I've heard," Mr. Tigwell tutted. "I trust your cousin has private means?"

"It was Lady Tallon's wealth that recommended her to him."

"Sir Edgar was far-sighted." He reflected on this for a moment, then went on briskly, "My client fortunately stands in no need of a rich wife, and I believe you may be the very lady he is seeking. I shall arrange a meeting. Where are you staying?"

"Fenton's."

"Your maid is with you, naturally?"

"I have no maid. Lady Tallon dismissed her months ago."

"Whatever for?"

Claudia shrugged. "To lessen my consequence. Oh, you need not fear Fenton's will turn me away as an undesirable guest. My standing is good there since my father's time, and I said I was obliged to send my maid home when she sickened on the journey. I am Miss Tallon, so naturally I was believed." She hesitated, then confessed, "It is as well because my means are limited. I could not afford to lodge a maid and cannot stay above three nights myself."

"There should be not difficulty," Mr. Tigwell assured her. "My client is anxious to get this matter settled."

It seemed extraordinary that anything as sacred as marriage should be referred to as "this matter," but as Claudia took a hackney back to her hotel she realized that Mr. Tigwell's businesslike attitude was the best one to adopt. It would be different if she were a fanciful miss with a head stuffed full of romantic dreams. She had been, once, but all that died with Tom at Corunna.

Her life prior to her father's death had not accustomed her to pinching pennies. She had unthinkingly bespoken a sitting-room as well as a bedchamber at the hotel, just as she had in the old days, yet she had cause to be grateful for her extravagance. While she was eating a light luncheon, a clerk delivered a note from Mr. Tigwell to say that his client would visit her at two that afternoon, if it was convenient.

Unseemly haste, Claudia thought it, however precarious her financial situation might be. Still, if she were to see "this matter" through, there was little point in delaying. She dashed off an affirmative reply and gave it to the waiting clerk. Then she glanced at the clock and saw she had little time to prepare herself for the coming ordeal.

Ordeal? She chided herself for that. A proper businesslike approach would be to regard it as nothing more than a necessary interview. Mr. Tigwell would have acquainted his client with her personal circumstances. It would be up to her prospective husband to acquaint her with his. All she had to do was accept or reject him.

She changed her walking dress for a blue gown of fine wool, which flattered the generous curves of her body better than she knew. She believed its high neck and long sleeves, decorated with white lace ruffles, made her look housewifely, which was no doubt the correct impression to give.

She sought to subdue the thick waves of her glossy hair into a chignon secured with pins at the back of her head. The overall effect of her efforts was not housewifely at all, but elegant and womanly. This, coupled with her natural grace and dignity, made it truly remarkable she had reached her twenty-sixth year without contracting a marriage of a far more conventional nature.

She went into her sitting-room and sat in an armchair close to the fire, enjoying the warmth and privacy, and feeling more like the privileged Miss Claudia Tallon of yore. As the clock on the mantelshelf chimed the hour of two she picked up a book, disposed herself more gracefully, and hoped she looked unconcerned enough to read.

Her eyes flicked constantly from the printed page to the clock, and her nerves tautened with every minute ticking by. At fifteen minutes past the hour she was annoyed, but when another fifteen minutes passed her mood veered. Like herself, it seemed the gentleman was suffering from cold feet.

She had no idea what she would do next, but she could not genuinely say she was sorry. She felt herself relaxing, and only then was she aware how much strain she had been under. A wisp of hair strayed across her cheek and she raised a rather limp hand to smooth it back into her chignon.

The door opened and, without ceremony or announcement, her prospective husband strode in and caught her in this little act of primping. She stared at him and suffered a severe shock. She had thought herself prepared for anything, but she had been wrong.

By no stretch of the imagination could she envisage this man needing to advertise for a wife. Indeed, he seemed the living embodiment of every woman's secret dream.

With his height and his width, in his many-caped greatcoat, he filled the doorway. There was a challenging moodiness about his brown eyes, his features were strong and handsome, and his complexion was so deeply tanned that he must have spent many years in the tropics. He carried a tall curly-brimmed beaver hat in his hand, and the dishevelment of his curly bronze hair, brushed in the windswept style, made him look for all the world like a pirate.

Claudia had thought herself safely beyond the age of romantic imaginings, but her heart was beating erratically. She was angry with herself, although it was not

14

merely his looks that made such an impact on her. There was an arrogance about him, a contempt, that struck her with almost physical force.

He repelled and attracted at the same time, a frightening and fascinating combination that would affect the most level-headed of women, which she did not feel just then. She sensed that, if crossed, he would be dangerous. She felt most unsafe, before he had moved or said a word.

At this point Claudia checked herself. She was letting her imagination run away with her, as though she were a silly young miss or a nervous old maid! And I am neither, she told herself crossly.

Her irritation shifted from herself to him as she became aware he was studying every inch of her with such clinical dispassion that she would not have been surprised if he had asked to see her teeth. Her eyebrows rose with the hauteur of a lady too socially experienced to be put to the blush by insolence.

"What are you thinking?" he asked abruptly.

She regarded him with disfavor. Had he no social polish, or did he disdain to use it? Well, he was not going to ride roughshod over her. She replied coolly, "I am thinking that you need only to affect an earring to look like a pirate."

"When you know me better, you will realize I never affect anything. Apart from that, many would say you are not far out." He closed the door carelessly and strode further into the room, putting his hat and gloves on a side table. "Have you strong nerves?"

Again that abruptness. Claudia's irritation increased. "It is to be hoped so. I suspect I shall need them."

"You will," he agreed. "I am Giles Verylan."

She was staggered. *Now* she understood why he needed to advertise for a wife. He had left no stone

15

unturned to make himself repugnant to a female of delicacy. How right she had been to perceive that the advertisement concealed far more than it revealed. No lady would dream of allying herself with such a scoundrel!

Like any member of the *ton*, she was only too familiar with his disreputable history. At nineteen he had eloped with a seventeen-year-old heiress, married her at Gretna Green and abandoned her and their baby daughter within two years. He had gone abroad to India, or was it China? Some outlandish place. Nothing more had been heard of him for several years, but his reappearance had coincided with her début Season, and Society had buzzed with his latest infamy.

He had not, as expected, become reconciled with his wronged wife but run off with somebody else's. The cuckolded husband, a baron who had been a friend of Claudia's father, had felt his shame so deeply that he had shot himself. Shortly afterward, Giles Verylan's own wife had died. From a broken heart, it was said.

Tales filtering back from India—yes, it was definitely India where he had taken the baroness—revealed his crowning infamy. He had not used his freedom to marry the lady he had ruined. He had left her, too. The last that had been heard of the unfortunate baroness was that she was wandering the Continent like some poor lost soul.

He was watching the play of emotions across her face, and said in his usual uncompromising way, "I see you know my reputation. It is deserved."

"I wonder you dare to admit it!"

"How very naïve of you. My reputation should warn you there is nothing I will not dare—if it is necessary or it amused me."

Claudia rose to her feet. "You do not amuse me.

16

Kindly leave, sir. We have no more to say to each other."

His heavy eyebrows drew together. "Don't be ridiculous! We have a great deal to say. I am not late by accident. I was giving you time to have second thoughts and flee, if you so wished, so that we wasted no more of each other's time. You are still here. Clearly your need of a husband is matched by my need of a wife. So sit down, Miss Tallon, and stop being missish."

Much to her annoyance, Claudia found herself sitting down, but she exclaimed, "How dare you!"

He shrugged off his greatcoat, put it on a chair and replied in a bored tone, "We have already established there is nothing I will not dare. Pray remember it. I don't care to repeat myself."

The wrath simmering in Claudia's bosom boiled over. "Mr. Verylan . . . !"

"You should rather say Lord Belgarrick."

She remembered then. His oldest brother, Viscount Belgarrick, had taken up the increasingly popular sport of yachting and had been lost at sea with his wife and only son. That had been two years ago. "You are the youngest brother," she said. "What happened to the middle one?"

"He also died two years ago, at Waterloo. Damned disobliging of him."

"*Disobliging?* How can you be so callous when your family has suffered such appalling tragedies?"

"It would be hypocritical to feel grief for a family that has treated me as a leper since I was nineteen. I am thirty-seven now. The years between made strangers of us."

"You are the most unnatural man I have ever met!"

Belgarrick regarded her enigmatically. "I can't abide females who delight in raking over old coals. Suffice to say, I never wished to inherit the title and all it entails.

17

It's damned inconvenient. However, I am a Verylan and I will do my duty by my name. That is where you come in."

Claudia rose to her feet. "On the contrary, my lord. That is where I go out."

"What do you plan to do?" he asked sarcastically. "Exit left with dancing bear? Why must women always introduce Drury Lane dramatics into a perfectly simple business transaction?"

"Marriage cannot be compared with a business transaction!"

"Why not?"

"Because . . . Because . . ." She broke off, confused, as she remembered that was precisely how she had intended to regard the marriage. But that was before she had met Belgarrick. What seemed reasonable then seemed sheer insanity now.

She had a chance to regain her composure when a knock sounded on the door and a maid entered with a decanter and two glassed on a tray. Claudia demurred, "There must be some mistake. I haven't ordered refreshments."

"There's no mistake. I have." Belgarrick signaled the maid to put the tray on a table and, when she left, he poured the amber liquid into the glasses and offered one to Claudia. "I thought we might stand in need of fortifying by now."

"If I needed fortifying I would take tea," she snapped.

"A mistake when dealing with me. Stop being silly and take it. A glass of Mountain Malaga will do you no harm. If I had immediate designs upon your person I would have ordered brandy."

"Thank you!"

"For you, not for me." He smiled suddenly, and Claudia's pulses fluttered. What charm he had when he cared to use it, and it was all the more effective for its unexpectedness. She understood all too easily now why first an heiress and then a baroness had ruined themselves for love of him. But she was Miss Claudia Tallon, full twenty-six years of age, and she knew him for what he really was. He could not intimidate her with his frowns or seduce her with his smiles. Could he?

## Chapter Two

Her sudden uncertainty made her every bit as angry with herself as she was with him. She took the glass he held out to her, saying bitterly, "I suppose I can always throw it in your face if your manners become even more impossible!"

"That will not do at all, Miss Talon. I advertised for an unquestionable lady, if you remember, and I have already noted that your own manners are not what they might be. Or is it only prospective husbands you keep standing?"

"Pray be seated," she replied, mortified.

He bowed. "After you."

She sat down and looked at him with dislike as he sat it the armchair opposite hers, and yet her feminine eyes also found much to admire. He was dressed correctly for the occasion in a well-fitting coat of dark blue superfine, pale pantaloons and gleaming Hessian boots. His neckcloth might have been tied with more impatience than precision, but it was spotless. He wore a large square-cut ruby ring—the family signet, she guessed.

She found herself resenting the way he stretched out his long legs and looked so very much at his ease. She

20

was far from easy herself, and this was her sitting-room. To look at him, one would have supposed it was his. Such was her rancor that, without realizing it, she drank half her sherry in one gulp.

He looked amused. "You *did* need fortifying. No, don't fire up at me! Now that we are through the preliminaries I mean to get to the heart of the matter. I will require two sons of you, Miss Tallon, to be produced as soon as possible. The recent rapid reduction in my family makes two a safer bet than one. I will be obliged if you do not delay the matter by producing daughters, which are of no use to me at all. I have as little love of England as England has of me, and the sooner I can go abroad again the happier I shall be."

She was getting used to his bluntness, but his utter lack of tact warmed her cheeks and made her exclaim, "I am not a brood mare! You also appear to have forgotten that your first wife had a daughter."

"I forget nothing. I was coming to Tansy. She is eighteen, and must make her début this year. It will be your duty to chaperon her and ensure she is creditably married, again as soon as possible. I wish to have her off my hands. It shouldn't be difficult. She is pretty enough and inherits her mother's fortune when she is twenty-one.

"You sound prepared to force her into a loveless marriage. I will not be a party to that!"

"I see we are back to Drury Lane, and quite unnecessarily. A girl of her age easily persuades herself she is in love. All you have to do is ensure it is with no one unsavory."

"Like yourself," she flashed.

"Precisely. Once Tansy is creditably established, my duty toward her will be finished. That just leaves you to throw two sons and I can be off."

"Th-Throw two sons!" Claudia stuttered, appalled. "I never heard anything so indelicate in all my life."

He shrugged. "I see nothing useful in mincing words. I shall return to England from time to time to confirm that they are being brought up according to my instructions. They must live at Belgarrick Towers, or they will have even less feeling for their inheritance than I have."

"They are likely to grow up with no feeling at all for their father."

"In that case, we are unlikely to disappoint each other. I set no store by family feeling."

"You are a monster! Don't you dare tell me we are back to Drury Lane, either."

"I never state the obvious. You become a trifle tedious, Miss Tallon, but no doubt my sons will hold it to my credit that I have put myself out to find a lady for their mother. You could also hold it to my credit that I have been honest with you; or would you have preferred me to beguile you with deceit?"

After a short struggle with herself, she admitted, "No."

"Good. We begin to understand each other. If you can be as honest with yourself as I have been with you, you will readily acknowledge the advantage of an absent husband in a loveless marriage. Once I have my sons, your bed will be your own unless you choose to share it with someone more to your liking than myself. For the children's sake you will have to be discreet— and for your own, careful. I will recognize no bastards."

Claudia, beyond words, just stared at him. After a pause, he continued, "Your reward for rendering the services I require will be handsome. You will be mistress of Belgarrick House in London, Belgarrick Towers in Kent and three lesser houses around the country.

In addition, you will be a viscountess and your quarterly allowance will be generous. A vast improvement, I would say, on your present life at Tallon Manor."

Claudia stood up and began to walk about the room, finding there was as little space here for pacing as there had been in her bedchamber at home when she had been agitated enough to answer Lord Belgarrick's advertisement. She was even more agitated now that she had met him.

He was all she had called him—an unnatural monster. A man who deserved his odious reputation. No lady of taste and refinement could possibly marry him. It was unthinkable. And yet . . . she could not deny her first impression of him. He fascinated her as much as he repelled. But didn't a snake fascinate a rabbit before it struck? She had never known such confusion of emotions. Her nerves were stretched to breaking-point, and yet her blood was pulsing through her veins in a way it had not done since Thomas died. She put her hand up to her brow in bewilderment. Was she, Claudia Tallon, seriously considering marrying this unashamed scoundrel?

"I would be mad to wed you!" she burst out.

He still lounged at his ease in the armchair, surveying her through slightly narrowed eyes. "You would be mad if you did not! Within two or three years our close association should be at an end and you would be set up for life."

"I might have daughters!"

"That is a risk we both have to take, but generally I am fortunate when I chance my luck."

Claudia took another turn about the room, reached the window and rested her hot forehead against the cold glass. She jumped when he said from right behind her, "Another fortifying glass?"

She turned, found him so close that she stepped back

and found herself pressed against the window. She was tall and built on too-generous lines to be considered fragile, yet that was how she felt as he towered over her. Involuntarily she took the glass he offered, holding it between them like some frail shield.

He looked amused and leisurely sipped his own sherry. "You need not fear my lust, Miss Tallon. I shall reserve that for my mistresses. The intimate side of our marriage will be approached in the same businesslike manner we have approached the rest. Does that reassure you?"

It didn't, but she could scarcely say so, and he continued, "I shall not pretend any emotions I do not feel and you will not be required to, either."

She found her voice, and protested, "I have not said I will marry you."

"You haven't said you wouldn't, nor have you swooned or had hysterics. That encourages me to think that, apart from uttering a few foolish sentiments, you are a sensible woman."

"A sensible woman would go home immediately!"

"Fustian! You remain because I can give you what you need, just as you can give me what I need. Marriages like this are made all the time, only they are not approached so frankly. *Our* marriage must succeed if we regard it in the right frame of mind."

Claudia was not at all certain of her frame of mind. She could only think: What about love? Was that not supposed to be all anyone needed? His cold-bloodedness might make him an exception, but she was not sure about herself. Her heart might be buried with Tom. Her body was not. And something within it responded to Lord Belgarrick in the most wilful and treacherous way.

"What is this?" he asked. "Maidenly misgivings? If so, you can do no better than trust yourself to an experienced man. I will also promise that you will be bothered no more than necessary."

Not for the first time, Claudia had to pull herself together. She said mutinously, "You have said a great deal about what you require in a wife. You haven't asked what I require in a husband."

He frowned. "I have already listed your benefits."

"I am not referring to worldly considerations. As a lady, I will require respect, courtesy and consideration from my husband."

"I shall make an effort, provided you are a dutiful wife."

Claudia's blue eyes flashed. "I can manage dutiful. A doormat I will not be."

He finished his sherry and walked to the table, where he put his glass down with a click. "I shall not bully you unless you force me to."

He made it sound like a major concession, and Claudia retorted bitterly, "No wonder you are still searching for a wife a month after the advertisement appeared! You would antagonize any woman. You are not the least bit conciliatory or sensitive. You . . ."

He took his watch from his fob pocket, looked at it, and interrupted, "If it will save time, I shall admit to being any kind of monster that you please. You are not required to have a good opinion of me, only to perform the duties I have specified. Perform them well and, as I have said, we shall soon be rid of each other. But understand me well. I have been at pains to make certain that you enter this marriage under no delusions about me. I will endure no recriminations hurled at me afterward. They could occur only because you have deceived yourself. Therefore the blame will be yours, not mine."

It was Claudia's turn to frown, and she replied, "I am not sure I understand you."

"Then I will spell it out. I know the ways of women. They must always search for a heart. Spare yourself the effort, Miss Tallon, because I don't have one. Do we understand each other?"

Claudia drew herself up to her full height. "Indeed we do. Lord Belgarrick, you have put your proposal in such a way that I have no choice but to refuse."

"Why?"

"Good heavens, you must know why!"

"I don't. You are six-and-twenty. On the shelf and gathering dust. You are dependent on relatives' begrudging charity. I can change all that."

"Yes, but . . ."

"You told Tigwell you have put romance behind you. Do you recant?"

"No, but . . ."

"Then why do you resent being taken at your word? Can't you see the benefit in not being obliged to pretend emotions you do not feel? If I required you to simulate love or passion I would understand your reluctance. As it is, I find you wholly incomprehensible."

Claudia thought it pointless to say she also found him incomprehensible, particularly as there was a certain awful logic in all he said. After her struggle to hide her hurts and humiliations these past months at Tallon Manor, would there not be a joyous relief in being honest? Her mind said yes, her wilful body wavered, and her heart made one last objection. "Perhaps I find a loveless marriage demeaning it itself."

"Then what are you doing here?"

That was unanswerable. Claudia walked to the fire and stood looking down at it. She felt battered and bludgeoned and nigh on exhausted, as if she had been hounded into a corner from which there was no escape.

"Well, Miss Tallon?"

There was only the truth left to her, and she said resentfully, "I was desperate."

"You are no less desperate now."

That, too, was the truth, and she liked it no better. In exasperation as much as anything, she fretted, "I don't like you."

"A perfectly understandable sentiment, but I have already pointed out that you are not required to like me."

Claudia capitulated. She must have, because she heard her voice saying, "Very well, Lord Belgarrick, I shall marry you."

He bowed. That seemed to finalize everything. Claudia felt curiously lightheaded. She drank her sherry, and it steadied her. Holding out the empty glass to him, she suggested, "The next time you feel I might need fortifying, you had better make it cognac. I have a feeling I shall need it."

"I shall remember." He took the glass, put it down and stood before her, searching her eyes for some moments. Then he held out his hand. "We will shake on our agreement, Miss Tallon."

She placed her hand in his and felt it gripped with more force than necessary. Again her blood stirred, and this time her breathing also quickened. Whether it was fascination or fright she did not know, but she tried to pull her hand away.

His clasped it more tightly still and said harshly, "I am a bad man to deceive. Was all you told Tigwell about yourself the truth?"

Claudia was nettled. "Of course it was! You're crushing my fingers."

He ignored her complaint and went on, "There is nothing else about yourself that I, as your betrothed, should know?"

As if one could possibly tell him anything he would

dislike hearing, she thought angrily. She gritted her teeth and, through them, said, "Nothing."

He released her hand. "Then it is settled. We shall be married as soon as I can arrange it. Tomorrow, possibly. There's time to get a special license today."

"Tomorrow?" she exclaimed, startled. "That's much too soon."

"Why?"

More than ever she wished he would stop firing his abrupt questions at her. They put her on the defensive when she had every right to object to his despotic decisions. "I traveled with nothing more than a carpetbag. I have no suitable clothes."

"What's wrong with what you are wearing? There's no need for bridal finery."

How like a man, she thought, and was incensed enough to persist, "I have little more than a toothbrush and nightgown with me. I shall need some sort of trousseau."

He took a drawstring purse full of guineas from his pocket and held it out to her. "Here. Buy what you need."

"No!" Her well-modulated voice cracked under her vehemence. "I cannot touch your money until we are married. It wouldn't be decent."

"Good God, are we out of Drury Lane dramatics and into a Cheltenham tragedy?" he exploded, dropping his purse back into his pocket. "You have refused a perfectly reasonable solution to your objection, so we may consider it no further."

"That wasn't the only objection," she said wildly. "The Tallons must be informed that I am about to marry."

"Why? You dislike them. Tell them by letter."

Claudia was aghast. "That would be improper!"

"It would be convenient, which is more to the point. Have you finished quibbling, Miss Tallon?"

She opened her mouth and closed it again. The entire circumstances of the marriage were so improper that her objections did, indeed, seem mere quibbling. Feeling as though she were once more driven into a corner, she grumbled, "You are a tyrant."

"You will find me so only when you are being foolish."

She was reminded of him saying he would bully her only when she gave him cause, but there seemed a world of difference between his notion of "cause" and hers. She was about to point this out when he continued, "In general, I see no reason why we shouldn't deal perfectly amicably together. Give me that ring you are wearing."

Instinctively, her left hand closed protectively over her right. He observed this and asked with a certain cynicism, "It has some special significance?"

"It was my betrothal ring."

"How touching. However, you now need another, and I must know the size of your finger. If you can bear to be parted from it for a moment I will draw its size on a piece of paper."

Feeling as foolish as he had called her, she slipped the ring from her finger and held it out to him. He took it to the little desk, placed it on a piece of the hotel's notepaper and, as he drew a ring around its inner circle, asked, "Did you select it?"

"No. It was Thomas's choice."

He came back to her, put the piece of paper in his pocket and dropped the ring in her hand. "I thought you would have better taste."

"What do you mean?" she was goaded to ask.

"Merely that an emerald is wasted on you. Your rich coloring cries out for rubies—although a lover, per-

29

haps, might be besotted enough to choose sapphires to match your eyes."

She was too angry to trust herself to answer. Instead she put up a hand to push back the wayward lock of hair that had once more strayed across her cheek. He caught her wrist. "Leave it. It looks charming."

Color flooded her cheeks. He was no lover, so she presumed he was mocking her, and she said icily, "The terms of our agreement do not require you to flirt with me."

He laughed. "If I were flirting with you I would have hold of something more relevant than your wrist. As it is, I am merely being courteous, as you required. I dare say I am out of practice. *Unquestionable* ladies do not come my way often." He raised her hand to his lips and kissed her fingers. "Thank you for doing me the honor of marrying me."

So . . . first he had crushed her fingers and then he had kissed them. What was she to make of such a man? He gave her no further time to come to any conclusion because he was gathering up his greatcoat, hat and gloves, and bowing. "Until we meet at the altar, then, Miss Tallon."

She inclined her head, but as he went to the door his arrogance piqued her into asking, "Are you so confident I shall be there?"

He checked and glanced back, eyebrows raised. "Certainly. An unquestionable lady cannot default on an agreement honestly struck."

"The whole world knows you for a scoundrel," she exclaimed wrathfully. "It is my position that is vulnerable."

"You cannot think I have gone to all this trouble just to jilt you at the altar."

"It isn't that. I have no way of knowing you will honor our terms once we are married."

His eyes smoldered dangerously. "I have been accused of many things, but never of reneging on my word. I will not dishonor our agreement unless you do so first. Try to bring yourself to trust me. It is a commendable quality in a wife." He gave a curt inclination of his head that was more of an insult than a bow, and then he was gone.

Claudia sank into an armchair and found she was trembling uncontrollably. "My God," she whispered, "what have I done? Whatever have I done?"

Such was her agitation that before long she was driven out of the comfortable hotel to walk the cold clean streets of this fashionable area of London. She tied the drawstrings of her hood tightly under her chin, clasped her mantle closely about her and welcomed the icy wind, hoping it would clear the numbness from her brain.

While the advertisement had not aroused any wild expectations in her breast, it had seemed reasonable to suppose that a marriage entered into with mutual respect and consideration might deepen by degrees into companionship and affection until some state of love was reached. Meeting Lord Belgarrick had made nonsense of such hopes. He neither sought nor offered love. He did not know what it was.

Claudia knew, and that was why she was so troubled. She had experienced the ecstasy and anguish of loving, and being loved in return. For a little while it seemed that she and Tom, in their perfect happiness, had frolicked with the gods, more than mere mortals. They had paid the penalty. Tom had died, and she had been condemned to spinsterhood, unable to compromise on a marriage made for anything less than love. Until now.

Suddenly Claudia knew why she was walking the freezing streets. It was to bring herself to let go, once and for all, of Tom and everything he represented.

Youth, dreams, ideals, perfection. All the aspirations of a hopeful heart. All the things Lord Belgarrick made a mockery of.

Just thinking of the man made her nerves jump. Her hands clenched, and her tight-fitting gloves drove Tom's betrothal ring into her finger. It seemed to reproach her, and rightly so. She was about to degrade herself by uttering sacred vows in a travesty of a marriage. She could not honor the man. She was not sure she could obey him. And as for love . . . it could not be *love* she felt for him.

Claudia gritted her teeth and strode on. What of it? At least he made her feel a woman again, and that was something no other man had managed these eight years since Tom's death. Was it *her* fault if, beneath her composed exterior, there lurked an earthier creature who had been re-awakened by a tantalising fluttering of the heart and senses?

It had been a shock to discover that Belgarrick could have this effect on her, and a greater one to realize that this primitive response meant more to her than the title and security he offered. It even made the fact that he was a scoundrel pale into insignificance.

She might be worried and not a little frightened but, like the heiress and baroness before her, she could no more stop herself being drawn to him than she could stop breathing. She was trapped by the excited beating of her own heart. She just wished she felt a little less ashamed of herself.

She had walked herself into no easier frame of mind, but the light was dwindling from the short winter's day and reluctantly she began to trace her steps to St. James's Street. She passed two crippled ex-soldiers sheltering in a doorway from the wind. One of them, not very hopefully, held out a begging hand.

She was almost past, but something about his sleeve

caught her attention. She stopped and looked more closely at the beggars, trying to identify the faded color of their tattered military tunics. Then she had it. She had been right. It was Rifleman Green. Tom's old regiment.

On impulse, she stripped off her glove, took Tom's betrothal ring from her finger, dropped it into the outstretched hand and hurried on through the gathering dusk. It was done. The break was made. Now she could betray nobody but herself.

## Chapter Three

Shortly before noon the following day Claudia arrived at St. George's, Hanover Square, to commit herself irrevocably to Lord Belgarrick's unloving arms.

A blizzard raged outside the church and, within, no braziers had been lighted to cheer the hasty ceremony. It was so cold that the bridegroom stood before the altar in his greatcoat, and the bride was shrouded from head to toe in her blue mantle. Her blue kid boots were stained with snow and nobody had thought to give her a posy.

There were no friends or relations to sustain her. The pews were empty. No organist had been hired and the choristers' benches were deserted. Hector Tigwell, little more than a stranger, had volunteered to give her away and Belgarrick's groomsman was unknown to her. Claudia had never attended a wedding ceremony stripped to its barest essentials, and consequently it had no reality for her. Hard as she tried, she could not summon up a proper businesslike attitude. Although she was a bride, she did not feel one, and so she felt robbed.

She stole a sideways glance at her bridegroom and found no comfort there. He looked, if anything, grim.

Her hand, straying unconsciously toward his for reassurance, fell helplessly back at her side.

She had great difficulty in concentrating on the time-honored words. Her mind, seemingly incapable of comprehending that they had anything to do with her, drifted away to more mundane matters.

She found herself recalling that when Hector Tigwell had arrived at her hotel that morning to tell her the ceremony would take place in a couple of hours, she had scarcely been able to believe that Belgarrick had indeed succeeded in arranging everything as speedily as he had hoped.

She had felt as helpless as a leaf in a stream, caught up in a current it was powerless to resist and being swept willy-nilly onward to an unknown fate. She was not even sure whether it was a source of wonder or shame that she had not struggled very hard to free herself, but she did know it was not a scrap of use wishing Belgarrick was a sight less captivating and a great deal more trustworthy. She was mesmerized by the man.

Most truly had she come to know how the rabbit felt before the snake struck. Only she was a willing victim, God help her, and there must be a hitherto unknown freakish streak to her nature because she actually *preferred* the present turmoil of her emotions to the flatness of her previous existence. Even so, it had been a shock to hear Mr. Tigwell say that when he took her to church, one of his clerks would carry her few belongings to Belgarrick house. There had seemed something so very final about that.

She had been pleased, however, to learn that he had succeeded in hiring a well-recommended maid for her, although only on a temporary basis in case they did not suit. Her name was Mellows, and she would be awaiting Claudia at Belgarrick House.

A look of gloom had come over Mr. Tigwell's face then and he had explained that the heavy fall of snow had overset Lord Belgarrick's plan to carry his bride directly into Kent. They would have to remain at the town house until the weather cleared. The servants, who had been packed to leave at dawn to precede the bridal couple to Belgarrick Towers, were now unpacking and hastily preparing the house to receive its new mistress.

Claudia, experienced in domestic matters, could readily understand the upheaval that must now be going on in Grosvenor Square. She stole another look at her bridegroom and wondered if having his plans changed by the blizzard was responsible for the frown upon his face.

She and Tom would have laughed at such an upset, not caring whether they slept in a castle or a cockloft so long as they were together, but this was not a love match. With a little ache she pictured how much happier Belgarrick must have looked when he had married for the first time. That union, from its very circumstances, must have been romantically inspired. His youthful bride must have had the joy of knowing what it was like to be loved by Belgarrick, if only for a little while.

Claudia sighed. It was more than she was ever likely to know.

Her wandering thoughts were checked by a movement among the small group before the altar: Hector Tigwell was stepping forward to give her away. She experienced a moment of panic, bit her lip to steady herself, and found she had at last won the attention of her moody bridegroom.

She met his questioning eyes and tried to smile, but it was a parody of the real thing. The service was a parody, too. The clergyman, shivering almost as much

36

as she was herself, hurried them shamelessly through their vows. Her hand rested in Belgarrick's only for as long as necessary, and when he slid the thick gold band on her icy finger, he might have been doing no more than trying it for size.

The clergyman was hurrying them through the blessing now, and Claudia realized despondently that there had been no moment during the ceremony that she could remember with warmth or tenderness. She bit her lip again. Belgarrick's ring still felt strange on her finger and already she was craving for far more than he had ever offered her.

He had contracted for a lady. She must remember that and stop being so much a woman. Survival in this union meant learning to be as detached as he was, however impossible it might seem at present. She wondered with an almost insane urge to giggle whether any other bride had ever had to lecture herself through a wedding before. Reaction to the strain she had been under must be setting in. She was feeling positively lightheaded. Was this being detached? She hoped so.

With a start she realized that the group before the altar was splintering into separate persons. So, the deed was done: she was Lady Belgarrick. This stranger at her side, unknown to her twenty-four hours previously, was her husband. It seemed too fantastic to be true, and yet the powerful presence of Belgarrick was real enough.

Once the register had been signed, the vicar did not encourage them to linger. On the contrary, he seemed anxious to get them off his hands. It occurred to Claudia that as this was a fashionable church he might well be aware of Belgarrick's reputation. Perhaps he believed that this hastily arranged marriage was due to her already being in an interesting condition. Embarrassment chased the pallor from her cheeks, and she

37

was grateful to find Belgarrick's hand under her elbow as he unceremoniously propelled her outside the church again.

The wind whipped the hood from her head. The blizzard was beginning to ease, but snowflakes settled like miniature stars on her rich dark hair. She blinked away more snowflakes from her thick eyelashes as she shook hands with Mr. Tigwell and Lord Charles Briddlesham, the groomsman. Each declined to return to Belgarrick House, pleading previous engagements they had been unable to cancel at such short notice. With something like incredulity Claudia heard them call her Lady Belgarrick and wish her future happiness. It drove home to her the fact that she was truly married in a way the actual ceremony had quite failed to do.

Belgarrick took her arm again and led her to his waiting carriage. The grooms, a splash of color in their scarlet and black livery, let down the steps and whipped the blankets from the horses' backs.

Claudia climbed into the carriage and relaxed against the scarlet squabs, relieved to be out of the driving wind. Belgarrick chose to sit opposite rather than beside her, the door closed, and the carriage moved cautiously forward at a snail's pace.

"Curse this snow," Belgarrick snapped. "It would be quicker to walk."

"Perhaps, but a great deal less comfortable," Claudia replied. She was still feeling lightheaded. Almost irresponsible. And why not? No *responsible* woman would have pressed on with this reprehensible marriage. She looked out at the snow and quipped, quite idiotically, "Happy is the bride the sun shines on."

"Happiness is something you must make for yourself. I did not guarantee it."

His abruptness brought Claudia down to earth with a thump. Clearly his wedding day had had no sweet-

38

ening effect on him. She wiggled her frozen toes within her boots, hoping to bring some life back into them, and retorted, "Happiness is often the sum total of many small things, and a few small considerations on your part would help. Had you thought to have the church warmed, and ordered hot bricks and rugs placed within this carriage, I would be a great deal happier now. Extremes of climate may not bother you, but you didn't specify that your wife had to be indifferent to personal comfort."

"Comfort yourself with the thought that you will be able to order things precisely as you wish in future."

"Precious comfort that will be if I die first of pneumonia," she grumbled, taking her lace-edged handkerchief from her reticule and dabbing at the rivulets of snow melting from her hair and running down her face.

"Good grief! We haven't been wed five minutes and already you are complaining."

"Only because you give me cause."

His brown eyes smoldered. "If I find myself closeted with a shrew, I'll get out and walk."

"I hadn't looked for such consideration," she retorted with heavy irony. "If anybody is to be put out in the snow, I supposed it would be me."

They glared at each other, and then, unexpectedly, he laughed. With his scowl gone, he was human and approachable. Claudia's wayward heart beat rapidly, and she was reminded of the reason she had married him. It was for moments like this, when he was devastatingly attractive.

He was still smiling at her and, delighted, she smiled back. It was the first time she had really smiled at him, and all the warmth of her nature lit up her face and transformed her from a handsome woman into a radiant one.

He stared at her and underwent another of his

abrupt changes of mood. The smile vanished, and his scowl returned to settle so heavily on his brow that she might never have succeeded in chasing it away. He said shortly, "You have a sharp tongue, madam."

"Claudia," she corrected huskily. "I might be a married lady now, but I find I don't care to be called madam in such a way."

The words cost her an effort but she was determined not to show her hurt. He had encouraged her to smile, so why should he react as though she had taken some diabolical liberty? She was bewildered, and yet she must not allow herself to be daunted. He was no longer a stranger she could walk away from. He was her husband . . . and tonight would be her wedding night.

Given his present attitude, it was hard not to be apprehensive at that prospect. Desperation caused her to search her mind for some innocuous topic of conversation that might build a bridge between them, however shaky, and she was driven back to the weather. "It is a pity the snow stopped us going to Belgarrick Towers. Is it all chaos at Belgarrick House?"

"I don't encourage chaos at any of my residences," he told her pithily.

Claudia felt he had not so much accepted her olive branch as slapped her in the face with it, and anger sabotaged her pacific intentions. "Your servants have been ordered to pack and close up the house, only to have the orders reversed at short notice. In addition, they have to prepare the mistress's apartment, which has no doubt been unused for two years. If you do not regard that as chaos, it must certainly have caused a considerable upheaval."

He shrugged, as though the matter were of no consequence. "The servants have been idle for two years. It won't harm them to bestir themselves."

"Idle for two years?" Claudia repeated, warming toward him again. "It was handsome of you not to have them laid off when you had no intention of returning to England immediately."

He shrugged again. "It was not handsome, it was obligation. They were born into service with my family, and most of them are too old to start afresh. Your apartment has been made ready, if that is what is bothering you, although you will have it redecorated as soon as possible. At the moment it is a nauseating green."

Claudia had no wish to start another fight, but he had no right to dictate what she did with her own apartment, and she objected, "It might be to my taste just as it is."

"It is not to mine and, as you will be receiving me there, the sooner it is changed the better. Order the work done while we are in Kent."

His dictatorial attitude and his tactless reference to her nightly duties goaded her into exclaiming, "You are a despot!"

"So I have been told," he responded indifferently.

"By your first wife, the baroness or both?" she snapped.

"Don't be impertinent!"

Claudia flushed scarlet. Her anger had betrayed her into an appalling lapse of taste, and she said with difficulty, "I beg your pardon, my lord."

He nodded, but his hard eyes did not soften at her apology nor did he say anything to make her more comfortable. She was not only humiliated, she was confused. She was his bride and yet he seemed to be doing his utmost to make her hate him. Or did she have it wrong and he was determined to hate her? Either way, it made nonsense of his confident assertion of yesterday that they could deal amicably together.

He was watching her, and when, this time, she did

nothing to ease the tension between them, he asked, "Sulking, madam?"

Her eyes flashed. "On the contrary, I was thinking that if this is dealing amicably, I hope we never fall to quarreling."

She had the satisfaction of seeing him taken aback, but then the carriage was stopping, and a footman was opening the door and letting down the steps. A path to the front door had been cleared in the snow and, for the moment, very little more was falling. She did not need to pause to study the house. She had visited it many times when the former viscount and his wife were entertaining, and was familiar with both its façade and its reception-rooms.

While the porter closed the door behind them and relieved Claudia of her mantle and Belgarrick of his coat, she made a quick inspection. Yes, it was all as she remembered. The black and white tiled floor, the marble busts set in niches around the hall, the graceful staircase curving in a gentle spiral to the top of the house.

She longed to warm herself by the fire that was casting a rosy glow over the magnificent white marble fireplace directly opposite the front door, but the servants were drawn up to meet their new mistress, and when Belgarrick took her arm she moved forward willingly. Accustomed to handling her father's staff for many years, this, at least, was one kind of ceremony that had no power to daunt her.

She shook hands with the portly, middle-aged butler and said, "No need to introduce you to me, is there, Hastings?"

He looked gratified. "It's good of you to remember me, Lady Belgarrick."

Again, it was a little shock to hear herself addressed by her new title, but she smiled and went on. "It would be difficult to forget. My father tried hard enough to entice you to come and work for us when our own Giddons retired, but nothing would shift you. I little thought then that I would live to be grateful for it."

Hastings looked even more gratified, and Claudia, knowing she had secured one friend at least in this strange household, moved on to Mrs. Binns, the housekeeper. This was another important personage. She was about the same age as Hastings, and even more portly, and she smiled when Claudia said she would send for her on the morrow so that they could have a longer chat.

And so Claudia went on down the line, a smile and a few words for each of the servants, until she reached the last of them and they were dismissed.

Belgarrick was leading her toward the stairs when a letter was delivered. They both looked back, saw the porter put the letter on a salver and paused as he came toward them. "It's for you, my lord," he said.

Belgarrick broke the seal, scanned the few lines and thrust the letter into his pocket, but not before a perfume more powerful than the subtle lavender she was wearing assailed Claudia's nostrils. She made no comment, but as they went on up the stairs together all her good breeding could not stop her wondering who would send Belgarrick a highly scented note on his wedding day, and was of sufficient importance to have it read immediately. He had no sister, no respectable lady friends among the *ton*, and that left only one possible conclusion—a conclusion that caused Claudia a searing pang of jealousy.

She knew it was a wife's duty to feign ignorance of certain facets of her husband's life, but not, surely, on her wedding day! She glanced at Belgarrick's profile. It was as classically sculpted as the marble busts down in the hall, and every bit as devoid of expression. He had something to hide, she was sure of it. Pride and breeding held back the questions she longed to ask, but her restraint cost her a considerable effort.

And in that moment she knew it was going to be hell being a dutiful wife. She was temperamentally and emotionally unsuitable for such a role. The tranquil years of half-living since Tom's death had duped her into believing that she might be, and she had been so wrong! How ironic that the passion Belgarrick aroused in her had destroyed the stoicism and composure she needed to survive marriage with him. It was, however, a jest she could not appreciate, and neither, if he ever discovered it, would he.

## Chapter Four

They passed the first floor where the reception and dining-rooms were situated and continued upward, Claudia so lost in her disquieting reflections that she started when Belgarrick said with his unnerving abruptness, "You will have to eat luncheon alone. I must go out on an urgent matter of business as soon as I have shown you to your rooms. You can occupy yourself this afternoon with writing whatever letters you thing necessary to your relations. I will be back in time for dinner."

Her thoughts flew to that horrid scented letter. That was the reason she had been brought a bride to Belgarrick House, only to be dumped. What power his mistress must have over him, but how dared she use it by summoning him to her on his wedding day!

Pride, jealousy, humiliation—all combined to make her voice shake as she exploded, "No! It won't do!"

"Won't do, madam?" he questioned, his eyebrows snapping together in a clear warning of danger. "You should learn immediately that I permit no meddling in my affairs, particularly by females."

Affairs . . . He had the right word there, but she was certain this one had nothing to do with business. She could cite neither pride nor jealousy for keeping him by her side, nor did she need to. There were more practical reasons within the terms of their contract that he could be forced to listen to.

She stopped on the stairs, looked up and down them to make sure no servants were within earshot, then began forcefully, "I am not any female, I am your wife."

"I do not need reminding," he broke in. "Nor do you need to make it more obvious that, *as my wife*, you stand in need of schooling."

"*As my husband*, there are some lessons you must learn first! You cannot go out as soon as you have brought me home. Servants can't be ignored. Think what gossip it will cause if it becomes known that your bride ate her wedding feast alone!"

"There is no feast. The servants have had no time to prepare one. A simple luncheon . . ."

"It makes no odds," Claudia interrupted. "Offend the *ton* in your treatment of me, and you will scarcely be thought a reformed character. Doors that are closed to you now will remain closed. Whatever you may think of me *as a wife*, I certainly will not go where my husband is not welcome. How, then, is Tansy to be established creditably? If the prospect of your wife and daughter skirmishing around the tattered edges of Society does not offend your dignity, I can assure you it offends mine!"

Belgarrick regarded her in fulminating silence for some moments, then gave vent to his feelings with a single word, "Damn!"

"I don't know what kind of females you normally associate with, but I'd be obliged if you didn't swear at me," she informed him icily.

"Don't push me too far, madam wife," he warned her softly.

"Don't threaten me for reminding you of your duties toward me and your daughter. A poor creature I would be if I didn't do so." Claudia turned her shoulder on him and began to walk on up the stairs.

He caught up with her, saying, "I can understand why you remained a spinster so long. You have a waspish tongue."

"I defend, my lord, I do not attack. If you have been stung, it is because you asked for it."

They had reached the second storey, and he led her along a passage expensively carpeted with Wilton. He stopped at a door, put his hand on the handle but did not turn it. Instead, he asked, "Do you make a virtue of always being in the right? No, don't answer that! It will take too long, and I have no taste for bickering."

Claudia's fine blue eyes sparkled angrily. "Mine is not a quarrelsome nature, but yours is enough to provoke a saint."

"If you say so. I have never had any dealings with one." He seemed to come to a decision, and went on, "Very well, you have made your point. I will remain for luncheon, and go out afterward while you are writing your duty letters. Only do not keeping me waiting long. My business is urgent."

He opened the door, gave her a bow that was little more than a nod, and walked off along the passage. Claudia went inside and, seeing a fire burning merrily in the grate, walked toward it with hands outstretched. She was still shivering, although not entirely with cold.

Her wedding day was not half over and she felt exhausted. Still, she had held her own in this last encounter, which made her more cheerful. He might be dictatorial but he was not beyond reasoning with, at least where his own interests were involved. How hateful, though, to hear him call her *madam wife* in that contemptuous manner.

She longed to hear her own name on his lips. She had the feeling he could make it sound like a caress, if he so wished. She cut short the sigh that came involuntarily to her lips. It was no use feeling sorry for herself. She might have done nothing but fight with him so far, but she was certain it was the best way. He would walk all over her if she let him, and probably never even notice he was doing it.

A second sigh came, more rueful than sad. She must set him an example which, she hoped, he would follow. She would start by calling him Giles, however much he scowled and snapped at her. It would make him seem more human, and he was a man very much in need of humanizing. In a few hours he would be sharing her bed and, as things stood, she was more likely to be trembling with terror than with desire.

Claudia turned away from the fire. Some thoughts were better denied than indulged. She was warm enough now to take an interest in her surroundings, and her first impression of her boudoir made her blink. The walls were painted a startling yellow, closer to buttercup than primrose, and the dominant shades of the thick-pile carpet were mustard and green. As if this were not enough, the graceful French sofa and its matching chairs were upholstered in green and yellow striped satin.

Dazzled and disbelieving, Claudia could not see herself retreating here for peace and solitude until it had all been changed. She could not imagine a more unrestful room and felt a nostalgic pang for the timeworn mellowness of Tallon Manor.

Not expecting too much, she walked into the bedroom and found the walls painted in a shade Belgarrick had quite rightly described as "nauseating green." The apricot carpet might have looked well enough had not the windows and bed been draped with a most determined pink. Assuming that the former Lady Belgarrick had not been color blind, she must have indulged her personal taste only in her private rooms, because, mercifully, the rest of the house bore witness to excellent taste. Either that of her husband or a professional decorator.

Claudia was just remembering her husband's command not to keep him waiting when a door opened on the far side of the room and a woman dressed with the neat stylishness of a lady's dresser entered. She stopped when she saw Claudia, and dropped a curtsy. "Forgive me, my lady, I did not know you had arrived. I'm Mellows, hired by Mr. Tigwell to serve you. I was hoping to have all ready for you, but the snow delayed my own arrival and I've scarcely had time to unpack your bag."

She was some ten years older than Claudia, almost as tall, although not so generously curved at bosom and hips. She had a pleasant open face, heavily freckled, and pale-lashed blue eyes.

Claudia greeted her civilly. She distrusted a man's ability to choose a suitable maid for a lady but she liked the looks of Mellows, and at least she had had the forethought to order a jug of hot water sent up.

While Mellows poured the water into a bowl, Claudia turned back her cuffs at the wrist and splashed the water over her face. She took the towel Mellows held for her and walked to the dressing-table while she patted herself dry. As she seated herself before the mirror, she saw that her own silver-backed dressing set had been put out.

"There isn't time to re-pin my hair. Just smooth the top where my hood has tousled it. I suppose you've been told that my baggage is being sent direct to Belgarrick Towers?"

"Yes, my lady. If you wish me to make any purchases for you, I could go to Bond Street this afternoon."

The offer was tempting, but Claudia thought it almost indecent to pledge Belgarrick's credit before his ring had properly warmed to her finger. She could not explain that, and so she replied, "Thank you, but I can manage. I'm sure you, like myself, have had enough of snow for one day. We'll both go tomorrow. We can stop each other slipping over if conditions haven't improved."

Mellows met her eyes in the mirror, saw she was smiling and, after a momentary hesitation, smiled back. Claudia was satisfied. The maid was deft enough at tidying her hair, but she appeared to be under almost as much stress as she was herself. Perhaps she was in distressed circumstances and hoped this temporary position would become a permanent one.

Claudia had not time to question her then, but when she saw the brush coming forward to swoop back the lock of hair that would stray across her cheek, she said, "No. Leave that."

The hovering hairbrush went back to the top of her head and if Mellows thought the neatness of the coiffure was spoiled, she said nothing. It was as well. Claudia could scarcely have told her that Belgarrick had said the curl on her cheek was charming, for which compliment she was only too willing to sacrifice neatness.

When Claudia stood up, she turned down her cuffs again, adjusted the ruffles at her neck and shook the soft folds of her woollen dress into place. She looked round the room once more as she did so, approving of the restrained Hepplewhite furniture, particularly the mahogany four-poster with its delicate flower carvings. Her eyes went to the door Mellows had come through, and she asked, "What is through there?"

"Your dressing-room, my lady. It leads to my lord's."

Claudia nodded as if this information were of no significance, although her pulses jumped in what was becoming an alarmingly familiar way. That, then, was the way Belgarrick would come to her tonight.

No, not Belgarrick, she chided herself. The name was somehow as uncompromising as the man himself. *Giles*, that was how she must think of him . . . to remind herself that he could smile and be human when it pleased him. Or, perhaps, when she pleased him. That was one of the many things about him she had to find out.

And it was time she joined him. She had lingered long enough—too long, he would probably say—and she did not want him to greet her with that heavy scowl upon his face. She picked up her reticule, and said to Mellows, "Have you eaten since you arrived?"

"No, my lady."

"Go downstairs now. I mean to write some letters after luncheon so I won't need you until later this afternoon. I would like a bath, at least three hours before dinner."

"I'll arrange it, my lady."

Claudia went outside, where a footman, clad in the scarlet and black Belgarrick livery, was waiting to take her down to the room commonly referred to as the breakfast parlor, in which the family took informal meals. He bowed her inside and withdrew, closing the door quietly behind him.

Belgarrick was leaning against the mantelshelf looking down at the flames licking greedily at a freshly-applied log, but he straightened immediately and came toward her. There was a scarcely disguised impatience about him, and as there were no servants in the room,

51

she said lightly, "I can see you are not well pleased. Am I to be hanged by my thumbs for taking too long?"

"Don't tempt me." He took her arm and guided her, not to the chair at the foot of the table as she expected, but to the one next to his at the top, explaining, "It will be more convenient if you sit here. We have things to discuss."

They were no sooner seated than Hastings entered with hot chocolate in a silver pot. When he saw she was not sitting where expected, he busied himself rearranging her place setting and the dishes on the table. Claudia, seeing his quickly suppressed smile, guessed he saw romance in the way they were seated, and avoided his approving eyes.

Instead, she studied the room. It was small enough to be cozy, as the breakfast parlor at Tallon Manor was cozy, but it was dominated by such large pieces of furniture that it merely looked crowded. Mentally, she removed two leaves from the dark mahogany table, reduced the twelve heavily-carved chairs round it to six, consigned one of the two massive sideboards to an attic, and found herself with a greatly improved room. Two compact armchairs could be placed on either side of the fireplace, and there would still be more space to move about.

Her housewifely reflections came to a sudden end when Bulgarrick asked, "Wool-gathering, Claudia?"

For a moment she was still, savoring the moment. There it was at last. Her name on his lips. He did not make it sound like a caress, although it was a great improvement on *madam*. Could she possibly be becoming real to him, a woman with thoughts and feelings, as well as a wife contracted for specific purposes? She dared to hope so, because she needed to, and she smiled as she replied, "I was thinking that this room would be better for less furniture. Would you object if I had one of those sideboards moved out, and perhaps some chairs?"

"You can throw the lot out with my good will. Living in India accustomed me to plenty of space in which to move about, and few pieces of furniture to get in my way. I have felt cramped ever since I returned to England. I can scarcely turn round without sending flying one of the side tables or spindly-legged chairs with which my sister-in-law saw fit to litter the place. I'm surprised Gervase didn't stop her. He was almost as big a man as I am."

Claudia saw that Hastings had finished arranging everything to his satisfaction, and nodded dismissal. She waited until he had gone out before she replied, "I dare say your brother and his wife put fashion before comfort, but that is no reason why we should. If you would just tell me what you like, I'll . . ."

"Arrange everything as you see fit," he interrupted, carving some slices from a large ham and putting them on her plate. "This house is nothing but a temporary inconvenience for me. It will be one of your homes for some years to come."

This harsh reminder of the nature of their marriage caused Claudia a pang, but she persisted, "It was one of your youthful homes. You must feel something for it?"

"Why? Nothing is as I remembered it. Besides, I was country reared. My time on the town, when I lived here, was brief, and ended with my elopement. The doors of this house were closed to me then and, but for a freak of fate, I would never have re-entered them. Do as you wish with the place and do not bore me with the details. Just have the bills sent to me." As though tired of the subject, he changed it by asking, "Would you like some of this game pie?"

Claudia, considering carefully all he said and won-

53

dering whether it sprang from bitterness or complete indifference, looked vaguely at the cold pie with its raised crust, then nodded. "A small slice, if you please, Giles."

They ate in silence for a while, then he said suddenly, "You may also do as you wish with your own rooms. I was wrong to order otherwise."

He was not by nature a conciliatory man, and Claudia guessed that the admission had not come easily to him. To meet him halfway, she replied, "You were right about the green, though. It is nauseating, and it will be changed."

He paused in adding home-made pickle to the cold meats on his plate and looked searchingly at her. She smiled, and he smiled back, and she felt the dizziest surge of happiness. The man was emerging from behind the monster.

Her euphoria lasted while she ate her meat and pie, a slice of rich fruit cake and a chestnut which she selected from a dish of assorted nuts. It ended as she peeled a second chestnut, and asked, "Who chaperons Tansy at Belgarrick Towers?"

"She is not there. She is at a seminary in Bath."

Claudia was shocked into forgetting how belligerently he reacted to criticism, and exclaimed, "Giles, no! Still at school at eighteen? That's monstrous! How could you have permitted it? Her friends of her own age must have left last year to make their débuts. The poor child! How neglected and unwanted she must feel."

He cracked the shell of a walnut between his fingers so forcefully that the nut within it shattered and the pieces fell on his plate. He pushed the plate away, and told her harshly, "Tansy is neither poor nor neglected, and if she is unwanted it is because she chooses to be."

"Much you know of the matter!" she retorted heatedly. "It's your boast that you have no heart. How could you possibly know what she is feeling? With you abroad and her mother dead, she has effectively been an orphan for years. She must have felt it, too, poor lamb, if the best arrangement you could make for her was to bundle her off to school."

"She hasn't been bundled anywhere. She went to the seminary at her own request. She wrote to me for permission and I gave it. She was unhappy living with her maternal grandparents, which wasn't surprising, when their treatment of her mother drove her to . . ." He broke off and glowered at her as though she had angered him into saying more than he wished.

". . . elope with you," Claudia finished for him.

"I was going to say throw herself at the first man who came her way, but that would be unchivalrous of me, wouldn't it?"

"It would indeed. She is dead, and cannot defend herself against any accusations you might make."

"The only person making accusations is you—at me."

Claudia's anger began to drain away and she realized she had been too hasty. Being honest, she admitted it. "I was making unconsidered judgments about a situation of which I know nothing, save for common gossip, and that years old. I beg your pardon."

The stormy look left his face. "You're fair, at any rate. That's rare in a woman."

Claudia could not permit that to go unchallenged. "If I have been guilty of an unconsidered judgment, you are guilty of a sweeping one. If you believe yourself justified in making it, I can only say that you must have been singularly unfortunate in the women you have known."

"I am beginning to think so, too."

Claudia's eyes flew to his, but he was standing up, and the moment was lost. "I must leave you to finish

55

your chocolate alone," he told her. "I did warn you that my business is urgent."

That letter, she thought. That horrid scented letter. It was claiming him again, just as ... Just as what? Just as there was something in his tone that had made her believe he was coming to see her as something more than a mere means of producing his sons? Yes, for a fleeting moment she had thought so, but now here he was, as abrupt and dismissive as ever. The closer she got to him, the further away he seemed to be.

He paused by her chair, and added, "By the way, Claudia, when you meet Tansy I think you will find she doesn't quite fit the picture you have painted of her. I visited her as soon as I returned to England, and told her I intended to marry and remove her to Belgarrick Towers while her début was arranged. She was not at all pleased. Far from fretting over her delayed début, she appears determined not to make one, and is most reluctant to leave Bath. She must be forced to, of course. She cannot be permitted to fancy herself a recluse, as her mother did, or I will never have her off my hands."

The callousness of this speech quite took Claudia's breath away, and all she could do was watch him as he walked to the door. He looked back as he got there, studied her expression, and said, "Yes, I can see you'll get on well with Tansy. She, too, thinks me a monster."

## Chapter Five

For some half-hour Claudia had been sitting at the desk in her boudoir nibbling the end of her quill pen. When she looked down at the blank sheet of notepaper before her, Giles's face appeared on it, scowling at her. Then he would smile and she would feel herself smiling back. It was absurd, but she couldn't help herself. The letters she had to write were difficult enough without this distraction. Hard as she searched for the right words, her brain was interested only in remembering everything Giles had said to her; analysing, dissecting, searching for meanings that had not occurred to her at the time.

Not that she came to any conclusions. The more he gave her cause to dislike him, the deeper her obsession for him became. It was a paradox, and it sprang from a conviction that there was a man behind the man, carefully hidden, for what reason she knew not. A man she could love as well as desire, if only she could find him. Although she was getting tired of sighing, she sighed again. She could not help that, either. She felt so frustrated. Occasionally she glimpsed the man she sought, only to have him disappear immediately into the harsh and uncompromising reality of Lord Belgarrick.

Her husband. He had given her a title and security. More than she had originally expected when she had answered the advertisement, less than she wanted now.

As a husband he was a fact. As a lover he was no more than a fantasy. But it was the fantasy she was obsessed with, and it was the fantasy that was causing her so much anguish. It had transformed her from a composed and rational woman past the first blush of youth into a fiery, fighting female chasing a shadow that might never achieve substance. Might, indeed, never exist outside her own fevered imagination.

He had told her bluntly enough not to search for a heart because he had none. What would he say if he knew she wanted him—heart, soul, body and mind? It was the only way she knew how to love. The only way Tom had known. Giles, of course, was an entirely different matter.

With an effort Claudia checked her rambling thoughts. These letters had to be written. She sought once more for words that would make her extraordinary marriage seem ordinary enough, and still they eluded her. The facts would have to suffice. She picked up her quill, and wrote:

Dear Sir Edgar and Lady Tallon,

This morning I married Giles Verylan, Viscount Belgarrick, at St. George's Church, Hanover Square. A private ceremony was deemed most appropriate as I am still in black gloves for my father. I would be grateful if you would forward my belongings to Belgarrick Towers in Kent. As soon as the weather permits, I shall send servants to fetch my mare and dog so that you will be put to no further trouble and expense.

Your respectful cousin, Claudia

She sat back and read over the letter. It was blunt to the point of rudeness. On consideration, she felt no shame for that. Neither of them had ever displayed any tact or delicacy in their dealings with her. She had no wish to be spiteful, but they could scarcely be surprised at finding themselves repaid in their own coin. If they chose to cause a fuss, she would refer them to Belgarrick, God help them.

There were no other relations on the paternal side she need concern herself with. However, her mother's sister, Aunt Adela, deserved better treatment. She had very nobly, considering her circumstances, offered Claudia a home if she should ever need one. Claudia had just as nobly refused. Aunt Adela was kindness itself, but, with two unmarried and one widowed daughter sheltering under her roof, she scarcely needed another surplus female added to her household.

Writing to her taxed Claudia's ingenuity to the limit. She deserved more than the barest details yet had to be spared the whole truth, which would shock her conventional heart to the core. In the end, she wrote that she and Giles had met by chance when he had returned to England some weeks before. He was a reformed character in his maturity, they held each other in mutual esteem and believed marriage would be beneficial to both of them. The letter was a mixture of half-truths and outright lies, and Claudia eased her conscience by telling herself it would spare Aunt Adela from going off into strong hysterics. It was, moreover, the story she thought best to be circulated among the *ton*.

As Claudia folded and sealed her letters, she perceived it would be no easy task to make Giles give credence to the story by behaving like a reformed character, certainly until after Tansy had had her Season.

This last thought raised twin worries in her mind.

Tansy must be saved from being so overpowered by her father that she married to please him rather than herself, and some way must be found to pluck the feathers from Giles's Bird of Paradise. He should have known before he married that an old mistress and a new bride would not do, not for a man with his past and his future hopes of launching his daughter into the first circles.

Claudia, intending to write a note to her old nurse living in retirement in Lincolnshire, picked up her quill and drew another sheet of paper toward her. This time, when Giles's persistent image appeared upon it, she scowled first. She had never expected marriage with him to be easy, but she had a right to some co-operation, and all he appeared to be doing was his damnedest to make it nigh on impossible. She burned again with the rage he could so readily evoke in her and for a few moments indulged a blissful vision of his unknown mistress drowning in her own horrid scent. God only knew she used enough of it!

Claudia flung down her pen in disgust, both with herself and Giles, and walked about the room to recover her composure. She told herself contemptuously that she had been doing a lot of this lately, far too much, and unless she learned to control the violence of her emotions she was likely to be doing a great deal more. Rage would not prise Giles away from his mistress. He had enough of his own, and the power to use it to greater effect.

She came to a halt in front of a cheval-glass and looked at herself with new eyes. The simple blue woollen gown with its prim white ruffles, which had pleased her enough before, she now found loathsome. Heavens, it only needed the addition of a matronly cap to her head to proclaim the female past the age or expectation of exciting a man.

That might have been how she saw herself before meeting Giles, but now—now she would throw the dress away as soon as she purchased some replacements. Giles's mistress, she was sure, would not be caught wearing anything so staid. Claudia's eyes kindled as she pictured the kind of gowns the woman of the overpowering scent would wear.

Who was she, and what did she look like? It was hard enough to have a rival, yet so much worse to know nothing whatsoever about her.

She stood for a moment irresolute, then, her jaw setting, she walked to her dressing-room. She went straight through it, sparing no glance for its many chests and hanging cupboards, to the door on the far side. She stopped and listened, but no sound came from beyond. She took a deep breath and entered. Giles was out, but if she came face to face with his valet she was not sure what she would do.

The room was empty. She walked through it into the bedroom and breathed a sigh of relief when she saw nobody was there, either. It was a magnificent blend of scarlet, white and gold, princely in its ostentation, and she could not imagine it being occupied by a lesser man than Giles. Yet, as she advanced across the thick carpet, a chill touched her spine. Only the brushes on the dressing-table, embossed with his initials, indicated that that was his room. There were no miniatures of loved ones, no favorite ornaments, no personal clutter—nothing to stamp his powerful personality on the room. But for its grandeur, it could have been a hotel room, hired by somebody who had no intention of staying.

Nothing could have brought home to her more forcibly the fact that she had more than a mistress to contend with. He had to be coaxed out of traveling on as soon as his mission here was accomplished. Claudia would readily have accompanied him anywhere, but he wanted his sons brought up at Belgarrick Towers. She found herself hoping she did not conceive too soon. Given enough time, he might come to realize that England was his true home, and overcome the dislike his past had given him for it.

All that, however, was in the future. Her immediate task was to discover where he had put that horrid letter. She would have smelled its perfume, surely, if it had still been in his pocket at luncheon? She quickly rifled through the two side cupboards of the Sheraton bow-front dressing-table and then tried the center drawer. It would not budge, but the key was in the lock.

She turned it and opened the drawer, and immediately the perfume she loathed wafted up to her. Obviously Giles had no secrets from his valet. The letter was there to be read by anyone who had the nerve, as she had, to sneak in and pry. That thought made her fully aware of what a contemptuous deed she was committing. How would she feel if she found Giles prying among her things? Outraged! Yesterday she would never have dreamed of such an act. Was it any defense that, as Lady Belgarrick, she had worries and jealousies unknown to the highly-principled Miss Tallon?

Claudia, letter in hand, fought with her conscience and won. She opened the letter and read:

Dearest Gilly,

A thousand kisses. The diamonds are magnificent. How churlish it would be of me now to refuse to do as you wish. I will be good and go to Paris. There will be no spicy gossip about us to ruin your rehabilitation with the *ton!* Poor darling, how bored you will be. Never mind. If I know my Gilly, your Society bride will soon drive you to join me in Paris. I'd go more willingly by myself if I thought it would be warmer than London. Yes, I know I am complaining again, but after Calcutta what can one do but freeze? Unless we are together, of course. Do I get a thousand kisses back for being a good girl? Only come to me quickly with the travel arrangements or I will change my mind and become a bad girl again!

Your own Lisette

Fresh wrath consumed Claudia. *Gilly*, indeed! How dared this Lisette have a pet name for him! It didn't even suit him. But that was a trivial matter compared with the confidence and intimacy the letter oozed. Even more worrying was that this connection had not been made since his return to England. They had known each other in India, and presumably he had brought her home with him. An affair that had endured for months, then, possibly years, and which the unknown Lisette clearly expected to endure a great deal longer.

Claudia locked the letter back into the drawer, a frown furrowing her brow. What weapons did she, a wife Giles had taken out of necessity, have to use against a woman he willingly embraced? She could think of none, but on one thing she was resolved. If anything drove Giles from his bride to Paris it would not, as his mistress so smugly expected, be boredom!

She went back to her room and wrote a careful letter to Lally, her old nurse, then rested on the day-bed for an hour to recruit her strength for her next encounter with Giles. Later she bathed, and Mellows washed her hair for her, rubbing it well with bay leaves, a formula of her own for making it soft and glossy.

Claudia sat by the fire to dry her hair, drinking tea while Mellows removed the ruffles from the blue gown and replaced them with a clean set Claudia had had the forethought to pack into her bag.

The afternoon and early evening passed peacefully in this way and Claudia felt a new woman when, wrapped snugly in a woollen robe, she sat before the dressing-table while Mellows brushed her hair. Under gentle questioning, her maid revealed that she had been forced to leave her previous employment because of the unwelcome attentions of her mistress's husband.

"He was shameless, my lady," Mellows told her quietly. "I feared my mistress would discover he was pursuing me and think I had encouraged him."

"A difficult situation," Claudia sympathized.

"I should have waited until I found other employment, but I feared for my good name and reputation. They were rich merchants who lived in grand style, and Mrs. Hewitt was a good mistress, but I didn't see what else I could do. I was at the agency when Mr. Tigwell called, and he interviewed me right away and hired me. That was good luck following bad, and I've always wanted to work for Quality."

"All's well that ends well," Claudia murmured. It sounded horribly mundane but she was unable to think of anything more original to say. Much as she appreciated Mellows's candor, with her homely features and rather spare frame, she was incapable of imagining her inspiring any man to unbridled lust.

She was hard put not to smile, but all amusement fled when the dressing-room door opened and Giles came in, strolling toward her with his customary assurance. Mellows curtsied, put down the hairbrush and whisked herself tactfully from the room, leaving Claudia feeling vulnerable and defenseless. Like a spinster shrinking from a dangerous male, she thought disgustedly.

In vain did she remind herself that a wife must expect such intrusions on her privacy. She did not *feel* a wife. Not yet. She felt like Miss Tallon, caught with her hair down and nought but a robe to shield her freshly-bathed and fire-warmed body, and she blushed.

He looked down at her with—what? Amusement? She thought it must be so, and blushed more fiercely.

"How novel," he said.

Her eyes widened. "What is?"

"A woman still capable of blushing. My compliments, Claudia. It becomes you."

What did? she wondered agitatedly. Her modesty or her heightened color? She picked up the brush Mellows had abandoned and began to brush her hair, grateful for something to do. Her gown was tightly belted and as she followed his eyes in the mirror she saw them drop to her breasts, which were outlined tautly against the soft wool by the movement of her upraised arm. She put down the brush in greater confusion than ever.

She jumped when he reached out and touched her sweet-smelling hair, his fingers lazily entwining it, and felt a fool when he said, "You are very much on your nerves. We *are* married, Claudia."

"Yes, but I—I am not quite used to it yet. It seems very strange, a man in my bedchamber."

"A natural maidenly reaction, I suppose."

She lowered her eyes and said nothing, and after a pause he added, "Don't fear me. There's no need for it. While you are fair with me, I will be fair with you. Why so silent, Claudia? Do you truly think me a monster?"

*While you are fair with me* . . . That rankled with her. Why should she be a saint when he had no scruples about being a sinner? What was fair about that? She raised resentful eyes and told him bluntly, "I think you are a bad-tempered, disagreeable, insensitive despot."

"Yes, yes," he agreed impatiently. "But a monster?"

She tried to free her chin from his fingers, but his grip tightened and she was forced to continue meeting his eyes. Their expression was so intent that she found

65

herself answering truthfully, although with heightened resentment, "No, I don't think that. At least, not yet."

He released her, and replied, "That's fair, at any rate. It encourages me to think we shall deal very well together."

"But we're always fighting!"

He shrugged. "That's the way it is between men and women."

"It doesn't have to be so."

"Then it is up to you to teach me otherwise."

He sounded neither autocratic nor dismissive, and Claudia's heartbeat quickened. It seemed that, this time, he was holding out the olive branch. She was wary of accepting it, mindful of previous snubs. He had a habit of crushing her whenever she softened toward him. She turned from him to the mirror, and said, "You do not strike me as a man willing to be taught anything."

He came behind her chair and put his hands on its arms, leaning down close to her so that she felt as if she were in his embrace. His cheek rested against hers as he met her eyes in the mirror, and he said softly, "Taught? Perhaps not, but I am a man, and I can always be tempted."

Claudia caught her breath. There could be no doubt—he was courting her, this harsh and difficult husband of hers! The impossible had happened. The wife of necessity had become a woman to him, and he wanted her.

She was as excited and, yes, awed as any green girl discovering for the first time she had the power to bring to heel a man she coveted. Then, as her euphoria reached its peak, it was destroyed. With Giles so close, a faint perfume assailed her nostrils. It was not as overpowering as it had been on the letter, but it was unmistakable, a potent reminder he had come to her straight from his mistress's arms.

Perhaps, Claudia thought bitterly, Lisette had urged him to get on with the business of making his wife pregnant so that he could follow her to Paris. And, under the terms of their marriage agreement, she herself could make no complaint. He had warned her strongly enough to expect no more than a title and security from him. Everything came back to that. It was like a rock she was beating herself against to no avail.

All the same, she rebelled. So, too, had she issued a warning—that she would be no doormat!

His lips were close to her ear, and a shudder of delight went through her as he breathed, "Well, Claudia? Are you in a mood to tempt me?"

She waited until she had the treacherous weakness of her body under control and then replied with a composure that pleased her a great deal more than it pleased him, "I find temptation difficult, when you smell of a perfume I don't care for."

He straightened up and in the mirror she could see his thunderstruck expression. She was a little frightened, but that was nothing to the unholy satisfaction she felt. Now he knew he could not have everything his own way.

To rub salt into the wound she went on calmly, so calmly that she sounded like a schoolmarm lecturing a rather naughty little boy, "You reminded me earlier that I have no right to meddle in your affairs. I would remind you that if your affairs are unseemly, you have no right to bring them to my notice. It would be more gentlemanly if, on certain occasions, you changed your coat before you came to see me."

As a setdown, it was masterly. Angry as he was, he had no cause to complain, and he knew it. A gentleman never brought his liaisons to the attention of his wife, and thus she permitted them. That was the way Society played the game, and if he insisted she stuck by the rules then so, too, must he.

Giles, temperamentally incapable of suffering attack without striking back, clenched his fists in fury. It had never been his intention to get himself into this situation. He had not expected to find her half clad, with her hair down, and beautiful hair at that, so that he would be beguiled into forgetting she was his wife.

Not for the first time in their brief acquaintance he found himself wishing she was a sour-faced spinster he could have molded more easily into the strict space allotted to her in his life. Nor did she ease his rage by asking, "Was there anything in particular you wished to see me about, Giles?"

"There was," he told her harshly. "I have some letters to be despatched. Do you have any you want me to frank for you?"

"Yes." The tension between them was so unbearable that Claudia was glad to get up and move away from him. She was picking up the letters from the desk before she remembered how her woollen gown, tied firmly at her slender waist, clung tightly to her generous bosom and hips.

She hesitated, but Giles was waiting by the dressing-table, his hand held out imperatively. She had no choice but to walk toward him. As he took the letters, his eyes traveled slowly and insolently over her, and he said, "You are very well formed. I believe you will bear me excellent children."

He had struck back, and with interest. Nothing could have been more calculated to put her in her place. He bowed and left her, apparently satisfied, and it was Claudia's turn to suffer all the agonies of rage and humiliation.

## Chapter Six

They dined tête-à-tête by candlelight, as a bride and groom should, but without the rapport necessary to overcome the formality of the occasion. The dining-room was large, with painted ceiling and painted panels on the walls, and Giles had not ordered her place set next to his. They sat at either end of the table, isolated from each other by such a vast expanse of polished Spanish mahogany that conversation was impossible. The liveried footmen, conscious of the butler's eagle eye, performed their tasks in a poker-faced silence more fitting to a wake than a wedding feast.

Claudia, miserably aware of the collapse of all the little bridges she had tried to build between Giles and herself before the marriage was consummated, had no appetite. Of the many dishes comprising the first course she accepted a little of the highly-seasoned mulligatawny soup, and then pushed a small portion of smelts about her plate.

She watched Giles eat dressed lobster and then a beefsteak with oyster sauce and vegetables before he signaled that he was ready for the second course. From this she managed to swallow a few slices of chicken

69

while he ate pigeons and a portion of apple pie, clearly unaffected by the apprehension that ruined her meal.

The third course was less of a trial. She waved away the meringue and sweetmeats and nibbled preserved fruits while she drank her hock. Giles also chose fruit, and French olives and nuts. Claudia, fearful he would be drunk when he came to her later, was relieved to see his glass re-filled but twice. He was not, then, a bottle-a-meal man, as her father had become in his last years, and that before the port and brandy were served.

She gave up any pretense of eating, and her eyes traveled the length of the table. By candlelight, Giles looked more piratical than ever. There was an air of brooding restlessness about him, as if these civilized surroundings were alien to him. His heavy tan was emphasized by the whiteness of his cravat and his tawny hair waved wildly about his forehead and ears.

There was something very untamed, very animal about him that issued a challenge Claudia's femininity could not resist. What a prize he would be if his disposition matched his romantic appearance! But, flawed though he was, he was the man for her. He could not have brought her back to life otherwise.

What a prim partner she must seem for him in her blue gown. Tomorrow it would be different, but tonight only the pearl necklace and earrings presented by her father for her twenty-first birthday dignified her appearance. Unlike Giles's mistress, she had no diamonds to flash. The Tallon jewelry, like the title and estate, had passed into her cousin's possession.

Her mood was deteriorating from miserable to morbid and she realized with relief it was time for the covers to be removed and the port placed on the table. She could decently escape the tedium of sitting there trying to look, for the servants' sake, contented with her lot. She rose to her feet, and a footman conducted her to the Blue Salon where generations of Verylan wives had waited, often hours at a time, for their husbands to join them after dinner. Giles, however, had no companions to share the port, and this was their wedding night. If he tarried too long, it could be an insult to his bride. Was he spiteful enough to think she deserved it?

She did not know, but was not prepared to take any chances. Having no embroidery to occupy her, and thinking a book too tame, she asked the footman to set up a card-table and fetch her a pack of cards. Scarcely had she set out the cards for patience when the door opened and he walked in. So, she had wronged him! The glow of pleasure that suffused her was quickly quenched when he frowned and came to her.

He put a hand under her chin, forced her face up to his, and asked with quiet menace, "Is this supposed to be a subtle way of informing me that you prefer cards to my company?"

What a touchy man he was, and how best to placate him? Claudia opted for honesty. "I thought it likely you would keep me waiting a long time. I was determined you wouldn't find me fretting on the edge of my seat."

"Why should I do that?"

"To punish me for angering you earlier."

He released her chin and walked over to the fire. "Spite is a woman's weapon."

"You delight in putting me in my place by reminding me why you married me. I call that spite."

"Good God! If this is an example of defense, you must be formidable when you are on the attack."

"I would have to be very formidable indeed to match you, Giles."

"So you would," he snapped. "Put those damned cards away. No, wait. Since we can't seem to exchange

71

a civil word, perhaps we'd be better employed playing cards. Have you a mind for piquet?"

"Certainly." Claudia swept the neat columns of cards together, then hesitated. "I might beat you, though. I'm very good."

Giles laughed, not sardonically, but with genuine amusement. "You have the knack of saying what I least expect, and just as I was becoming convinced it was beyond the power of any woman to surprise me. Might beat me, you think? Let's put it to the test."

He drew up a chair and sat facing her, smiling still. As Claudia removed from the pack the cards not needed for piquet her hands trembled slightly. With delight, not nervousness. The man she found irresistible was emerging again. She must not lose him this time.

She could have screamed with vexation when Hastings entered, bowed and said apologetically, "I'm sorry, my lady, but a Mrs. Hewitt has called to see you. I've told her you will not wish to be disturbed, but she is most insistent."

Claudia was about to deny any knowledge of the woman when she suddenly recalled Mellows saying she had been employed by a Mrs. Hewitt. What on earth could her maid's previous mistress want with her at this time of night?

"Who the devil is she?" Giles asked, and Claudia could not help but be happy that he appeared to resent the intrusion as much as she did.

"Nobody you would know. However, I'd better see her. Her business must be urgent if she insists on seeing me at this hour on my wedding night." As she passed him, she put her hand on his shoulder and pressed it briefly, adding softly, "Don't be cross. I won't be above a few moments."

The gesture was impulsive, but when she followed

Hastings from the room and along the passage she found herself worrying whether Giles would resent it as unwarranted familiarity. He was so prickly, there was no telling. Nor was that her only worry. What must Hastings be thinking at finding the bride and groom playing cards on their bridal night?

"Mrs. Hewitt will not be inclined to linger," Hastings told her in a colorless tone. "I have shown her into the Yellow Salon. The fire has not been lighted."

Claudia's worries receded in amusement. Servants had their own way of dealing with people they disapproved of. When she was in the room and Hastings had closed the door behind her, she paused to study her visitor.

Mrs. Hewitt had the over-fed and over-dressed look of an affluent middle-aged woman with little taste and less self-discipline. Her slightly bulbous blue eyes peered through pouches of flesh that hung both above and below them, and her cheeks and chin showed a similar tendency to sag. She was expensively clad in an orange pelisse trimmed excessively with chinchilla, and ostrich feathers dyed a matching orange quivered on her formidable gray bonnet. She looked so very nervous, all but wringing a handkerchief between her gloved hands, that Claudia's ready sympathy was aroused.

She went toward her with her hand extended, saying more cordially than she had intended, "Mrs. Hewitt? I am Lady Belgarrick. How may I be of service to you?"

Mrs. Hewitt touched her fingers briefly, then uttered disjointedly, "So kind! So civil! And you just married. I did not know until your butler told me. So impertinent of me to intrude like this. I am covered in mortification, 'pon my word I am, but I cannot go away until I have told you. I wouldn't get a wink of sleep otherwise, though heaven knows I've forgotten what a night's rest is like. How to find the words I do not know, but I must, I must! I will not shirk my duty as one wife to another, one Christian to another, even though I be exposed to gossip and ridicule. Lady Belgarrick, be warned! You have a serpent under your roof!"

Claudia, listening to this outburst in amazement and making no sense of it, could only think that Mrs. Hewitt was more than agitated, she was deranged. "Madam, are you quite well?" she asked politely. "Will you not sit down? I will send for a cordial . . ."

"No, no! There is no cordial that will calm me, and I have no wish to be a nuisance. I shall go the minute I have discharged my painful duty. You must cast this serpent from your house as I cast it from mine. Before you, too, are undone."

"I haven't the faintest idea of what you are talking about. What serpent?" Claudia asked, bemused.

"Mellows!"

*"Mellows?"* Claudia echoed, incredulous that her quiet and efficient maid, with her homely and honest face, could be described in such a way.

"Ay, you might stare! I, too, would have done so, had I been warned when she came into my employ two years ago. So proper, so anxious to please. I treated her well—and she seduced my husband! She was the Delilah to his Samson, the sinner who cast down the saint, the . . ." Words failed Mrs. Hewitt, and she buried her face in her handkerchief.

"Mrs. Hewitt, I think you must be imagining . . ."

She gave a hysterical laugh. "I wish I were, but there's no mistake. I came upon them together, saw with my own eyes—oh, I will spare you the details. Twenty-five years of faithful marriage destroyed by that wanton. I dismissed her instantly. Was she repentant? Not her! She laughed. She said it was always the same.

74

Wives got the fine houses and respect but it was mistresses who got the passion and jewels. I shudder at such depravity. You must turn her off before she works her evil in your household."

Claudia looked calmly at her, not believing a word of her extraordinary outburst. Mrs. Hewitt was not tearful now. Her eyes were glittering in a way Claudia recognized. So, too, had Lady Tallon's eyes glittered when she had been jealous. No doubt Mrs. Hewitt had become aware of her husband's *tendre* for Mellows and had blamed the maid for it. Her intrusion here tonight was ample evidence of her vengeful nature.

"Mellows has only just come into my employ. How could you know of it?" Claudia asked.

"It seems she left some belongings with a housemaid and returned to collect them this morning. She boasted that she had secured a fine position as Lady Belgarrick's dresser. I heard of it only this evening, and came immediately to put a stop to her games."

"She was hired by my husband's man of business. He would demand excellent references."

"If she produced one from me, it is a forgery. I would not put my name to lies."

"I shall look into it." Claudia extended her hand, her overwhelming wish to be rid of the woman. She had told Giles she would be only a few moments, and she had been a great deal longer than that. The irony was that Mrs. Hewitt could have no idea how handsome her husband was or she would realize that a woman as plain as Mellows would never have a hope of enticing him.

Mrs. Hewitt shook her hand. "You will get rid of her?"

"Your information was not entirely correct. She has been hired only on a temporary basis because—because the snow stranded me in London without my maid," Claudia replied evasively.

"Do not be soft with her. She will take advantage. However, that is your concern. My duty is discharged now. Any grief that comes to you will not be upon my head." With these dramatic words, Mrs. Hewitt strode toward the door.

Thankfully, Claudia followed her. Hastings, hovering at the end of the passage, took charge of the woman, and Claudia was able to return to Giles. When she went into the Blue Salon, he had left the card-table and was lounging in an armchair by the fire. He was looking moody again.

Her heart sank, but she had no intention of losing whatever chance remained of re-establishing companionship between them by discussing Mrs. Hewitt and her jealous imaginings, so she said brightly, "I'm sorry I was so long. It was an unnecessary visit on a matter of no importance. I shall not bore you with the details."

There was no response, so she went to the card-table, picked up the deck of cards and let them slip invitingly through her fingers. "Are you still willing to risk being beaten?"

She was never to find out. Another tap on the door heralded the arrival of the tea-tray. Thwarted again, Claudia sat across the hearth to Giles and ordered the tray set on a table beside her. When they were alone, he said, "No milk or sugar for me."

Claudia poured tea straight into his cup, looked at it dubiously, then handed it to him. He smiled at her expression. "It's a taste I acquired in the East, along with a love of highly-spiced food; not that I'll be tasting any until I'm back in India. God, it irks me to be chained to England!"

*Thank you*, Claudia thought, but her voice did not

reveal her chagrin when she replied, "You are chained by circumstance, not by me. Or have you forgotten the terms of our marriage?"

"I forget nothing. Always before, when circumstances were not to my choosing, I was able to alter them. This time I can't. That is what chafes me."

His bitterness was evident and, seeking to soften his mood, she said, "Life hasn't been too kind to either of us lately, has it, Giles?"

"Produce the sons I want promptly and I'll consider my luck has changed." He saw embarrassment stain her cheeks with pink, and added irritably, "I see I am too blunt for you."

"Would you like more tea, Giles?"

"No, I wouldn't like more tea, and don't be so damned polite, Claudia!"

She poured herself another cup, and then met his eyes squarely. "Perhaps you shouldn't have married a lady. I can't help but be offended by your indelicacy and your swearing."

He glared at her, but she did not flinch, and he underwent another of his lightning changes of mood. He leaned toward her, clasped her hand briefly, and said with a gentleness she had not heard in his voice before, "I married you for your virtues and now blame you for them. That's scarcely fair, is it? I'm sorry. You're a good sort—and I'm the monster you called me."

*A good sort.* Not exactly a fulsome compliment, but she treasured it. Fearful of scaring him away by responding too warmly, she said, "I stand by tyrant and despot but you must be forgetting that I conceded earlier that 'monster' might be one epithet too many. It's merely on the reserve list, in case future need should arise."

He laughed, and lounged back in his chair, saying

77

companionably, "Speaking of the future, what is the name of your attorney?"

"Jeremiah Figson, my father's man of business, has been handling my affairs for me. Why do you wish to know?"

"So that Tigwell can consult with him. We married too hastily for the usual settlements to be agreed, and your attorney will want to ensure that your future is provided for should anything happen to me."

On her wedding night, it was all too mercenary for Claudia, and she protested, "There is no need for us to speak of this. I'm sure you will make adequate provision and that Figson's intervention is unnecessary."

"You can be sure of nothing unless it is in writing. You married me for security. You would be stupid to shrink from ascertaining whether you have received it. As things stand, if I should be succeeded by my cousin, you will find history has repeated itself and you are once more dependent on charity. You wouldn't like that, would you?"

"No," she agreed reluctantly.

"Then I shall instruct Tigwell to see your man tomorrow. What's the matter, Claudia? Are you so much of a lady that you find discussing anything as base as money repugnant to you?"

"On my wedding night, yes! It makes me feel very cheap."

This time it was her bluntness that nettled him, and he retorted, "Not cheap, my dear wife. I am not niggardly when I purchase something I want. You will find I have been more than generous."

"It is not the amount that concerns me, it is the fact that you should discuss this with me at all. It isn't seemly!"

"I see. It is not indelicate for a lady to marry for money but it is indelicate for a gentleman to refer to it. What curst hypocrisy!" He stood up and glowered down at her. "Well, you'll get no hypocrisy from me. My reason for marrying you was to breed sons. So off to bed with you, my lady. I'm not a patient man."

Claudia rose from her chair, her face flaming, shocked to the core by his vulgarity. As she passed him, he slapped her familiarly on the buttocks.

It was the final affront. She turned and glared at him, her blue eyes disdainful, her head held proudly.

He put his hands on his hips and laughed mockingly. "That was to remind you, if further reminder be necessary, that though I am a gentleman by birth, I am not by inclination."

"You are not *any* kind of a gentleman!"

"Take care, madam wife," he warned her softly. "You will find it difficult to look down your proud nose at me when we are in bed together."

His words fell like chips of ice on her spine, causing her to shiver involuntarily. But she did not flee. Instead, she stepped toward him. She put her hands behind his head and pulled his face down to hers, her soft body resting briefly against his. Then she kissed him full on the lips.

He was too stunned to respond, but when she released him and stepped back, he said, "What the deuce did you do that for?"

"Because I am not very brave. I would be too frightened to get into bed at all if I thought a monster was coming to me. I had to reassure myself that, somewhere inside you, there is a man."

And then she turned and left him.

## Chapter Seven

Whatever ordeals were behind her, Claudia knew she faced worse. Outwardly she was composed as she entered her bedroom, but beneath the soft folds of her dress her legs were trembling so that it was with difficulty that she walked at all. She wanted nothing more than to sit down, bury her face in her hands and give way to her overwrought emotions.

This solace was denied her. Mellows was awaiting her in a state of agitation so acute that it almost matched Claudia's. "Oh, my lady," she exclaimed, her hands clasped so tightly that her knuckles gleamed white in the candlelight. "Hastings was saying in the servants' hall that your evening was interrupted by a Mrs. Hewitt. I don't know how it could be, but—but was it my former mistress?"

Claudia sank into an armchair by the fire, leaned back and closed her eyes. She was drained. So much had happened that she felt she had lived a year in one day. "Not now, Mellows," she murmured. "I have other things on my mind."

Mellows came close to her and saw the trembling Claudia could no longer control. She took the thick shawl from her own shoulders, wrapped it around her mistress and chafed her hands. "You are as cold as a tomb. What has Mrs. Hewitt been saying to shock you so? I knew she would tell you wicked slanders, I knew it!"

She fetched Claudia's own shawl to drape over her knees and then hurried away. When she returned she had a glass of wine in her hand. "Here, my lady, drink this. It will make you feel more the thing."

Claudia opened her eyes and made an effort to pull herself together. She looked longingly at the wine but waved it away. She would need a clear head to deal with Giles.

"Just a sip," Mellows coaxed. "It will do you no harm."

Claudia resisted a hysterical urge to giggle. Giles had said much the same thing yesterday. Within twenty-four hours he was her husband. A few additional hours was all it had taken for him to reduce her present state. Just because of a sip of wine that would do no harm.

No, she chided herself, the wine was not to blame. It was her own blind passion that had drawn her into his power and, the truth be told, she would rather be trembling here than snug in her spinsterish bed at Tallon Manor.

"Please, my lady," Mellows coaxed, pressing the glass into her hand.

Claudia was touched. It was a long time since anyone had cared enough to fuss over her. She sipped the wine, and after a while her nerves steadied. She sat up, watched the maid put another log on the fire, and said, "I am better now. It's time I prepared for bed."

Mellows poured hot water from a jug into the flower-painted wash-bowl. "It was Mrs. Hewitt who upset you, I know it, and I blame myself for that. I—I shall pack my bags. I have nowhere to go tonight, but I shall leave first thing tomorrow."

Claudia put aside the shawls and stood up so that she could be disrobed. "What makes you think you deserve dismissal?"

"I lied to you. Not as much as Mrs. Hewitt, I'm sure, for she swore she would prevent me ever finding respectable employment again, but enough to make you think I'm untrustworthy."

Claudia realized it would be cruel to keep Mellows on tenterhooks all night, not knowing whether she could be turned off without a chance to defend herself. The matter would have to be discussed now, inconvenient though it was.

There was nothing to be gained from beating about the bush, so as she went to the wash-stand and picked up a bar of sweetly-smelling soap, Claudia said, "Mrs. Hewitt believes you seduced her husband. She said she came upon you in circumstances too delicate to relate."

Mellows gasped. "How could she say such a thing! She is hounding me, as she promised she would. The truth is that Mr. Hewitt waylaid me in a passage. I was trying to fight my way free when Mrs. Hewitt came upon us. Such names she called me! My face burns to think of them. It was Mr. Hewitt who brought me to such a pass, but he would not aid me by telling the truth. Indeed, he condemned me to save himself. He said I'd faulted myself before him until he'd succumbed, as any man would under such temptation. I was dismissed instantly. Without a penny or a family to go to."

There was silence while Claudia rinsed soap from her face and reached for the towel. "And then?" she asked.

"I was dazed. Mrs. Hewitt had always been so kind before. I couldn't believe the creature she became. She said the street was the place for a harlot. I don't know what would have happened to me if I hadn't chanced to meet Mr. Tigwell at the domestic agency."

"Why weren't you honest about this before?"

"Mrs. Hewitt didn't believe me. I feared nobody else would. I still can't credit how she changed. Jealousy does terrible things to a woman. You just don't know."

Claudia did. She had experienced Lady Tallon's jealousy at first hand, and this very afternoon her own jealousy of Lisette had caused her to stoop to prying. She finished washing, and when the maid slipped a nightgown she had been warming by the fire over her head, she asked, "Surely Mr. Tigwell required a reference from Mrs. Hewitt?"

Mellows bowed her head. "I wrote one. I cannot excuse myself. I can only say it seemed better to be a liar and a forger than a woman of the streets, as Mrs. Hewitt predicted. I was desperate, my lady, and a desperate woman does desperate things."

Nothing could have struck a deeper chord of sympathy. Claudia knew well enough what it was to be desperate, and her own slate was not entirely clean. However, she was responsible for the moral welfare of her servants, and if she had believed Mrs. Hewitt's story, she would have dismissed Mellows. She looked into the maid's pale blue eyes blinking anxiously, and though it farcical that she could be branded a temptress.

"Must—Must I go?" Mellows faltered.

"I cannot condone forgery and deceit, but since you were the victim and not the villain of the circumstances that lost you your job, there is some excuse for your behavior. We shall speak no more of it. I shall judge you only by what I observe myself."

Mellows's face quivered. "Oh, *thank* you, my lady! A fresh start is all I ever hoped for."

Claudia nodded. Another time she might have smiled

at her own pomposity, but her mind was already sliding back to her immediate problems. The most imminent was that Giles could walk in on her at any moment, and possibly in the devil's own mood. *I'm not a patient man,* he had said, and she had gone on to provoke him further. Where had she got the nerve? She only prayed it would not fail her when she needed it most.

She looked round anxiously when there was a knock on the door, and relaxed when she saw it was a house-maid with a pan of hot coals to warm the sheets. While this was being done, Claudia sat at the dressing-table to enable Mellows to unpin and brush her hair.

The house was very quiet, then came the sound of a door being carelessly shut, followed by a murmur of voices. Giles had returned to his apartment and was talking to his valet. Soon he would be here to claim his conjugal rights. Mellows apparently thought so, too, because she put down the hairbrush and asked, "Is everything to your satisfaction, my lady?"

Claudia nodded, anxious to be rid of any witnesses to my lord's mood when he joined her. She went over to the bed, waited while the housemaid removed the pan of coals, then slipped between the sheets.

"Shall I extinguish the candles, my lady?" Mellows asked.

"Except for those beside the bed. Do not draw the curtains on that side, either." She wanted to see by Giles's face what sort of humor he was in before he climbed in beside her. "When I ring for you in the morning I will want only hot chocolate. I prefer to get up for breakfast."

Not until the maids had curtsied and withdrawn, did she think, What about Giles? He might like breakfast in bed. It was then that she realized he might not remain all might. He might intend only to act the stud.

For all she knew, his own bed was being warmed at this moment against his early return.

Claudia's eyes kindled with something close to mutiny. She wanted to be desired, to be loved, not merely made pregnant. That was outside the terms of their contract, but the contract made no allowance for feelings, and she appeared to have more than her womanly share. Was it her fault if she found it too degrading to lie submissively while Giles did his damnedest to perpetuate his line?

He might not think so, but she did. Too degrading to be endured, and yet she must endure it. She had promised to be dutiful.

She looked at the plump snowy pillow beside her, which would soon know the indent of Giles's head, always assuming he bothered to make himself comfortable before he mounted her. And then she thought that somewhere, on another pillow, Lisette was lying. No doubt smiling as she imagined Giles performing his duty to his noble house, and anticipating the boredom of it all driving him speedily back to her.

"No!" Claudia exclaimed aloud, flinging back the covers and scrambling out of the great bed. She would rather risk his fury than submit passively to being impregnated. At least there was passion in anger, and if that was all she could wring from him, she would wring every last drop. She would keep the vow she had made earlier. He would not, regardless of what happened, be bored!

Her sudden movement had caused the candles on the chest of drawers beside the bed to flicker wildly. She snatched up the candelabrum and stormed over to the cheval-glass, where she held it aloft to study her reflection.

Her full-sleeved nightgown was tied modestly at her neck, but it was of the finest lawn and her skin glowed

85

through when her movements disturbed the full folds falling from lace insets at the shoulders. Superficially modest, she could make it as seductive as she wished by the way she turned her body. She tried several effects, her expression intent, her aim as ruthless as any harlot's.

Giles might have no heart, but he had a body—and it was all male. She would use her own to make him aware of it! And so she practiced her poses, grimly aware that she appeared to have cast off her modesty with her maiden name. Claudia Tallon had ceased to exist, and Claudia Verylan did not mourn her.

When she was satisfied, she moved to the dressing-table, put down the candles and leaned forward to study her face. There was nothing composed and ladylike about it. Her rebellion had brought a glow to her eyes and complexion so that she looked and felt more vital that she had ever been since . . . Well, it was best not to think about since when.

Her rich dark hair fell in thick lustrous waves to just below her shoulders, and she teased some wisps forward to curl about her forehead and cheeks. When she was down, she studied the effect carefully.

Then she nodded to herself, satisfied. All day, prim in her blue gown and with her hair pinned up, she had looked the wife. Tonight she looked the mistress. Convention prevented her from confronting Lisette face to face, but she could be challenged here by transforming Giles from a husband to a lover.

The task did not seem as impossible as it had earlier. He was not a man of ice. He was a man of fire. He could be ignited. If she, a woman in full bloom and desiring him as she had desired no man since Tom, could not do it, she deserved to lose him to Lisette.

Her reverie was interrupted when his careless manner of shutting doors warned her that he was on his way. She hurriedly put the candelabrum back beside the bed and fled toward the fire, casting a last look at herself in the cheval-glass as she did so.

The fire was burning brightly enough to light this part of the room. She positioned herself before it, knowing full well how its glow would silhouette her curvaceous body. She had no time to still her hasty breathing before Giles came in, clad in a silk dressing-gown and carrying a decanter and two glasses.

He checked when he saw the empty bed, looked long and hard at her, one of his arrogant eyebrows lifting in silent question. At this point, Claudia's bravado deserted her. Everything seemed different now that he was actually in the room with her. His dominating presence was responsible for that. His power seemed to drain hers, so that she no longer felt assured, far less wanton.

He looked again at the bed and, mesmerized, she did so, too. It no longer seemed a trap but a haven where she could hide her near-nakedness. Not for the life of her, however, could she take a step toward it.

Giles put the decanter and glasses on a lowboy and came closer to her. "You are a constant surprise to me, Claudia," he said.

'Am—Am I?" she stammered, because her throat was dry, and nervously she licked her lips.

"Yes." His eyes roamed over her, missing nothing. "I expected you to be under the covers, feigning sleep. It is what any other woman in your position would have done. Why are you so very different?"

'I—I hadn't the courage." It was the first thing that came into her head, and was not entirely a lie.

"Cowardice, you mean. I have yet to observe you take the craven way out of any situation! That might annoy me at times, but I don't dislike you for it."

"Nor like me for it." Now that they were talking,

87

Claudia's spirit was reviving. "That is why I am not in bed. We have quarreled all day, and I feared you would leap upon me without—without sensitivity or understanding."

"Leap? I am not an acrobat."

She blushed fiercely under his mockery. "You know what I mean. I have my pride, and there are certain things I cannot endure."

"I thought I made It perfectly plain yesterday that I meant you to—ah—*endure* as little as possible."

Her receding color was overcome by a new wave, and she said hotly, "Yes, but I cannot summon up a proper businesslike attitude. I am not like you. I am a woman!"

His glance went slowly over her. "That, my dear Claudia, is one issue that is not in doubt."

She had wanted him to look at her, to appreciate her, but now that he was doing so she was, most contrarily, full of indignation. "If you are any kind of a man, you will make some allowance for my feelings!"

"I have made allowance for your preferences." He went over to the decanter and poured dark liquid into the glasses. "Brandy, as you requested when next you needed to be fortified."

"I do not need to be fortified. I need to be reassured!"

"First things first," he commanded, offering her a glass, and sipping his own.

She took it with a scowl. "I suppose, if I drink this, I shall be a *good sort?*"

"Did that rankle? It was not meant to. Drink the brandy, Claudia. It will do you more good than a string of meaningless compliments."

"A great deal you know about women!" she scoffed, drinking the brandy straight down and gasping as it seared her throat.

He looked amused. "You can, at times, be most diverting."

"Are you mocking me?"

"You cannot seriously expect me to believe you have reached the age of six-and-twenty without learning the difference between mockery and praise?"

If he was not harping on his reason for marrying her, he was harping on her age! Her resentment came to the boil, and she snapped, "If you want something to marvel at, only consider what a miracle it is that I can get about without a walking-stick."

He threw back his head and laughed. Claudia's hostility vanished, as it always did when he showed his human side. She found herself smiling back at him and told herself disgustedly she was no better than a pet dog fawning over its master when it received unexpected approval. Even so, she wanted—needed!—the approval to continue.

He took her glass and put it down with his own, which was almost untouched. "Claudia, I forget how many times we have fought each other to a standstill today, but don't you think that now is the time to call a truce?"

She wanted more than a truce, but it was a beginning, and so she nodded.

"Then let us go to bed," he said.

If he had held out his hand, she would have taken it. He didn't, and she found herself incapable of moving toward him on her own. Much as she desired him, she still dreaded the marriage being consummated until she was certain he desired her, too. She was still too much the woman, too little the wife. Difficult, in fact, when she was required merely to be dutiful.

His eyebrows rose. "What do you fear? Rape? A husband cannot rape his wife, you know."

She replied miserably, "I think perhaps he can."

89

"You are unwilling?"

"N-No, it isn't that."

"Then what is it?" He came to her, took her head between his hands and slowly ran a thumb back and forth across her lips. "I told you yesterday that you can do no better than trust yourself to an experienced man."

She longed to kiss the thumb that so tantalized her lips, just as she wished she could tell him what was troubling her, but he would think she was searching for his heart, which he had expressly forbidden her to do. She was beyond prevaricating or lying, so she could only raise troubled eyes to his and say nothing.

"Poor Claudia, you do need reassuring." He bent his head and kissed her lips. "There, your own kiss back again to reassure you that it is a man who comes to you and not a monster."

"Oh!" His gentleness, so unexpected, filled her eyes with tears, and to hide them she leaned her head against his shoulder. She went on in a muffled voice, "You must think me very foolish."

"I think you have too much sensitivity. You must think I have too little." His arms went round her, drawing her closer to him. "We shall both have to make allowances."

She nodded against his shoulder, not risking one word that might mar the magic of this moment. Because magic it was. Their bodies were attuned in a harmony that made a mockery of their opposing aims and temperaments. Only this seemed valid now, the touching of flesh on flesh in mutual need and pleasure.

Claudia closed her eyes in ecstasy, glorying in the strength of his arms about her, the hardness of his muscled body. Gone were her fears and worries, vanquished like so many nebulous wraiths by the reality of their passion.

She melted as his hands moved over her, skillfully seeking a response and then, as his own need grew, demanding one. She felt his lips on her hair, her face, her throat. These were no kisses of gentle reassurance. They were wild, inflamed, and she relished and returned them with abandon.

He was pulling at the ties that secured her nightgown across her bosom, and she moved slightly so that he could reach them more easily. The fine lawn slipped from her shoulders, was caught at her wrists, but she pulled her arms and trampled the gown underfoot as it fluttered to the floor.

His hand clasped and coiled in her hair, jerking her head back so that he could gaze down at her. She did not gasp with pain, scarcely heeding it as she met his gaze with eyes smoldering with equal desire.

"Wife . . . woman . . . witch . . ." he muttered huskily. "The devil take it, which are you, Claudia?"

His lips came down on hers, crushing any answer she might have made; were she capable of answering at all. She wound her arms round his neck and clung to him, blissfully certain that her heart was passing into his safe-keeping and that she was receiving his in return.

With a smothered oath he caught her up in his arms, carried her to the bed and placed her on it with such care that she felt as though she had become very precious to him. He stripped off his dressing-gown, his eyes not leaving her for a moment, then dropped within the circle of her arms as naturally as if this were the hundredth, and not the first time they had come together.

Claudia moaned with something close to anguish as his hands and lips explored her full breasts, her slender waist, her curved stomach and her shapely thighs. Sometimes, when the torment became too great, she seized his hair and pulled him up to her so that she

91

could press ardent kisses on the lips that were giving her so much delight. It was she who was demanding now, and he who was holding back, prolonging his pleasure until she was driven near to madness.

"Giles, for God's sake . . ." she breathed.

He raised himself, and looking at her with a smile that would have crumbled her last defenses had they not already fallen. "Whose sake?"

"Mine!"

"In that case, *madam wife* . . ." He said the hated words so caressingly that she loved them, and then he smiled again, so that she loved him, too. Then he moved over and into her, and she held him against her fiercely, her body moving with his, seeking a climax to the desire raging through her. When it came, she gasped and fell back, and when he fell panting upon her she clasped him as tightly as ever, doubting if she could ever let him go.

She was sated, and so supremely happy that tears seeped from her eyes and trickled slowly down her cheeks. She was his, and he was hers. The miracle had happened. Her harsh husband had become her caring lover. Against all the odds, she had triumphed. Relaxing, she sank blissfully into the euphoria that followed a perfect union. She felt as if the gods had at last relented, and once more permitted her to frolic with them. If that were so, their benevolence was short-lived.

She fell from heaven into her own private hell when Giles thrust himself from her and said with loathing, "An unquestionable lady? I have been cheated. Good God, madam wife, you are nothing but a strumpet!"

## Chapter Eight

His words smote Claudia like a series of blows, hurting her more cruelly than if he had struck her with his fists. The filthy name he had called her, the contempt in his *madam wife*—how could this be when they had just shared such supreme joy? She shrank from him in shock and bewilderment, scarcely crediting her ears, and thinking him deranged. In his fury he certainly looked it, and what sane man could turn from a lover to a raging demon within the twinkling of an eye?

Dear God, had she truly married a monster?

She could think of no other explanation, except—yes, maybe there was one way in which she could have given him a disgust of her. She was his wife, and wives, perhaps, were expected to behave differently from mistresses. Moistening lips parched by shock and fear, she said, "If . . . If my abandon displeased you, then I am sorry, but it was you who aroused me to such passion. Why did you do so if you were then to hold me solely to blame?"

"You were certainly not solely to blame for the loss of your virginity." He threw back the covers and flung himself out of bed as though the proximity and sight of her were not to be borne. He picked up his dressing-gown, shrugged himself into it, and then his hard eyes raked her cowering form. "I did not take it. Who did?"

The color drained from Claudia's face and her eyes dilated with horror. Oh, God, he *knew!* It was nine years since she had lain with Tom, so long ago that it might have been another lifetime. Certainly it seemed so to her. She had had no mother to confide in, no friend close enough to consult, and in her ignorance she had imagined any damage done then would be healed by now. But it couldn't be so, because he knew. He was not deranged. He was a deceived husband, and his fury was not as unreasonable as she had at first supposed.

Yet he had come to care for her. In a moment he would calm down and give her the chance to explain, as she would him, if anything occurred to threaten their new-found happiness. "Giles . . ." she said softly, reaching out to clasp his arm so that her touch would rekindle the feeling they had shared, which would surely plead her cause more eloquently than any words.

He threw off her arm, and thundered, "Don't *Giles* me, madam! My title will serve when you wish to address me. My given name is for my friends, and I've yet to call friend anybody who has deceived me."

"I have not deceived you. At least, not—not intentionally."

"Nothing was ever more intentional," he contradicted her angrily. "Our acquaintance has been brief, but you never deviated from the role of modest paragon. How magnificently you have played the lady, how swift to reprove me whenever I was less than the gentleman. My compliments, madam. You are a consummate actress. You actually had me believing you—I, who have long since stopped believing in any woman. God, what a mortification! That I, who of all men should have known better, could be so duped. You actually had me feeling guilty and wondering how I could make myself more acceptable to you. What a rich jest! All the time it was you, madam wife, who was the unacceptable partner."

His contemptuous eyes seared her as much as his words, making her blushingly aware of her naked state. There was no glory in it now. She felt ashamed and defenseless, and reached down to pull the covers over her.

He seized them and flung them back. "It's too late to play the modest maiden now. You forgot your clever act at the most critical time."

She curled herself into a ball, trying to hide her more vulnerable parts from him, and protested, "It isn't as you think."

"It is as I *know*. When I came here tonight, I thought you too innocent to realize that, with the fire behind you, I could see straight through that gown of yours. The rose-tipped breasts . . . the long white thighs . . . the so-intriguing shadows. More than enough to beguile the most reluctant of husbands. But how artfully you trembled, persuading me you were the most unsuspecting of temptresses. Hell, I should have thrown you on the bed at once and been done with it!"

"Why didn't you?" she was goaded to retort. "You are being enough of a beast now. What stopped you from being a beast then?"

He laughed in humorless self-mockery. "My own idiocy. I actually believed what I saw, a shrinking maiden desperate for—for reassurance, was it not? It seemed criminal to take what should be coaxed. I thought no man ever had a more apt pupil, until I realized at the last that you had had enough experience for both of us!"

Claudia's head shook from side to side on the pillow in denial. "That isn't true!"

"Isn't it?" He bent down, flipped her on her back and covered her breasts with his hands, massaging them with a deliberation that revolted her. "You see," he went on, "your body needs no tuition. It expects—demands!—satisfaction."

It was true that her nipples had hardened instantly to his touch, but this was no caress, it was a cynical manipulation that made her feel defiled. "Don't," she pleaded, trying to cringe from his all-knowing hands. "Please don't."

"Then stop playing the innocent. It is insult on injury. What is a man to think when he marries a woman who can give him no proof of her virginity and behaves, moreover, like a Covent Garden whore? Well, madam? You are usually swift to defend yourself. Why so silent now?"

He released her. Claudia clasped her arms over her aroused breasts in shame, and begged, "Please . . . let me cover myself."

"Strewth, if you knew how your coyness sickens me, you wouldn't affect it, but—" he tossed the covers over her "—it gives me no pleasure to look on a woman who has deceived me. God knows, women—even beauties—are two a penny to men who can afford them, but I thought I had something additional in you. You led me to believe you possessed honesty and integrity, twin virtues and I thought alien to the female of the species. Well, more fool me! It didn't take me long to discover you are as deceitful as the rest of your sisterhood."

Claudia's senses swam under his invective, but she insisted, "I have not deceived you."

He seized her hair and twisted it cruelly so that her face was forced up to his. "I contracted for an unquestionable lady and now find myself tied to a highly questionable one. Do you not call that deceit?"

"You never stipulated that I had to be a virgin."

"Dammit, that went without saying! What could a respectable spinster be but a virgin? Only a widow would have no cause for shame in your used state."

*Used state!* Claudia flinched. How carefully he was choosing his words to pile humiliation upon humiliation on her. Her spirit, shattered by the unexpectedness and ferocity of his attack, began to revive, and she said bitterly, "What right have you to demand purity when your name is synonymous with depravity?"

"It was honesty I demanded. I was at pains to ensure that you were neither duped nor deceived. Yet, when I asked you yesterday if there was anything else I should know about you, you said no. Did you think the possibility that you are already carrying another man's seed within you was of no significance to me?"

He threw her from him in a fresh spasm of rage and she fell back against the pillow, stunned that he could believe such a thing of her. She tried to find words of denial, but they would not come. It was all too incredible. What kind of women had he known if he could think her so despicable?

He paced up and down beside the bed as though his anger would not permit him to be still, then went on harshly, "It all makes sense now, that which I could hardly comprehend before. A beautiful woman, well-bred, well-connected, willing to wed a man such as I, and without even a lawyer to haggle first for her full worth. It had to be too good to be true, of course, although your story of Lady Tallon's ill-treatment seemed feasible enough. Now I can see a likelier reason for your desperation. You were in urgent need for a man's name—any man's!—because you are already pregnant."

"No!" Claudia whispered, aghast. "All I told you is the truth!"

"Spare your breath, madam. You will never find me

97

so gullible again. If every word you have uttered is the truth, then the untruths must lie in what you haven't told me. The best you can hope for is that you have not conceived this night. I will not acknowledge as a Verylan a child who could be anybody's."

His callousness, his readiness to believe the worst his warped mind could imagine about her, brought Claudia out of her disbelieving daze. She sat up, clutched the covers about her bosom, tossed back her tousled hair from her face, and told him furiously, "Do that, and you will deny your own child. It is nine years since I have lain with a man, and that man was Thomas, my fiancé."

"An alley-cat like you," he scoffed. "Spin me no fairy-tales! Once awakened, you would not slumber on for nine years. You forget, madam, that I have a lifetime's experience of such women."

"It is not a fairy-tale! Tom and I did not come together to seek sensation, which is the way you approach love-making because you know no other. With us, it was different. He was leaving the next day for the campaign in the Peninsula. We needed to—to *belong*, before we were parted for heaven knew how long. And—And that's the way it was, a giving and receiving of love."

Her voice faltered. She swallowed, raised her head proudly and met his scornful look with eyes bright with cherished memories. Then she said slowly and distinctly, "I have never regretted it. Nothing you can do or say will make me regret it now. I am glad it happened. Do you hear me, Belgarrick? Glad! I was only seventeen, but I learned what pure happiness is, and that is something you will never know because you are a stranger to love."

He folded his arms and stood looking down at her, his expression unreadable. When he spoke, she knew she had made no impression on him because he ridiculed, "Very pretty, but one coupling does not make a woman as experienced as you are."

She clenched her teeth with exasperation, and said through them, "I am not experienced. To say so is to deny your own skill. It was *that* I responded to, and now you hold me depraved because of it. I am not a strumpet, but if there were a male equivalent of the word, you would merit it a thousand times over. If anything is sickening here, it is your hypocrisy!"

"Then hypocrisy must breed hypocrisy. I concealed nothing when we arranged this marriage; the concealment was all on your side." He laughed suddenly, but without mirth. "I noticed you had removed your beloved Thomas's betrothal ring. I thought you were being tactful, but you had good reason, did you not, for removing anything from your person that would remind me of other men? What a crafty little jade you are!"

Her control snapped so suddenly that she surprised them both by lashing out at him, catching his face with a stinging slap. As she brought her hand back to slap his other cheek, he grabbed her wrist and dragged her to the edge of the bed. He used his other hand to catch hold of her hair and twist it so that her face was forced up to the candlelight. He seemed to her like some avenging demon as he stared into her eyes and commanded, "Now, madam, unless you have a taste for further violence, swear you did not marry me to give a name to another man's child."

Claudia's face contorted in pain from his rough handling, and she said, "I swear."

Even that did not appease him. He threw her from him as though her touch was loathsome. "I waste my time. No woman's vow is worth the breath it is uttered with. I've never yet known one who wouldn't swear the devil out of hell to gain a mean advantage."

"Giles . . ." she began.

"Belgarrick! There can never be any friendship between us now. I shall never forgive your duplicity."

"You don't know the truth when you hear it, because you don't want to know! Your mind is warped, your thinking twisted. Hatred and distrust are more natural to you than love and trust. You can call me filthy names and bully me and I can't stop you, but, of the two of us, it is you I pity, Belgarrick. *You!*"

He was a dangerous man at any time, but in this mood his rage flared to a red heat. He seized her shoulders, pulled her into a sitting position and shook her mercilessly. "Save your pity for yourself, madam. You do not yet know how much you will need it!"

The shaking stopped, and his hands went from her shoulders to her throat. Claudia thought her last moments had come, but she was so angry herself that she would not give him the satisfaction of screaming or pleading. She closed her eyes and waited. For death or sanity to return to him. In her wretchedness she did not care which.

But his hands did not squeeze her throat. He used them to hold her captive, while he ordered, "Look at me, madam."

She looked at him, her eyes dull with indifference. If there was any emotion she had not experienced this night, she did not know about it, nor did she wish to.

She heard him say, his words ringing like a death-toll over all her dearest hopes, "I shall not touch you again until you can give me proof that you are not pregnant. If you are, there can be no certainty that the child is mine, and I shall divorce you. I don't care how many years it takes, but I shall start again with an honest woman who can give me a true heir. If you are *not* pregnant, then we shall begin again to produce the children this marriage was made for. You shall have your quarterly allowance, but no widow's portion if I should pre-decease you; what children we have will be governed by trustees other than yourself. You, madam wife, will be left as I found you—without a penny. It is a pity you did not heed me yesterday when I told you I was a bad man to deceive. Now you know that, of the two of us, I was the one who spoke truly."

He took his hands away from her throat and stood up. She did not move. The covers had fallen to her waist, but she made no attempt to cover her bare breasts. When she finally raised her head and looked at him, her rich hair fell down her back and the candlelight revealed the marks on her throat, shoulders and arms from his harsh treatment.

In such dire straits, the dignity which was so much a part of her came to her aid. She held her head at a proud angle and, curiously, had never looked more the lady as she told him, "I do not believe that anything I might have said or done yesterday, or today, would have made any difference. The *real* truth here is that you were always determined to hate me. Now that you have found cause, be satisfied and rejoice elsewhere. It is an oddity of mine that, when I cry, I prefer to cry alone."

She turned her back on him, lay down and covered herself. She sensed him standing there, staring at her, and thought he was not satisfied at all and meant to torment her further. She could not stop herself from shuddering with sobs waiting to consume her, but she made no sound.

After what seemed an eternity, she heard him go away, and then came the click of the dressing-room door closing. She could let go at last. The tears, when they came, were prolonged and painful.

101

## Chapter Nine

Either Mellows expected a bride to rise from the nuptial couch very much the worse for wear or she was the soul of tact, for she kept up a flow of innocuous everyday chatter that covered her mistress's subdued state, and made no mention of the bruises on her tender flesh.

Claudia was grateful, feeling unequal to questioning or solicitude as she bathed and dressed. After a night of tossing and turning and broken patches of sleep, exhaustion had finally forced her to accept that what had happened between herself and Giles was unalterable. It was pointless wearing herself out wishing that this or that had happened, or not happened, because there was no changing a single ecstatic or anguished moment of it.

There was another fact, just as unpalatable, that she had had to force herself to accept. Giles loathed her—and she loved him. What manner of love it was she did not know, only that it existed. He could never have hurt her so much otherwise.

The bruises on her skin would soon heal. The bruises on her heart would last a lifetime. Like a wounded animal she must hide them, the better to survive. If Giles suspected her vulnerability he would pounce, as he had last night, and destroy her with his mockery and contempt.

As Mellows coiled her hair and pinned it to the top of her head, Claudia felt as if she had gone to bed young and hopeful and arisen old and defeated. She had found the sublime lover she desired, and watched him turn into an implacable enemy. How curious she should desire him still, when she should be every bit as disgusted with him as he was with her. It seemed that she had lived for twenty-six years without learning anymore about her true self than she knew about Giles's! Was it possible that she had known more about love at seventeen than she did now and, in losing Tom, had lost her way? She found the thought as chilling as Giles's eyes when last she had looked into them, but she had wallowed in despair long enough for a reaction to set in. It was as she had told him. She had never felt guilty over the consummation of her love for Tom, and she did not feel so now.

She would *not* hide herself away in her bedroom as though she had some terrible sin to expiate. She would treat this, the first day of her married life, as no different from any other. If Giles wished to avoid her, he could put himself out to do so. As for herself, she would go down to breakfast as she always did.

Her defiance was not as brave as it seemed, for she was relying on the presence of servants to act as a restraint on him. When she entered the breakfast parlor, her back was straight, her head high, and if she would have adopted the same stance to mount the steps of a scaffold, then only she knew about it.

Giles was sitting at the head of the table, eating his way through a steak that almost filled his plate, a newspaper propped up against a jug of ale before him. Claudia greeted him civilly, and received just as civil an answer. She was relieved. So he meant to keep up appearances before the servants, no doubt mindful of what she had told him yesterday.

Then she saw with dismay that Hastings, who was fussing over the chafing-dishes on the sideboard, had set her place next to my lord's. Giles, of course, would not have been able to order her removal to the bottom of the table for this informal meal without giving rise to the sort of speculation they were both anxious to avoid. She would have to sit close to him, the last thing she wanted. Already she was having to struggle to maintain her hard-won composure. Just looking at Giles made her vulnerable again. Nothing he said or did appeared to lessen the fatal magnetism he had for her.

She became aware that Hastings was beaming at her and she bade him good morning, grateful for his ignorance that anything was amiss, then thanked him when he said he would fetch her hot chocolate directly. His departure meant she was alone with Giles, and she moved to the sideboard and removed the lid from the nearest chafing-dish. Soused herrings. She put the lid back hurriedly.

Her outward calm must have been achieved at the cost of inner turmoil, since the sight of food caused her stomach to churn uncomfortably. She should eat. She had scarcely touched her dinner last night, yet the deviled kidneys in the next dish failed to tempt her and she did not investigate any more. She took her place at the table and helped herself to a slice of bread and butter.

Hastings returned, put a silver pot of hot chocolate beside her cup and regarded the bread and butter on her plate with disapproval. "Shall I order something special from the kitchen?" he asked. "An omelette, perhaps?"

"No thank you, Hastings. I am not hungry this morning. Doubtless I shall make up for it at luncheon."

He bowed and left them, but Giles did not remove his attention from his newspaper. So . . . she was to be ignored. She tried to tell herself it was better than being shouted at, although it did not seem so. Even at Tallon Manor, under Lady Tallon's resentful eyes, she had not felt quite so unwanted.

Claudia stretched her arm for a dish of blackberry preserves and, in doing so, brushed Giles's newspaper. He glared, and she apologized, "I'm sorry. That dish is beyond my reach." Then she realized he was staring at the bruises on her wrist. The ruffles on her sleeve had fallen back, exposing them.

His hard eyes met hers, his expression unfathomable. Faint color tinged her cheeks. He had caused the bruising but hers was the embarrassment. She did not know why. Hastily she shook the ruffles forward, and murmured her thanks when he passed the dish of preserves to her. Shortly afterward he left the table and the room.

Claudia gave up all pretense of eating and stared numbly into space. She found his wrath easier to endure than his silent hostility, and yet, now that he had gone, she felt strangely bereft. Exasperated, she read the newspaper he had left behind and found within it the formal announcement of their marriage. She could imagine with what incredulity it would be read by her friends. Claudia Tallon, confirmed spinster, wed to Giles Verylan, confirmed rake. They would be even more incredulous if they knew the marriage was already tottering, not because of his past but because of hers.

Her chocolate was cold, her appetite non-existent, and if she did not take care, she would be sinking into self-pity. A shopping expedition was definitely called for. Half an hour later she was on her way to Bond Street. It was snowing lightly, but the fierce wind had dropped, and she had chosen to walk because she felt the exercise would do her good.

It was a year since Claudia had last replenished her wardrobe. Those clothes had never been worn, because her father had died before the London Season started and she had gone into mourning. It was only recently that she had begun to wear colors again, albeit dark ones, so that when her belongings were delivered to Belgarrick Towers she would find herself in possession of what amounted to a perfectly good trousseau. Today she needed to purchase only a few gowns to tide her over . . . and cheer herself up.

For years she had been a discerning and free-spending customer and, as such, was valued by the fashionable modistes of Bond Street and its environs. Today, however, she was treated with extra deference. They had read the announcement of her marriage. In their eyes, Giles's scandalous past was outweighed by more important factors. He was a viscount and a nabob—as a gentleman who made his fortune in India was called—and the twin appeal of title and fabulous wealth ensured Claudia fawning attention.

She might also have received sympathy if she had tried on the gowns she liked, but, mindful of her bruises, she ordered some half-dozen to be sent to Belgarrick House so that she could make a selection at her leisure. Nightgowns, pantalettes, silk stockings and a fringed shawl completed her shopping. She visited Hookham's library to select some books, and by the time she and Mellows returned to Grosvenor Square her purchases had been delivered.

For luncheon, she wore an elegant york wrapper, a high-necked dress of jaconet muslin buttoned at the back and decorated at the front with diamond-shaped panels of lace and needlework. Her hair was loosely

106

tied into a knot at the back of her head, from which it fell freely in thick ringlets.

She had the confidence of knowing she did not look at all like a bride who had been roughly used by her bridegroom, but if he noticed her improved appearance, he made no mention of it. He did, however, carve some slices of beef and ham for her plate before returning his attention to the paper he was reading.

Claudia saw that it was *Lloyd's List,* and inquired, "Do you have an interest in shipping?"

"Yes, madam," he replied unencouragingly.

"In the cargoes or the ships themselves?"

"Both."

She ignored his obvious efforts to snub her and continued, "You do not take an active interest, do you?"

"Until I returned to England, extremely active. Now, for the most part, I employ agents. What is the matter, madam? Distressed to find your husband is tainted with trade?"

"On the contrary; in these depressed times it is a comfort when one's income doesn't depend entirely on agriculture."

His eyes settled on her, frankly sceptical. "Don't try to grovel your way into my good graces. It won't work. I am aware that the root of your antagonism with Lady Tallon was because she was of merchant class."

"The antagonism was hers. She *chose* to feel inferior. Frankly, I was in such dread that the manor would go under the hammer that I would have welcomed money from any source. So, too, would you, had you ever been pinched for a penny."

"*Pinched for a penny?* There have been times in my life when I've had nothing but the clothes I stood up in!"

"Were you happier then?" She saw his astonishment,

107

and explained, "You are rich now, and as cross as crabs. I thought perhaps, when you were poorer . . . ?"

"Were you happy when you were poor?"

"No."

"Then don't ask stupid questions." He turned over the list of shipping and began to read the financial and commercial information on the other side.

Claudia calmly added some pickle to her plate and began to eat. She had succeeded, at the cost of having her head snapped off, in getting him to utter more than monosyllables to her, and that was no mean achievement. To submit tamely to being ignored was not only craven, it was tantamount to admitting she had something to feel guilty about. If she continued to force herself upon his notice, he might come to wonder whether he had been wrong in his judgment of her. It was a slim chance, but, all in all, she would rather endure his active wrath than his soul-destroying silence.

Claudia, her strategy decided upon, carried it out with a determined cheerfulness which proved to Giles, if nothing else, that she was a difficult woman to crush. They rarely met except at meal-times, and whenever the servants were out of the way, they invariably clashed. She was the goad and he the rogue bull, ever ready to charge.

She did not permit the hours between their encounters to lie heavily on her hands, dreading idleness because it encouraged her to dwell on how miserable she really was. Instead, she inspected the house from top to bottom, finding everything in excellent order. The stocks of linen, china and cutlery were plentiful and of the finest quality. Few things in the house were old, and she came to the conclusion that her predecessor must have been obsessed with keeping abreast of the latest fashions in all things.

Mrs. Binns, the housekeeper, confirmed that this was so, ut warned Claudia she would find a very different story at Belgarrick Towers. The town house had been kept in tip-top condition at the expense of the country residences. The former Lord and Lady Belgarrick had been no lovers of rural life, preferring to divide their time between London and the fashionable resort of Brighton. They had taken up yachting simply because it was the fashionable thing to do, and it had cost them their lives.

The housekeeper ran on in this vein for some time, ending with the anxious hope that she would not be held to blame for the many shortcomings Claudia would find at Belgarrick Towers. There was a limit to what the most diligent servants could achieve when no expenditure would be authorized, particularly when a house was ancient and in desperate need of renovation.

Claudia made haste to reassure her, although privately she was dismayed. She already had a brooding, despotic husband with a reputation for ruthlessness she could not help but believe was deserved. If she was also to find herself living in a crumbling ruin, she would be hard put not to believe she had strayed out of reality and into the realms of fiction—of the more lurid Gothic kind that was so popular among ladies of the *ton* at the moment. Then her sense of humor reasserted itself, and she asked, "Does it have a ghost?"

"Certainly not, my lady," Mrs. Binns replied forcefully. "It might be in need of repair, but it's a respectable house."

"A respectable ghost, then?"

"If a ghost were respectable, it wouldn't wander about frightening the wits out of honest folk!" the housekeeper exclaimed, then she saw the quizzical gleam in Claudia's eyes, and laughed. "Shame on you, my lady. You're teasing, and here was I thinking someone must have said something about Belgarrick Towers to give you a dislike of the place."

"You're fond of it yourself?"

"It's my home," Mrs. Binns replied simply. "I grew up there, as did most of the rest of the staff. We all hope it will become the principal residence again."

"That is what his lordship intends," Claudia assured her.

Mrs. Binns was so pleased that she entered fully into Claudia's plan to reduce the clutter of furniture in the town house that so annoyed Giles. The breakfast parlor was tackled first, then the superfluous side-tables, low-boys and cabinets from the reception and sitting-rooms were carried up to the attics. The result might not have been strictly fashionable, but Giles was able to stride about less like a caged tiger and, as the housekeeper pointed out practically, the housemaids' daily cleaning was made a great deal easier.

Claudia visited the more fashionable warehouses to select wallpapers, carpets and curtains for the refurbishing of her own rooms and arranged for the work to be done while they were in Kent. January was not a popular month for residing in London but the few acquaintances of Claudia who were in town visited her, avid for the facts that lay behind the announcement of her wedding in the newspapers.

She kept to the story she had invented for her duty letter to Lady Tallon and managed to convey the impression that she was very well pleased with her marriage. When Giles was at home, he played his part civilly and correctly, so that even those who were sceptical about his reformation had to concede that he was trying.

All in all, their enforced stay in town was not such a trial as it might have been, and Claudia, looking ahead a few weeks to Tansy's introduction to Society, thought it might actually prove a benefit. The ice had been broken and Giles's necessary re-establishment had begun. He was titled, rich, handsome and assured, but, as far as the high sticklers of the *ton* were concerned, none of these considerable assets was sufficient to weigh the scales against his reputation.

No, it was the fact that he had married Claudia that made them pause and reconsider. She was respected and well liked. He could not be cut without also cutting her. Nobody was prepared to do that, not without waiting to see how the marriage turned out.

The weather turned milder, the icy roads thawed and the servants prepared once more for the journey into Kent. On the day before they left, when the greater part of the house was shrouded with dust-covers, Hector Tigwell called to see Claudia. She had him shown up to her private sitting-room. She guessed why he had come, and once he was seated and each had inquired courteously about the other's health, embarrassment caused them both to fall silent.

He was wondering what on earth could have happened to make Lord Belgarrick cancel immediately after the marriage the handsome sum he had settled on his bride in the event of his death; Claudia was wondering how best to gloss over the shameful facts.

In the end it was she who took the bull by the horns by asking, "You have come to discuss financial matters?" When he nodded, she went on, "Have you seen my man of business?"

"No. I did mean to, but . . ."

"You are worried by the alteration Lord Belgarrick has made in his provision for me, and think it best we should talk first?"

"Yes," he agreed worriedly. "I helped to bring this marriage about and I know full well that you entered into it for security. Your future was secure, too, and

111

when his lordship came to me the day after the wedding and cut you out of his will, you could have knocked me down with a feather. I tried to reason with him, but to no avail, nor could I discover what had come over him."

"That's explained simply enough." Claudia spoke lightly, as though the matter were more of amusement than concern. "He lost his temper with me, and his pride is such that, once he makes a stand, he finds it difficult to climb down. He is also fair, however, and will put things right as soon as his pride permits. Pray do not concern yourself."

"If you are sure . . ." he said doubtfully.

Claudia adopted an air of candor and leaned confidingly toward him. "Mr. Tigwell, you must understand that both his lordship and I are—how shall I put it?— *positive* people, and also rather set in our ways. It is inevitable that we should clash sometimes. We both need to adjust, and we shall do so because it is in our interest to make this marriage work. I thank you for your concern but, as I said, given time, I'm sure he will do the right thing."

Privately she thought: He very nearly murdered me and doubtless, at the time, he thought that that was the right thing . . .

Her public face so convincingly concealed her personal misgivings that Mr. Tigwell was reassured, although he had one last worry that he was not slow to voice. "What *will* I say to your lawyer?"

"Nothing at all. Do not contact him."

"Will he not contact me?"

"Not unless I tell him to. He was, after all, my father's lawyer, and the only dealings I had with him were when my father died. I do not wish for unnecessary fuss. Nobody can prevail upon my husband to

112

change his mind until he is ready to do so, and opposition now will only make him more stubborn."

Mr. Tigwell, much struck by her wisdom, thankfully left the thorny subject and tackled the more agreeable one of her quarterly allowance. This was so generous that Claudia was struck speechless, until she recollected that she was the wife of a very rich man and that Society would expect her to act and spend accordingly. It would reflect badly on Giles if she did otherwise, and it must be for this reason that he had not canceled or reduced it.

When the business was concluded and Claudia was pouring the lawyer a glass of excellent sherry, pale and dry, she said, "By the way, Mellows is proving to be an excellent maid. Efficient, industrious and with that rare talent of knowing when I wish to chatter and when I wish to be silent. You made an excellent choice, and it made me wonder whether you could also find me an Indian cook."

Mr. Tigwell choked on his sherry. "A *what*, my lady?"

"An Indian cook."

"You would employ a *heathen* in your household?"

"I would employ the devil himself if I thought he could sweeten my lord's mood upon occasion," Claudia told him frankly.

Mr. Tigwell could not believe her to be serious and laughed jovially. "Oh, very good, but you must not tease me, Lady Belgarrick."

"I assure you I am in earnest. His lordship has spent half his life in the East. He has become impatient of English customs and English tastes. I have watched him closely, and I believe he is not so much readjusting to old ways as reacting to *alien* ways, and reacting unfavorably."

Mr. Tigwell looked so uncomprehending that Claudia went on bluntly, "He feels restricted. Caged, if you like. I have thrown out a lot of furniture so that he has more space, and . . ."

"Th—Thrown out furniture! But everything in this house is of the finest. No expense has ever been spared."

". . . and now something must be done about his lordship's food," she continued inexorably. "I have spoken to Émile, and he refuses to co-operate."

"He is French. You cannot expect him to cook heathen food!"

"So he informs me. Therefore an under-cook must be hired. I shall require him to produce one Indian dish for each course at dinner that his lordship can actually enjoy, as opposed to tolerate because he must eat."

"Émile will walk out rather than permit a foreigner to meddle in his domain."

"He is foreigner himself."

"He is French, and a *cook*," Mr. Tigwell replied, much shocked. "That makes a vast difference."

"So he appears to think. I have acquainted myself with his circumstances and learned that he has had a comfortable and lucrative position in this household since the previous Lord Belgarrick brought him back from Paris during the Peace of Amiens in 1802. For the past two years he has not had to exert himself at all. If he continues to refuse to exert himself now, he must go. I will not have a cook, French or otherwise, dictate what his master should or should not eat."

The note of steel that entered Claudia's voice impressed Hector Tigwell as much as the force of her argument. Here was no hesitant bride afraid of taking on an entrenched household, set in established ways, but a wife determined that her husband's comfort should be put above all things. Which was only as it should be, now that he came to consider it, and his opposition to her scheme died forthwith.

"You put forward a convincing case, my lady, and I shall do my best for you. It will not be easy. An Indian cook is unlikely to be on the books of the regular domestic agencies, and where I must look for one I cannot, for the moment, think."

"Try Whitechapel. That is the dock area, is it not, and the place where foreigners are most likely to congregate?"

"Nobody in that area would be fit for your consideration. I am sure they would have no references!"

"Then we must dispense with references." She saw the fresh dismay that flooded over Mr. Tigwell's plump features, and smiled. "Have no fear, my dear sir. This is such a large household that I doubt very much if one foreigner could succeed in murdering us all in our beds. Or carry off the family silver, for that matter! There is far too much of it."

It was this tendency toward levity, Mr. Tigwell thought, that must have brought about the clash between his client and his bride and, if this were so, more disciplining was clearly necessary before his lordship could safely relent. For his own part, he could do no more than bow over Lady Belgarrick's hand, promise he would do his best to carry out her unusual commission, and take himself off thinking that perhaps he had been pitying the wrong partner in this unconventional marriage.

As for Claudia, she could only wish the bland assurances she had given Hector Tigwell that Giles would soon relent were true, but there was no sign of it. The following day, when they set out for Belgarrick Towers, she had the comfort of a warm rug over her knees and a hot brick at her feet. From her husband she had no comfort at all.

He chose once more to sit opposite her so that there could be no possible physical contact between them. There were no servants within earshot to be considered. He dealt with her attempts at conversation by telling her to spare him the boredom of having to listen to social inanities.

Unlike the weather, his lordship had not thawed. It seemed to Claudia, wistfully regarding his handsome face, that he was more encased in ice than ever. A shaft of that ice pierced her heart every time he scowled at her, adding a sharp spasm of anguish to the dull ache of unhappiness that had become her lot.

She would have given anything for one of his sudden smiles, but she had only the memory of them to sustain her. And memory was not enough.

## Chapter Ten

Within a few hours Claudia was to fall in love again, this time with a pile of gray Kentish stone that had been the country seat of the Verylans since the reign of the last Plantagenet. The house had endured in its present form since early Tudor times, and the Verylan responsible for extending the original castellated building had clearly been uncertain whether he wanted a fortress or a residence. The resulting compromise, however, was a happy one and by fortunate chance succeeding Verylans had been content—or uninterested enough—to let it mellow in unadulterated splendor.

The towers that gave it its name guarded the arched entrance to the arcaded courtyard round which the house was built, and there was a further tower at each corner of the quadrangular building. The whole was set in a huge park, well wooded with oak and elm and beech, and the damming of a stream some generations previously had provided an ornamental lake which looked entirely natural.

The weathered stone of the house, its air of permanence and security, reminded Claudia so much of Tallon Manor that she truly felt as though she were coming home. "It's perfect," she breathed.

But Giles's eyes as he gazed at his childhood home were nothing so much as brooding, and he said cynically, "The prodigal returns. Fortunately with enough money to provide the fatted calf for himself. Gervase was a rack-renter, extracting what he could from his estates to support his gambling and other dissipations. He had no head for cards, or anything else, for that matter. George was hardly better. He was all but ruined when Waterloo put an end to his problems. It's cost me a tidy sum to square his accounts. Gervase would not have helped him. His sympathy never extended beyond his own immediate needs."

"You should not speak so harshly of your brothers. They are dead."

"It is hard to do otherwise when I am left to unravel the muddle they left behind them."

"It is still better than being dead."

"The point, madam, is that there should be no muddle. Gervase inherited everything in good order from my father, and George inherited my mother's fortune."

"You are not exactly a plaster saint yourself."

"Nor am I in the company of one," he snapped back.

It was as well, perhaps, that the carriage sweeping through the archway and drawing up in the courtyard ended the conversation. Their arrival must have been watched for, because a pair of massive oak doors were thrown open immediately. Most of the servants had traveled down the day before and Hastings was there to greet them.

Claudia found herself in a paneled vestibule with a great oak staircase facing her, several doors on the left and a magnificently carved screen on the right. Hastings was bowing them through an opening in the screen and into the original medieval great hall with its lofty hammer-beamed roof and minstrels' gallery.

The family coat of arms was carved in stone above

118

the massive fireplace. An ox could have been roasted there, and probably often had been, and what seemed like half a tree-trunk burned there now. The heat was so fierce that the armchairs grouped about the fireplace had been pulled back for comfort.

Hastings ushered her to one of them, saying, "I have prepared some mulled wine to warm you after your journey, my lady. My lord, would you care for a glass also?"

"Thank you, Hastings." Giles sat down, and when Hastings had given them their glasses, he left them.

Claudia looked about her, feeling very much at home. As at Tallon Manor, to step into Belgarrick Towers was to step back into the fourteenth century, albeit on a grander scale. It was only when she looked more closely that she saw the differences. Her father had spared no expense in maintaining the manor in excellent condition, but here the energetic efforts of the servants had been unable to hide years of neglect.

The oak tables, chairs and chests gleamed with polish, the suits of armour and ancient weaponry were burnished like new, but the tapestries on the walls were so dirty that it was difficult to detect their designs. Claudia rather thought they were hunting scenes, although it was impossible to be sure. And it was so long since the white paint on the stone walls had been renewed that it was yellowed and flaking. There was, as Mrs. Binns had warned, much to be done.

Claudia, sipping her wine and mentally putting the hall to rights, was suddenly conscious of a dull ache in her head and a nagging pain in her back. She must have been more on edge than she knew during those long hours in the carriage with Giles. Normally she was a good traveler. She loathed feeling unwell or lethargic, and to buck herself up she once more attempted to make polite conversation.

Giles was sprawled in his armchair, his booted feet stretched toward the fire, and he looked sufficiently at ease to encourage her to ask him, "Is it good to be home?"

He looked at her, his eyes as cold as his voice as he replied, "It might have been, if you were all you were supposed to be."

She flinched. She could not stop herself, and for one terrible second she thought she was going to burst into tears. With a great effort she rallied, and retorted, "It's my belief you carry your own misery around with you and need a scapegoat to blame it on. You are a spiteful bully, Belgarrick!"

His title came readily to her lips. She did not, then, feel the slightest inclination to call him Giles. For good measure, she repeated, "A spiteful bully."

He tossed back the last of his wine and stood up. "There are some women who do not think so. You might have been among them."

"I doubt it." Claudia also stood up. "I have no penchant for cheap perfume."

His brown eyes began to smolder, and he said with dangerous calm, "It is not cheap, I assure you."

"Obvious, then. A very obvious perfume for a very obvious type of woman."

"You must not despise a woman who flies under her true colors. It is the one who pretends to be one thing and proves to be another who is to be deplored."

"Bruises are not enough for you, are they? I believe you would brand me if you could!"

They faced each other, white with anger, and after long tense moments it was Giles who stepped back. "You had best go to your rooms, madam. I don't think you are quite—safe—with me just now."

She was dismissed and should be thankful for it, but she was not. She felt the wildest urge to go to him, to put her head on his chest and tell him she would be sorry for anything he wished, if only he would love her. The urge was so strong that she took a step toward him, only to be brought up short when he said, "If you have it in your mind to strike me again, I would advise against it. You will not catch me that way twice."

Claudia turned away. What was the use? She could not appeal to a man without a heart. She could only destroy herself by trying, and she was not quite ready for that. Not yet.

She loathed herself for her craven retreat, but she was too fatigued and despondent to battle on further. She was very conscious of Giles's eyes on her back as she went out of the hall, and it was all she could do to keep her shoulders from drooping. It was a relief to find the housekeeper waiting in the vestibule to show her the way to her rooms.

As they went up the staircase and along a paneled passage, Mrs. Binns was much inclined to chatter. Claudia could not pull herself together enough to answer. The heels of her kid boots clicked against the polished floor and each step she took jarred her throbbing head.

It was only when Mrs. Binns had turned into another passage and stopped at a door a little way down that she became aware of Claudia's silence and looked closely at her. "Merciful heavens, you're as white as death!" she exclaimed. "The journey has quite knocked you up."

"It is only the headache and, perhaps, a little fatigue."

Mrs. Binns ushered her into her sitting-room and straight through to her bedroom, where Mellows was not slow to express her own concern. Between them they offered her a posset, a saline draught, hartshorn, laudanum and smelling-salts. Claudia, wishing for

121

nothing more than to be left alone, declined all these comforts, saying that a wash and a rest would soon put her right.

Mrs. Binns curtsied and left, having satisfied herself that the jug of water, placed in the wash-bowl and covered by a spotless towel, was still hot. Mellows soon had Claudia stripped to her chemise, the water poured into the bowl and another towel warming by the fire. It was during these ministrations that Claudia discovered the reason for her malaise. A full week early, she had the proof Giles required that she was not pregnant. It seemed that he could upset the regular rhythm of her monthly cycle as dramatically as he could upset the rhythm of her heart!

She truly did not know whether she was glad or sorry. She would be able to vindicate herself from the worst of Giles's suspicions; on the other hand it would not be long before she could expect his attentions again, and this time they would be far from loving.

Not until another twenty minutes had passed, and she had packed Mellows off to the servants' hall to refresh herself after her own journey, did Claudia gain the solitude she so much needed. She had refused to lie either in her bed or on the day-bed, preferring the armchair by the fire. She had much thinking to do.

She was wrapped in her robe, her feet were on a footstool, a rug was over her knees, her head rested on a soft pillow and the pins had been removed from her hair. She was relaxed as much as she was likely to be, and yet she still could not think straight. Her eyes closed, opened and closed again. The days without eating properly, the nights without rest, took their toll at last and she sank into the sleep of exhaustion.

Country hours were kept at Belgarrick Towers and dinner was at six. It was while Giles was changing for the occasion that he learned from his valet that Claudia would not be going down to dine, since she was indisposed after the journey from London.

A flicker of annoyance crossed Giles's face, and he ordered a brandy posset, sweetened with sugar, to be sent up to him.

"For you, my lord?" exclaimed Jedson, surprised out of his customary calm.

"For Lady Belgarrick. I shall take it to her myself."

When Giles entered her bedchamber a little later carrying the posset, he found the room lit only by the flickering light of the fire and a single branch of candles on the mantelshelf. Claudia was not, as he had supposed, hiding in her bed. She was reclining in an armchair, her face turned toward the fire, away from him.

"In need of fortifying again, madam?" he asked, walking toward her. "Take this. The brandy is hot this time, and I pray it will work all the faster. You must practice what you preach, and acknowledge it will not do to have the servants say you declined to dine with me on your first day here."

When she did not move, he said more harshly, "This will not do, either. I've less patience with a sulk than I have with a shrew." When she still did not respond, he pushed back the soft hair screening her face and turned her face toward him.

Claudia, drifting up through layers of sleep, opened her eyes. Delighted that her dream was so very real, she smiled and murmured huskily, "Giles . . ." Then her eyes fluttered shut again and she sank back into oblivion, her face resting trustingly against his hand.

Giles stared at her, his expression inscrutable, and carefully withdrew his hand. Her head lolled back toward the fire. She sighed and stirred in her sleep, and her robe, loosened by her movement, fell open to expose one bruised shoulder and the swelling curve of

123

her breast. He was leaning forward to cover her up when a voice said, "My lord, pray do not disturb her."

It was Mellows standing in the doorway, silhouetted by the light streaming through from the sitting-room. Giles straightened up sharply and strode toward her, asking, "What ails your mistress?"

"It is her troubles, my lord."

His eyebrows snapped together. "What troubles?"

Mellows was more specific. "Her woman's troubles. The headache, the backache, the lowness of spirits and the fatigue that must be expected when the time of month is come."

Giles stiffened and looked back at Claudia. Mellows, misunderstanding his thoughts entirely, went on soothingly, "You must not take it as a personal slight, my lord. Rare indeed is the bride who fulfils her husband's dearest wish in the first days of her marriage."

"Are you sure that is what is wrong with her?"

"Positive," Mellows assured him serenely.

"Then why is she not abed?"

"She would not hear of it. She said a short rest by the fire was all she needed to put her to rights."

"Why, then, did she send a message to the kitchens saying she would not be dining?"

"I did that. My lady fell into such a deep sleep that I was loath to wake her. Nature's own cure, as they say. I shall have a tray sent up later unless, of course, you wish me to awaken her now."

"No, but see that she eats and is kept properly covered."

Mellows curtsied. "Shall I take that posset from you? It was a kind thought, not that she would drink it if she were awake. Neither Mrs. Binns nor I could prevail upon her to take any restoratives. She said peace and quiet would do her more good than anything, and I daresay she was right. I have observed, my lord, that

124

she is not a lady to mollycoddle herself, although anybody can see she is not made of iron."

Was that a reproof for his rough handling of her? Any criticism, even if only implied, had its usual effect on him. He gave her the glass, snapped, "Indeed!" and strode back across the bedroom to the dressing-room, which led to his own as it did in the town house.

Mellows watched him go, her expression as inscrutable as his own had been. It would do him no harm to know that his bride could not be used for the next few days to assuage his bruising passion. It was patently obvious, she thought, that he had lusted his bride into this exhausted state.

She sighed, not in condemnation but in envy. Any woman would welcome the attentions of Belgarrick, however punishing they might be. Not for the first time she thought it would be kinder if a woman born without beauty, as she was herself, was also born without the desires that only the beautiful could fulfill.

Mellows went softly across the room to the chevalglass. The light was too poor to see her reflection properly, but the shadows were flattering. In any case she already knew that time had not improved her homely countenance or softened with generous curves her gaunt frame. Still, she also knew that gentlemen starved of love were not inclined to be over fussy, particularly on dark and lonely nights. It did not seem likely that my Lord Belgarrick would ever fall into this category, but one never knew.

Smiling to herself, Mellows lifted the warm brandy to her lips and sipped it appreciatively. One of the perks of the job, she told herself, and if she were watchful there might be greater rewards to come. She had a good mistress and, if gossip could be believed, a womanizer for a master. Things could not have worked out better if she had planned them so.

Mellows had gone down to her own meal and returned by the time her mistress awakened at ten o'clock. Claudia was still so drowsy that she wanted nothing more than to climb into her bed, but Mellows, moving round lighting more candles, told her that my lord had expressly commanded that she be made to eat something.

Claudia's sleepy brain grappled with this information, then she asked, "Lord Belgarrick was here?"

"Certainly, my lady. He fetched you a brandy posset."

"Why should he do that?"

"To brace you up for dinner, I suppose. I'd informed the kitchens you were not well enough to go down."

Claudia was thinking more clearly now, and she came to her own conclusions. Brandy, which she had requested when she was in need of fortifying. Of course! He had come to gloat over her craven retreat from him earlier, and doubtless he thought she had not recovered enough to face him over dinner. He had wanted to *enjoy* her humiliation, damn him!

"You should have woken me for dinner," she said crossly.

"I would have done had my lord bade me to, but once he knew the nature of your malaise he agreed it was best to let you sleep."

Claudia stared at her. "What exactly did you tell him?"

"That it is your time of the month. Did I do wrong?"

Claudia ignored the question because she had a more important one of her own to ask. "What did he say?"

"He asked if I was sure."

He would, of course, Claudia thought bitterly. He would not easily believe that his nasty suspicions were unjustified.

"I told him I was positive," Mellows went on. "He looked—I can't exactly say *how* he looked, my lady—but I thought he must be disappointed. Men always expect to get their brides pregnant immediately, if you'll excuse my frank speaking. I told him that was rarely the way it happened, and he bade me keep you warm and see that you ate when you awoke."

Claudia, putting her own interpretation on these snippets, guessed that Giles's reaction was as equivocal as her own, and they neither knew whether they were glad or sorry. Still, if he had ordered her to be looked after, he must have decided it was in his favor to be proved wrong in this instance. In a few days he could try again to make her pregnant, certain that the child would be his.

Her blood ran cold at the thought of how he would approach her then. She would have to hide her love. He might, or might not, try to hide his loathing. Such an encounter could only be distasteful to both of them. The continuance of a dynasty wrapped up in legalized rape!

"My lady, you have gone quite white," Mellows exclaimed. "You must be faint with hunger. I shall have a nourishing broth sent up immediately."

"I loathe broth! All I want is my bed."

"There was turtle soup for dinner, made a special way with Madeira wine. Very nourishing. Will you not try some of that?"

"Oh, very well, if it will get me to my bed sooner!" Claudia exclaimed, then her conscience smote her. She was behaving like the kind of female she detested—peevish, vaporish, and venting her ill humor on a servant. She added contritely, "I'm sorry, Mellows. I am not myself."

"Quite understandable, my lady," Mellows replied

with an indulgence that set her mistress's teeth on edge, then she went off to order the supper tray.

It was not *understandable*, Claudia thought resentfully. Nothing had been understandable since Giles had walked into her life, unannounced, unashamed and more handsome than any man had a right to be.

She looked round for the posset he had brought her. It was not to be seen. Mellows must have thrown it away. Not that she wanted to drink it. A cold posset would be more abominable than a hot one. No, she merely wanted to touch the glass *he* had touched, and such maudlin sentiment only sickened her the more.

If there were a posset to cure her of Giles Verylan, that she would willingly drink—hot or cold, abominable or not . . .

She drank her soup valiantly, nibbled at the crusty bread accompanying it and had her reward when she was tucked into a warmed bed and left to dream the dreams that were so much happier than her life. They were so real, too. While she had been asleep in the armchair she could have sworn that if she'd reached out her hand she could have touched Giles's face. And she had wanted to so much. There had been no hate on his face at all. No, he had looked . . . How had he looked?

She fell asleep trying to remember a moment that might have been so promising, but was gone for ever.

## Chapter Eleven

It was Giles who set the pattern of their life together at Belgarric Towers, and it was one of avoidance. When Claud went down to breakfast, he was out riding. Sometimes he appeared at luncheon, more often he did not. The only time she could be certain of seeing him was at dinner, and he appeared to resent having to spend an hour or so with her afterward.

To Claudia, loving him as she did, the days passed in a kind of purgatory. She was waiting for better things, a smile, a softening of his mood, but she waited in vain. There seemed no way she could expiate her sin, and she was forced back to her original conclusion, that he wanted to hate her and was glad she had given him cause. Yet at the same time she was certain he had, as he had asserted, intended an amicable relationship. Why, then, should he *want* to hate her?

It was all so contradictory that there was no fathoming it. Living with Giles was difficult enough. Living with an enigma as well was one cross too many to bear— but she had to bear it, every waking hour.

If her heart was obsessed with Giles so, too, was her mind. No matter what she found to occupy herself, her thoughts were always with him, worrying away at the riddle he represented without ever solving it. She began to realize that she would never be at peace with herself until she was at peace with him, and there was no prospect of that.

Her life had become a burden she could not ease because she loved him. If she was in purgatory with him, she would be in hell without him. She could not suddenly decamp, as she had from Tallon Manor. There she had been fleeing a miserable situation. Here she would be fleeing herself. It could not be done. She was trapped, not only by a wedding ring, but by her whole being.

She was completely in his power, and there was no condition more pitiful than to love a man like Belgarrick and not be loved in return. Her plight was worsened by the need to keep up appearances. She could not mope or confide in anyone. She was a bride in a marriage that could afford no gossip.

Any interested onlooker would have thought that everything was as it should be. Giles was meticulously correct, Claudia gracious and pleasant. If they were rarely together, the explanation was not hard to find.

Giles's estates needed his most urgent attention. Nothing had altered on his lands during a time when agricultural methods had improved tremendously. The livestock had been allowed to dwindle, with never a thought given to improving meat and dairy yields by improving bloodlines. The grain, hop and fruit fields were in similar decline, while the cottages of the laborers who toiled in them were crumbling about their ears.

Yes, there was much to be done, and Claudia was just as deeply involved within the house in putting to rights the neglect of a generation. They were thought of as an industrious, caring couple, and if they displayed more care for their duties than for each other, there was nothing remarkable in that. It was an age when a public display of affection would have been regarded with disgust. Civility was the thing, and within the thick walls of Belgarrick Towers this code was rigidly observed.

It was only when they were alone that the mire beneath the smooth surface was allowed to show. Claudia refused to knuckle under. She could not buy peace at such a price. When he snubbed her, she fought back. When he ignored her, she forced him to talk to her. He had to, or knuckle under himself, and she knew full well that the towers around them would fall before that happened.

There were many things they needed to discuss, although he refused to acknowledge it, and one of them was Tansy. Claudia asked him one evening when she would be joining them, and would not be fobbed off being informed that the matter was in han ... one ... him forthrightly, "Tansy should not still be at the seminary. She should be here."

"So she would be, had she not written asking permission to extend her holiday until the end of the month."

"What holiday?"

"Her Christmas holiday."

"I thought she was at the seminary."

"She has been in the habit of spending her vacations with the Granthams at Keynsham, a few miles from Bath. The daughter of the house was at the seminary with her. I gather that they are—what is the revolting term?—bosom bows. She preferred her company to mine over Christmas, at any rate."

"Very fortuitous," Claudia observed drily, thinking of Lindson.

"Extremely, since I had no proper chaperon for her. I only wish I could be sure I have a proper one now." He watched the angry color flood her cheeks and, apparently satisfied, went on, "She was due to return to the seminary until I married, but when I wrote that the event had taken place, she asked if her holiday might be extended. Whether that sprang from tact or a desire to avoid me as long as possible I do not know, but since she appears to have dropped her opposition to a London Season I granted her request."

Possibly the poor girl dreaded the entry of a step-mama into her chequered life, Claudia thought, but Giles was asking pointedly, "Is the inquisition over?"

"It is not an inquisition, it is concern for your daughter," she flared. "Who are these Granthams? I have never heard of them."

"That is not to be wondered at."

"Why?"

"The father is an obscure squire with no taste for fashionable life. A very forgettable man. He is dull, and far too proper to afford any but the meanest hospitality to a black sheep like myself. When I visited him to see what company Tansy was in, he did not invite me to stay overnight. I count that one of the few mercies to come my way since I returned to England." A cynical note entered his voice as he went on, "If you are about to point out what a sad reflection it is upon me that Tansy should prefer his roof to mine, spare your breath. I am aware of it."

"You do not mind?"

"I do not require affection from my daughter, only obedience."

"Poor Tansy," Claudia exclaimed involuntarily.

"On the contrary. She is very rich."

"Wealth is not everything."

"Fine talk from a woman who married for it."

"I did not!"

"Ah, you *did* fear you were pregnant, then! What a relief it must have been to discover you were not. Or did you feel you had jumped out of the frying-pan into the fire for nothing?"

Claudia jumped to her feet, her fists clenched. "Stop it! You know very well I married to escape Tallon Manor."

"What will you do to escape me? Run off with the next buck who ogles you?"

"I will not *run* anywhere. If I leave, it will be because you have *driven* me. Is that what you want?"

"You know what I want, madam. Sons. And preferably without the quarrels."

"You can begin to try for your sons next Tuesday," she shouted at him. "About the quarrels, I promise nothing. And if you are satisfied that you have humiliated me enough for one day, I shall seek my bed while it is still, mercifully, my own."

She went out and slammed the door behind her. As she stalked to her own rooms, rigid with anger, she half expected him to follow her to have the last word, as usual. He did not, but she was not conscious of any relief. He was impossible to live with, impossible to live without. What possible relief could there be for a woman in her situation?

Claudia slept badly and awoke early, pale and with shadows under her eyes. When she pulled back the bed-curtains and got up, she saw that a servant had already been in to clean the grate and light a new fire. She tied her robe about her, thrust her feet into her slippers and, deciding not to summon Mellows to dress her yet awhile, went over to her desk.

The announcement of her marriage in the newspapers had brought her a flood of letters from relations and friends and now, she thought, was as good a time as any to begin answering them. She must not risk alienating anybody, because she would need all the support she could muster if Tansy were to be creditably launched in the spring.

One person, however, was alienated for life, and that was Lady Tallon. The letter from her had been full of hysterical abuse. Claudia was a snake in the grass. She had repaid their kindness and their charity by making the family an object of speculation and gossip of the worst kind. She had allied herself with a rogue and would, Lady Tallon confidently predicted, live to rue it. Such was always the fate of stupid spinsters who permitted themselves to be seduced by nefarious rakes. Hole-in-the-corner marriages could result from no other circumstance, as the whole world knew, and she could count herself lucky to have a ring upon her finger, even if it had been placed there by a scoundrel. She would wish Claudia no joy, since none was to be expected of an infamous union, and washed her hands of her. So did Edgar. Henceforth, the family connection was cut. There was much more in the same vein. Three sheets of it in all, for which Claudia had had to pay the privilege of reading. Sir Edgar, not being a peer of the realm or a member of parliament, was unable to frank his wife's letters. In truth, the closely-written invective was but a thin disguise for Lady Tallon's fury that Claudia was now above her on the social scale, and for her awareness that her neighbors were rightly blaming the precipitate marriage on her treatment of Claudia.

The letter was consigned to the fire. Aunt Adela's, full of wonder, curiosity and exclamation-marks, was more balanced. Claudia was wished every possible happiness and once more offered a refuge if she should need one. Lally—Miss Laleham, Claudia's beloved old nurse—wrote more hopefully. Reformed rakes, she believed, often made the best husbands, and if her dear Claudia saw enough merit in Lord Belgarrick to enable her to marry him, then merit there must be.

The other letters were of lesser importance but they all had to be answered, and Claudia had made a dent in the pile before Mellows appeared to dress her. By this time the bedchamber was nicely warmed. It was much smaller than the one in the town house and cosily furnished with rose damask drapes, a rosebud-patterned carpet and gleaming Jacobean furniture. It was so much like the bedchamber Claudia had grown up in at Tallon Manor that she felt at home here, at rest.

When she went downstairs, she took her completed letters to leave in the library for Giles to frank. She knew he spent a great deal of time there but not at this hour in the morning, when it was his custom to go out riding. All the same, she looked cautiously round the door and entered only when she was certain it was empty.

Her housewifely heart was wrung when she saw the disorder within. Papers overflowed from the desk to nearby chairs and the floor and the sofa were littered with scrolls that looked like rolled-up architectural plans. It seemed that Giles had too much work to do and not enough space to do it in, and yet the room was a large one.

She placed her letters on a pile of papers in the center of the desk, where he could not miss them, and slowly looked around. There was nothing wrong with the room, which was lined on three walls with finely carved oak bookcases. It was the furniture that was inadequate. It was modern and extremely elegant, but scarcely suited to a man of Giles's proportions or the amount of estate work he had to do, and there were his business interests besides.

She did not have to wonder long why he had not made himself more comfortable. The answer was obvious. He did not *want* to be comfortable. He was determined to look on his sojourn in England as nothing but a temporary inconvenience. He was taking great care not to be trapped here by anything, including the charm of his old childhood home. He must feel something for it, or he would not be so angered by its neglect and work so hard for its future preservation. Perhaps he was afraid of what he felt and was resisting anything that might make him feel more deeply still.

Claudia's eyes gleamed. If this house could hold him where she could not, then damme if she wouldn't make him comfortable in it, even against his will! It might not be the way that Lisette would make him comfortable, but Claudia was resigned to fighting with whatever weapons came to hand. A much-loved home and a much-needed son. Such a combination might do the trick. If Giles could be made to feel content, then surely he would look more favorably on the woman who had made him so? The prospect did not seem too hopeful; still, it offered a small crumb of comfort. Claudia had already discovered that living on any hope, however ill founded, was better than living on none at all.

She ate her breakfast and read her mail absently. The letters all stemmed from the announcement of her marriage, and all would have to be answered guardedly, which was becoming tedious. Her mind was still on the problem of the library, and she decided to seek out the housekeeper at once to see what could be done about it.

She was just about to rise from the table when Giles walked in. She gave a start of surprise. Usually he was at pains to avoid her at this time of the day. She sank back into her seat. He would take it the wrong way if she left the moment he entered the room.

His eyes flicked over her, missing nothing, including her expression. It prompted him to say, "I disturb you, madam?"

"Of course not." She reached for the silver pot and poured herself another cup to make it look as though she had a reason for remaining. She watched him covertly as he filled a plate from the contents of the chafing-dishes, unable to keep her eyes from him whenever he was not looking directly at her, although she feared he was once more spoiling for a fight.

In this she was wrong. When he took his place at the table, he neither buried his face in a newspaper nor snubbed her desperate efforts at polite conversation. He was not forthcoming, but he was not rude. After a while she was encouraged enough to ask, "Have you been successful in finding a new steward, my lord? I gather the old one died before you came home."

"India is my *home*," he corrected her. "But, no, none of the candidates Tigwell sent down impressed me."

"I'm sorry. It would help you a great deal to have the day-to-day running of the estates taken off your hands. What sort of man are you looking for?"

"One who can be trusted not to line his pockets at my expense when I return to India."

He sounded testy, as though the answer were so obvious that the question should never have been asked, but Claudia leaned forward eagerly. "Will you consider my father's steward, Charles Reveson? He is an excellent and dependable man."

"Do you seriously consider I would employ the steward of a bankrupt estate?" Giles asked, his eyebrows rising.

"Things would have been much worse if it hadn't been for Charles. Sir Edgar acknowledged it by keeping him on although the rest of the senior staff were dismissed. His presence here would make a great deal of difference to me. We worked closely together for the last ten years when my father lost interest in everything

137

but pleasure. If you remain determined to go abroad again, I shall feel much easier having a steward I know and trust."

Her eagerness to impress him had brought a glow to her pale cheeks, and Giles looked at her for some moments without saying anything. Then he asked, "How old is he?"

"He is in his middle years. That is why he remains at the manor, thinking other employment difficult to find at his age, although he is as active as he is able."

Giles's face remained as inscrutable as ever, and Claudia had the hollow feeling that he would never consider any recommendation of hers. She had probably damned Charles just by speaking up for him. It seemed she was right, too, for Giles said, "Tigwell thinks he has found the right man for me at last. I will let you know."

She knew it was useless to argue Charles's case further. It would only lead to another argument she could not win. The glow faded from her cheeks, and a few minutes later she quietly excused herself.

She took her letters to her apartment, then sought out the housekeeper, doggedly determined in spite of her unhappiness that however much Giles might dislike her as a woman, he would be made ultimately to appreciate her as a wife. It was with this aim in mind that she went with Mrs. Binns to a storeroom to inspect the furniture that had been in the library when Giles was a boy. She emerged dusty but pleased, having ordered the furniture to be prepared for removal back to the library when an opportune moment occurred.

She was walking along a gallery overlooking the courtyard when a rumble of wheels over cobbles made her glance out. A carrier's cart was just coming through the arched entrance. It must be her baggage arriving at last, and much needed it was, but it was not that

that made her pick up her skirts, race along the gallery and down the stairs. "Saba!" she cried joyously, and a red setter curled up on her corded trunks launched itself off the cart and streaked across the courtyard toward its mistress with shrill yelps of excitement.

Heedless of her gown, Claudia sank to her knees and threw her arms around the dog, sinking her face into the soft fur and gasping, "Oh, Saba, if only you knew how *pleased* I am to see you!"

Saba's welcome was no less rapturous, and Claudia's eyes filled with tears. How starved she was of love, even a dog's. She looked up, straight into Giles's eyes, who must have been attracted by the commotion. She fancied he looked as disapproving as ever and, brushing away her tears, she rose to her feet and said laughingly, "Yes, I know! *Maudlin nonsense,* and you are quite right, only I make no apology because it is so good to see my dog again. Saba, stop frisking and come to be introduced."

Saba advanced on Giles in a reasonably decorous manner, apart from her still frantically wagging tail, and offered him a paw. He shook it, stroked her silken head and commented, "A fine animal."

"She is a perfect lady. At least," Claudia amended hastily as Saba, deciding Giles was a friend, jumped up at him, "she is when she is not over excited."

"She has much in common with her mistress, except that . . ."

The flush of happiness died from Claudia's cheeks. "Must you always taunt me, Belgarrick? There must be something wrong with you if you can take such pleasure from destroying mine. Heaven knows I've had little enough of it since we married."

There was an infinitesimal pause, then he continued as though she hadn't interrupted him, ". . . except that Saba is already breeding."

Claudia forgot her anger at his gibe in her concern for her dog. "Oh, no! She is only eighteen months old herself. I have not tried to breed from her yet."

"Then you have left it too late. When was she last in season?"

"Two or three weeks before Christmas. Curse Lady Tallon! It is all her fault. She would not have a dog in the house and poor Saba was banished to the stables, which was not at all what she was used to. One of the stable dogs must have got to her. I only hope it was the spaniel. The puppies will be decidedly odd if it was one of the collies." Another thought occurred to her and she asked, "Do you object to dogs in the house, my lord?"

"I can remember a time when this house was never without them." Giles looked moodily about him at the gray stone walls, punctured frequently with arch-shaped mullioned windows. "That was when this place was like a home."

"It will be again."

"For you, madam, certainly."

For both of us, she vowed silently, but Saba's arrival had cheered her too much to risk an argument. Instead, she said laughingly, "Belgarrick, for all your frowns, you cannot be all bad. Saba would not like you so much otherwise."

He looked down at the dog, who was rubbing her head affectionately against his leg. "I wouldn't take that as a recommendation! Her condition proves she's not at all fussy what company she keeps."

Claudia laughed again, then turned away. "If you will excuse me, I must find out how she came to travel by carrier's cart when I sent a servant to fetch her to me by stage."

The carrier, a squat but hugely muscled man, had approached closely enough to overhear and, doffing his cap, said, "Begging your pardon, my lady, but it was the missus at the manor as said I was to bring that there dog. As good as gold it's been, a'setting atop your trunks and a'guarding 'em whether they needs guarding or no. Only I'll have to charge extra for her feed. The meat what was provided lasted no more'n three days and we'm been on the road for five, having other calls to make twixt there and here. I don't know about no servant sent special-like. Belike we left afore he got there."

Claudia was torn between amusement at hearing Lady Tallon referred to as "the missus" and anger that her precious Saba had been dispatched without proper provision or protection from the elements, but Giles was saying, "When you have unloaded Lady Belgarrick's luggage, which looks like thirsty work, go to the kitchens for refreshment. The housekeeper will settle your account."

"Thank you kindly, my lord," the carrier replied, beaming broadly and taking himself off.

"I wrote instructing Lady Tallon to keep my animals until I sent for them. How like her to rid herself of Saba at the earliest opportunity. I suppose I should be thankful that my mare was not tied on the back of the cart!"

Hearing her name and anxious at having herself discussed, Saba returned to her mistress. Claudia stooped and fondled her ears. "It's all right, Saba. You won't have to get on that horrid cart again. This is your new home and you are safe now. Lady Tallon's spite can't reach you here."

"Or you," Giles observed coolly.

"She is doing her best! She wrote me the most odious letter, saying she wished me no happiness in my marriage." The indignation that led to this little outburst was swamped by embarrassment as Claudia realized

141

she was airing her grievances to the wrong person. Giles scarcely wished her happiness, either! She went on awkwardly, "If you will excuse me, I must see Émile. Saba's night-bed must be arranged, and she was used to sleeping in the kitchens before Lady Tallon turned her out."

A few minutes later she discovered that Émile shared Lady Tallon's antipathy to dogs. The ensuing argument was conducted in French, Émile being adept at forgetting all his excellent English when it suited him. Claudia's fluency in his native tongue neither impressed nor swayed him. In the kitchen he reigned supreme, and eventually both she and her dog were repulsed.

Mrs. Binns, succumbing to Saba's affectionate ways, suggested a bed beside the fire in the servants' hall and set a carpenter to making a suitable box right away. With this Claudia had to be satisfied, although the hall was far too large and draughty for her liking.

It was only later when, writing more letters in her sitting-room with Saba dozing happily at her feet, Claudia realized that she and Giles had conversed almost amicably in the courtyard. True, there had been that one taunt—but only one! It set her thinking once more how different everything might have been if she had entered this marriage as a virgin.

But in a few seconds she realized that the sigh she uttered was one of regret. Instantly she felt guilty. Had she not vowed never to regret her love for Tom? Frantically she tried to conjure up Tom's image, but it was hazy. The more she concentrated, the more it blurred. Finally it reformed as Giles's face.

Tom was gone from her, as truly gone as the ring she had given away. She was filled with an inexpressible sadness, and something else beside. She was unsure whether it was fear or resentment, or perhaps a combination of the two, for it seemed there was no part of her—even her past—that Giles could not reach and destroy at will.

*Chapter Twelve*

The following day was Tuesday, but it proved so full of incidents that Claudia had little time to brood over what kind of mood Giles would be in when he came to her bedchamber that night. At any event, the day started happily enough with the arrival of Dusty, her speckled gray mare, brought down by easy stages from Tallon Manor.

With her luggage unpacked, her own prized possessions about her, her horse in the stables and Saba at her heels, she was somewhat cheered and began to feel at home at Belgarrick Towers, even if Giles could not.

A little later, the mysterious disappearance of the servant she had sent to bring Saba to her was explained when he arrived heavily bruised and deeply apologetic. The stagecoach he had been travelling on had been involved in an accident and he had been obliged to rest up at an inn until he was fit enough to set forth once more.

The post brought her a letter from Hector Tigwell. He had been unable to find an Indian cook with dependable references but, one foreigner being much like another to him, he asked if my Lady Belgarrick might consider a Chinaman. He spoke English in a recognizable fashion, wore decent English clothes and had been re-named Bertie by the English master he had served for fifteen years. This master, a merchant, had traded in Canton and Calcutta before retiring and bringing Bertie to England with him. As a result, Bertie was experienced in Chinese, Indian and English food. The death of the merchant was the cause of his looking for new employment. Whether he was a fit person to be allowed within the kitchens of a noble household it must be for Lady Belgarrick to decide. The tone of the letter suggested that he, Hector Tigwell, remained unconvinced.

Claudia was not so proud. As far as she was concerned, there was a place in her kitchens for anybody who could stop Giles frowning at his food with disfavor. He never complained, but it was obvious that he ate for nourishment and not for pleasure. Excited at the change she hoped to bring to this, she dashed off a few lines to Mr. Tigwell requesting Bertie to be sent down for a trial immediately.

There was to be more good news. As she came out of her sitting-room to take the letter downstairs, she encountered Giles in the passage. He had just interviewed another prospective steward, found him wanting, and would interview Charles Reveson if she would find out what date would be suitable for him.

Delighted, Claudia tried to express her thanks, but Giles cut her short and went on his way, saying she had best point out to Reveson that an interview was no guarantee of employment. Claudia was left trying to talk to the empty air, no new experience with Giles, and she went back into her room to write another hasty letter.

After lunch she went to the portrait gallery, on what was becoming something of a daily pilgrimage. What drew her back time and again was a portrait of Giles painted when he could have been no more than eighteen, and certainly before he had become the family outcast. There was no trace in that unlined countenance of the harsh and unforgiving man he was to become. His eyes were merry, his lips smiled and, although Claudia could readily believe he was capable of any amount of high-spirited pranks, she searched in vain for a hint of the depravity for which he was to become notorious.

She had not known him then, but every time she stood before the portrait her heart ached with a terrible sense of loss. She was grieving for the carefree laughing boy who had gone for ever, and she was also grieving for the unsmiling and suspicious man he had become.

Giles, the untried boy, looked happy. Giles, the grown man, behaved as though he did not know what happiness was. He had not matured so much as soured, and Claudia, sighing, thought it a sad waste of so much promise.

Her eyes moved on to the portraits of his brothers. George, in the Light Dragoon uniform he was to die in; Gervase, the foppish man about town. Both were handsome, but they lacked the magnetism of their younger brother. Had they resented him before he had given them cause to turn their backs on him? Certainly they looked insufferably vain, and that was one fault she could not lay at Giles's door.

She felt, without quite knowing why, that the answer to the enigma Giles had become lay in these three portraits and that one day it would be revealed to her. That was why she came back so often, but today, as on her previous visits, she went away unenlightened. She had the strangest feeling that their painted eyes followed her, triumphant, perhaps, that she had pried loose none of their secrets. It was easy to be fanciful in Belgarrick Towers.

The rest of the afternoon she spent more prosaically answering her letters, as good a way as any of keeping her mind off the fact that it was Tuesday. Her nerves began their attack when she bathed. Naked, it was all too easy to remember how it was to be in Giles's power. She still bore faint traces of their last encounter. There was no comfort in recalling that her bruises had been caused not by his loving but by his anger. She did not expect him to approach her in either love or anger this time.

His love had been lost to her in the moment she thought she had gained it. His anger he had under control, so she could not depend on that sparking off any genuine emotion in their union. She could only fear that he would approach her at night as he approached her by day—cold, soulless and indifferent. Such an encounter would wound her far more deeply than mere bruises, only there would be no marks to bear witness to her pain. It was small wonder she trembled.

"You've stayed in that water too long. It's gone cold," Mellows said in concern. "You'll catch your death."

Claudia, wishing she could stay in the bath until she turned to ice and therefore could feel nothing, obediently rose to be enveloped in a warm towel and have the life rubbed back into her shivering limbs. She could not confide in her maid that it was her spirit and not her body that was chilled. Much as she longed to unburden herself to somebody, her pride as well as her loyalty to her husband would not permit it.

When she was wrapped in her robe and seated before the dressing-table so that Mellows could dress her hair, she said, "That's a fine brooch you are wearing. An amethyst, is it not?"

The remark had been made more to make her appear at ease than anything, but the brush in Mellows's hand stilled for a second before continuing its vigorous work. Then she replied, "Yes, my lady. My first mistress, an elderly woman who lived in a villa at Highgate, left me a few pieces of her jewelry when she died. It was most unexpected. I had served her only three years."

"Then the diamond brooch and the pearl I have seen you wear are both genuine?"

"Yes, my lady."

"You have been fortunate. How many ladies have you worked for?"

"Six. You might think that a lot, but I have always tried to better myself."

Claudia smiled. "You will seek to serve a duchess next."

"No, my lady. I am content now, if—if you are satisfied with me?"

"Perfectly, Mellows. You suit me very well."

"Then I may look on this position as permanent?"

"Of course. I would have made fresh arrangements otherwise."

"*Thank* you," Mellows said warmly, deftly winding a strand of Claudia's wavy hair around her finger to form a soft ringlet.

Claudia was always meticulously dressed, but tonight she had taken extra care and she knew she was looking her best. She was wearing a chemise gown of sapphire-blue silk, chosen to enhance her fine dark-lashed eyes. It was buttoned down the front, and the back trailed behind her in a small train. A frill fell from the low-cut neckline and the short sleeves were melon shaped. It was a style favored by fashionable women, but few had the height and figure to wear it to best advantage. Claudia, possessing the right attributes, looked both dignified and desirable where others might have looked dumpy and over-dressed.

She wore pearls at her throat and in her ears, and her ringlets were arranged simply, à l'anglaise. Saba, sleek and glossy, walked by her side and Claudia was grateful for her company. She knew from bitter experience that Giles could make her feel more alone while she was with him than when she was, indeed, by herself.

When she entered the Blue Salon, Giles did not pay her the compliment she craved. His eyes did rest on her for several seconds before he resumed pouring sherry but, hard as she searched, she could detect no gleam of approval in them. His face was as much a mask as ever. Her careful toilette, then, had been in vain.

Saba, lacking her mistress's inhibitions, frolicked and fawned around him. Claudia, seating herself by the fire, commented, "She appears to regard you as a friend already."

"I am certainly not her enemy," he answered curtly, giving her a glass of sherry.

"No," she sighed. "All your enmity is reserved for me." The remark had come out unbidden from the deep well of bitterness within her which she usually managed to conceal. She regretted it instantly, and was once more made wearily aware of the strain imposed on her by living a life where she could have no unguarded moment.

"Spoiling for a fight, madam?" Giles asked silkily, taking his sherry to the fireplace and leaning his broad shoulders against the high mantelpiece as he sipped it.

"No. I spoke without thinking. I did not mean it."

"I think perhaps you did."

The anger that seemed inextricably bound up with

her love for him flared anew, causing her to exclaim, "It is you who are spoiling for a fight!"

"You are confusing contempt with contention. I have no patience with a woman who wallows in self-pity when she is caught in a situation entirely of her own making."

Claudia could have disputed that. Yesterday she might have, tomorrow she probably would, but tonight the fire to fight him would not burn. That one brief flare, then nothing. Perhaps she was too weary. Perhaps she was too intimidated by the night that was to come. Whatever the cause, she did not defend herself.

Apparently Giles did not care to be robbed of his right to bludgeon her with words, for he challenged her, "What's the matter, madam? Have you nothing to say for yourself?"

"What can a wife say when her husband believes her to be a whore?"

The ugly word lay between them, suspended in a silence that was broken only by the ticking of the bracket clock upon the mantelpiece. Claudia looked at Giles and thought he had whitened beneath his heavy suntan. She wished it might be with shame but knew it must be with anger. She went on bitterly, "Now what is the matter with *you?* Shocked that I should use in my drawing-room a word you use freely in my bedchamber? Or are you angry that I will give you no more entertainment by defending myself in an argument I cannot win? Accept my apologies. This *madam* is not in the mood for quarreling tonight. I shall try not to disappoint you tomorrow."

"Claudia . . ."

Had it been anybody else speaking, she would have thought her name was said uncertainly, but this was Belgarrick. The heavens would fall before he was guilty of uncertainty like lesser mortals. So positive was she of this that her anger returned and, with it, her spirit. "Oh, no, not *Claudia*," she mocked. "Don't use my name after all this time. You will make a human being of me, and before you know where you are I might expect to be treated as one. I might even begin to believe we can deal amicably together, and what a fool I'd be to make the same mistake twice! That would never do, would it? No, best to keep it simple. Stick to madam, whore—anything that will remind me what an imperfect mate I am for the mighty Belgarrick!"

"Good God, if ever a woman asked to be beaten . . . !"

"For quarrelling with you? I thought I would be commended. It is what you wanted, what you always want! You believe you got a bad bargain in me, and so I must pay for it by being made as miserable as you are yourself."

"You are over-indulging your taste for dramatics again. Before you write me as the villain of the piece, remind yourself that none of this would have happened had you been honest with me at the start. Or do you suffer from that most common of women's complaints— a convenient memory?"

"I suffer from nothing but a surfeit of the Right Honorable the Viscount Belgarrick! As for honesty, do you think it is easy to confide *anything* to that scowling face of yours? It is impossible! Besides, I don't believe you ever intended an *amicable* relationship. You were always looking for a flaw, and when you found it you attacked, and have been doing so ever since!"

"Have you done, madam?" he asked with savage scorn.

"No, madam is not done, but what's the use? You and I cannot talk to each other. We never could." She turned away from him in disgust, her breasts rising and falling with her agitated breathing, her face as flushed as his was pale beneath his tan. Then the release of the

151

emotions that had been pent up for days carried her further than she intended, and she went on, "It is as well we do not need to talk to make babies! I agree with you that the sooner they are born and we are done with each other, the better."

She regretted the words, spoken in bitterness and not in truth, as soon as they were uttered. Giles, however, did not give her the opportunity to recant. He bowed formally. "So be it. Would you like another glass of sherry, madam?"

"Thank you, no," she replied with the same icy civility.

Hastings, mercifully, entered at that moment to announce that dinner was served. Claudia remembered little of the meal but, for once, she was thankful that such a vast expanse of table separated her from Giles. Several times she was conscious of his eyes on her but she avoided meeting them. They would be full of hostility, and it was enough to know she would have to meet them in much more intimate circumstances in a few hours from now.

When the covers were removed she was able to escape to the Blue Salon where Saba, stretched out before the fire, greeted her by thumping her tail and raising her head sleepily. Claudia sat in a fireside armchair and reached down to stroke her pet's silky ears.

"You know what is the matter with us, Saba?" she said softly. "We are questionable ladies, both of us, and we must be made to pay for it, however impeccable our lineage. Where am I to place your puppies, whose father is unknown? And what am I to do with my children, whose father might just as well be unknown for all the interest he means to take in them?"

Saba yawned.

Claudia said sarcastically, "Thank you. I knew I might depend on your concern. Only—Only what if I don't have any children? What then? Giles will despise me twice as much. Or will he in some twisted way be glad I have been a further disappointment to him? *Why* is he so set on hating me? We are married. We have to make the best of each other. It is not rational to deny me a second chance, yet men are supposed to be the rational ones."

Saba was asleep. Claudia continued talking to her, but the pattern of the thoughts she expressed aloud was depressingly familiar. Always questions. Never any answers. She wished she could shut off her mind, although it would be more to the point to shut off her feelings.

Giles joined her when the tea-tray was brought in. It was purely for appearances. He did not have anything to say to her. She could not bring herself to say anything to him. The barrier he had erected between them was taking effect. Her efforts to break it down had been in vain and she could no longer appeal to him to be human. She could not find the words. His silences, his disapproval, were freezing all her natural responses. She was retreating into herself, as he had, but her isolation did not give her the satisfaction it appeared to give him.

She could imagine no worse fate than to love a man and be unable to reach out and touch him, or even talk to him. Unless, of course, it was to bear his children without that love being acknowledged and expressed. She did not know how she could do it, and yet she must. She wondered if that was why girls of her class were taught more about duty than they were about love. Did their mothers know that perhaps, one day, duty was all they would have to sustain them?

Another question, and Claudia was sick of them. She rose abruptly and tugged the bell-rope for a footman to take Saba to her night-bed. Then she went to bed herself. The next move was up to Giles, and he would make it regardless of what she thought, felt, said or did not say.

She had a wide choice of night clothes now that her baggage had arrived, but she made no objection to the voluminous fleecy gown Mellows had warmed for her. It was designed to combat a cold night rather than to inspire passion, and left no part of her exposed save her face above the high ruffled neck. She even permitted the maid to place a frilly night-cap over her glossy hair and tie it demurely under the chin.

A quick glance in the mirror revealed no trace of the temptress who had awaited him on their wedding night, then she slipped quickly into the warmed bed. Mellows drew the curtains round the bed, doused the candles and went quietly away.

Time passed, but Claudia lay wide-eyed, alert to every sound. She was certain Giles would come to fulfill his duty to his line. Whatever the animosity between them, he would make sure he got what he wanted from this marriage, and as soon as possible. He was that sort of man, and in her anger she had condoned his attitude.

She loved him and so she could not fear him, yet still she dreaded his arrival. She did not see how she could lie passive in the arms of the man she loved, and yet if she abandoned herself to the passion that stirred within her at his slightest touch he would again liken her to a whore.

She must be passive. Dutiful, as he would be dutiful. The prospect made her cringe. It seemed a denial of all that she was. All that he was. Two people sharing a lust that was distasteful to both because only one of them loved . . .

For all her waiting and worrying and wondering, she was unprepared when he did come. There seemed not a second's space between the sound of his footsteps, the opening and closing of the dressing-room door and the swishing back of her bed-curtains. If she did not know what she intended, he was in no doubt.

His weight on the bed beside her was purposeful, and even more purposeful when he was on top of her. Without a kiss, a caress, a word, he sought to impregnate her. For Claudia, the nightmare she had dreaded on her wedding night—and averted—became a reality. Nothing could have been more businesslike or, for a woman in love, more soul-destroying. She kept her eyes firmly closed as though, by not seeing anything, she was not a party to it.

But there was no escaping the fact that it was her body, and it was being used, not loved. She did not feel wifely or dutiful. She just felt defiled. She had the feeling that the act was every bit as odious to him, and that made her feel worse. Could he truly loathe her so much that only the need to beget a son could force him to touch her, and then as little as possible?

When he withdrew from her she rolled on her side, her back to him, her eyes still tightly shut. She felt the bed lighten, heard the curtains swish and the door close. He was gone, as he had arrived, without a word.

Still she could not open her eyes. She was his wife, and so it could not be, but she felt as though she had been raped. She had been right, then, when she had told him she believed such a thing possible between husband and wife. She wished she had been wrong. As it was, she began to shudder uncontrollably. Her teeth chattered, and she could have felt no worse if a complete stranger had violated her in the night.

She had promised to be dutiful, but if this was what it meant, then the promise would have to be broken. Never, ever, would she endure such an experience again. She could not. She was still more of a woman than she was a wife, and it was the woman who was outraged. Nothing Belgarrick had said or done had altered that—and that was why the marriage had always been doomed.

Eventually, when there was no other recourse left, she wept. It did her no good. The loss of romance and the acceptance of reality was too harsh a blow for even tears to soften.

## Chapter Thirteen

When Mellows brought her hot chocolate the following morning she also delivered a note from Giles. It was, like the man himself, abrupt to the point of rudeness. Scanning the sparse lines Claudia learned he had gone up to London on an urgent matter of business. It was signed simply: Belgarrick.

Her immediate feeling was relief that she would not have to nerve herself to face him before she had in some part recovered from the trauma of last night's coupling. Then she was suspicious, and asked Mellows what time his lordship had left.

"At first light, my lady."

Claudia leaned back against her pillows and sipped her chocolate. Giles had made no mention yesterday of a trip to London and he had left before the arrival of the post. How, then, had he known an urgent matter of business had cropped up?

The more she thought about it, the more certain she became that business was not the cause of his sudden departure. It was herself. She must have been right in thinking he had been as revolted as she last night, and he wanted a respite before facing a further attempt to impregnate a despised wife. Either that or he hoped his duty was done and he had gone not to London, but to Paris and the welcoming arms of Lisette. His reward for all he had endured for the sake of perpetuating his noble name . . .

Jealousy stirred anew within her. So . . . all she had endured herself had not cured her of her mindless obsession for the man—and it must be mindless for her to still want him so. If she had any sense, the only passion she would feel for him would be hatred!

Claudia flung back the bedclothes and got up. When Giles returned, it would not be to a wilting and self-pitying wife. She would fight for as long as she had the strength to do so. She would prove, if nothing else, that she would not willingly lie down for Giles and his mistress to walk all over her.

In this martial frame of mind Claudia began what was to be an extremely busy week. An army of workmen arrived to put right the neglect the house had suffered during Gervase's indifferent ownership. Some of the roofs needed attention. There were warped or rotted window frames to be replaced, floorboards and wall paneling to be inspected for worm or rot. The great hall had to be repainted and the tapestries removed for expert restoration. More ambitiously, the kitchens were to be modernized and water-closets installed for the servants as well as the family.

Amid all this bustle the Chinese cook arrived, a tall, thin, scholarly-looking man whom Claudia hired immediately. Émile, true to his word, packed his bags and left. If he could not cook for the master, he would cook for nobody. The under-cook, a woman born on the estate, stepped smartly into his shoes, scarcely believing her luck. With a cheerful face and competent calmness, she continued to produce the excellent dishes the household was accustomed to.

Thus it was that Bertie, who spoke English with a

strong North Country accent learned from his previous master, was assimilated into the servants' ranks with precious little fuss. He might be a heathen, but nobody was murdered in their beds and, more importantly, he made no attempt to usurp the position of the new head cook. This made him an acceptable novelty, and Émile's tyrannical disposition ensured that his departure was not lamented. Saba's exile in the chilly servants' hall also came to an end and she was allowed a warm night-bed by one of the stoves.

Claudia was able to turn her mind to other matters. The furniture Gervase had installed in the library was carried up to a storeroom, and the massive oak desk, deep armchairs and couches it had replaced were brought down. When everything was in place, she inspected the result with the housekeeper. The room looked much more comfortable, but a vague dissatisfaction made Claudia ask Mrs. Binns, "You're sure this is how it was when his lordship was young?"

"Except for the paintings, my lady. The old lord bred his own racehorses and he had his favorites painted by Stubbs. They were all hung in here, but Lord Gervase had them taken down when he inherited. He had no love of horses and preferred the scenes from mythology you see now."

"I *knew* there was something wrong," Claudia breathed, "although I could not for the life of me say why. What happened to the Stubbs paintings?"

"I expect they are in a storeroom. I couldn't say which one. There are several of them, and many are choked with the clutter of centuries."

"Have a search made," Claudia ordered. "If the paintings are still in this house, I want them found."

Found they were, but not until after two servants had spent the better part of the day searching for them. Hastings, a keen horse fancier himself, remembered precisely which painting had hung where and he supervised their restoration to the light of day. When they were all in place, and the mythology paintings put aside until a suitable place could be found for them, Claudia was satisfied. She did not know what Giles would think, but, as far as she was concerned, the atmosphere in the library was exactly right now.

The hammering and upheaval caused by the workmen continued over the next few days and Mrs. Binns always seemed to be appearing with a list of linen, china or cutlery to be checked and the purchase of new stock authorized. Claudia did not know it, but her lack of resentment at the demands all this domesticity made on her time was rapidly endearing her to her servants. She was felt to be a great improvement on the previous Lady Belgarrick, who had never wanted to be bothered by anything.

In fact, Claudia enjoyed running a house again and she liked to be busy. With her mare to ride and her dog to exercise, it was only in the evenings that time hung heavily on her hands and she was hard put to hide her loneliness. True, when Giles was home she saw little of him, but knowing he was somewhere close was a solace to her heart and spirit. She tried very hard to convince herself he was indeed in London, but as day after day passed with no word from him it was hard to believe he was not with his mistress in Paris. The anguish and jealousy this caused her did not lessen with the passing of time.

Then, eight days after his sudden departure, he was just as suddenly back. Claudia, who had been out walking Saba, was in the courtyard about to enter a side door when his traveling chaise drove under the archway and drew up by the main door. Giles jumped down without waiting for the steps to be put in place, and Claudia's heart lurched at the sight of him. She would forgive him everything, she knew, if only he would smile at her.

She was wearing a warm green pelisse trimmed with sable, her complexion was glowing from the vigorous walk and her dark hair sparkled with the fine rain that had begun a few minutes before. Saba left her side and bounded toward Giles with excited yelps of welcome. He bent to pat her, then straightened to watch Claudia approach more circumspectly. He did not smile but subjected her to one of his searching looks. Her heart sank. Absence, it seemed, had not made his heart grow fonder.

"You look well, madam," he said, taking the hand she extended and kissing her fingers perfunctorily. "The Kentish air appears to agree with you."

"And London air with you," she responded.

"Somerset more latterly," he corrected, and turned back to the coach. It was then Claudia saw that the footman had put the steps in place and was assisting a female to descend, and for a second her heart stopped. Surely not even Belgarrick would dare to bring his mistress home!

Then Giles was saying formally, "Permit me to present your new daughter to you." He led the girl forward. "Tansy, make your curtsy to your new mama."

Tansy obediently curtsied. She was dressed in an expensive but plain brown pelisse and her bonnet had a simple braid trimming. Her likeness to her father was stunning. Tall, brown-eyed, tawny-haired, she was every inch a Verylan. Only her manner was different. She exhibited none of Giles's restless energy. She was composed and self-contained. Tranquil where he was striking. Old beyond her years, Claudia thought, and on the defensive.

Her ready sympathy made her move forward to embrace the girl warmly, kiss her on the cheek, and say, "Welcome home, Tansy."

"Thank you," Tansy replied politely, but she stiffened slightly and Claudia instantly released her and stepped back.

"You are thinking a girl of your age cannot have a new mother," she said frankly, "and in your position I would think the same. I shall be satisfied if you can come to look on me as a friend."

Tansy smiled. She was still wary, but Claudia thought she was partially disarmed. She tucked her hand companionably in Tansy's arm and led her into the house. "You will be thinking me the *wicked* stepmama if I keep you standing about in this cold much longer, and that will never do. The housekeeper assured me there are no ghosts in this house, and I'd prefer there to be no ogres, either—or perhaps I should say ogresses."

She chatted on lightly in this way while the porter relieved them of their coats, and they walked up the stairs to a comfortable sitting-room which had become Claudia's favorite because it was not too large to keep warm. It was only when they were drinking the tea Hastings brought them and she was still talking that it occurred to Claudia she was speaking mainly for her own benefit. Tansy did not need putting at her ease. She was perfectly composed. Definitely older than her years, Claudia decided.

An eighteen year-old straight from a seminary, unused to Society, finding herself closeted with a new mother and a father little more than a stranger, should exhibit some kind of nerves. Tansy, however, was politely—politely what? *Indifferent* was the word that slid into Claudia's mind. She was taken aback. Then she realized that Tansy, not wanting to be here but having no choice, had sensibly bowed to the inevitable. Claudia herself at eighteen would not have been half as sensible, or half as composed. It did not seem right, somehow, and it spoke volumes for the kind of life Tansy had led if she could take in her stride situations that would annihilate other girls of her age.

Gathering her scattered wits, Claudia tried once more to pierce Tansy's guard by saying, "I have had the yellow bedchamber prepared for you. I thought it the prettiest. If there is one you like better, pray let me know. I want you to be comfortable, and you must be better acquainted with this house than I am."

"Indeed I am not, Lady Belgarrick. This is the first time I have been here."

"Good God! Surely your uncle, Lord Gervase, invited you here?"

"No. I never met him. My birth five months after my parents' marriage was, I believe, as much an embarrassment to the Verylans as the elopement. Don't look so shocked. We are one family now and have no need to mince our words. Indeed, my father and I go on better for plain speaking. I believe my uncle coped with the scandal by ignoring it. He certainly ignored me."

"You poor child," Claudia breathed.

Her compassion was not appreciated. Tansy told her briskly, "We would have had nothing in common. He and my aunt were town people. I most definitely am not. I will endure a Season in town because my father orders it. I do not expect to enjoy it."

Claudia looked fearfully at Giles, expecting a burst of temper, but he did not look at all put out by his daughter's plain speaking. It was almost as though he approved of it, although he said, "You cannot speak with authority on something of which you know nothing. A few balls, a few beaux and you will enjoy yourself as much as any débutante."

"I know myself. However, I will not argue over a

matter that is already settled. Getting over the heavy ground as lightly as possible, as the military would say."

"Oh? And what do you know of the military?"

"Sally's eldest brother was in the army until the Peace. Some of his expressions rubbed off." Tansy turned to Claudia and explained, "Sally Grantham is my particular friend. It is her family I have been staying with at Keynsham."

Giles said, "I trust you have no interest there. The son of a squire will not do for you."

"I have no interest, apart as a friend." Tansy looked again at Claudia, and asked, "If the housekeeper could be summoned to show me to my room, I would like to put off my traveling clothes."

Claudia stood up. "I will show you myself—if you will excuse us," she said politely, looking at Giles.

He nodded. "I shall be in the library to see what letters have accumulated during my absence. I would like to see you there when it is convenient."

"I shall not be long." Claudia led Tansy out of the sitting-room, but her heart was sinking. What now? Giles never spoke to her privately if he could avoid it. Tansy's presence had helped to overcome the constraint of meeting him again for the first time since . . . Claudia closed her eyes briefly. She preferred not to think about since when. But to be alone with him would bring the awkwardness, the embarrassment back. At least for her. She had no idea how he felt. She never did.

Not only that, but the pile of letters awaiting Giles's attention was proof that he had not been where he said he was. Had he indeed been working in London he would have stopped his mail being forwarded to Kent. Nor would he have spent the last eight days at Keynsham with Tansy. He had made it plain enough that he had no welcome there. So . . . it had been Paris and

164

Lisette. She wondered why she had not realized before that the mail was proof of her doubts. But then, she supposed, no wife liked to have her suspicions confirmed, particularly one foolish enough to love her husband.

Claudia hid her misery beneath polite questions about Tansy's journey and received equally polite answers, and she was sensitive enough to perceive that the girl was little happier than herself. They were both playing roles and for the same reason—to pacify Giles, in whose power they were.

She stopped suddenly in the corridor and placed her hand on Tansy's arm. "I know your life has been altered out of all recognition by your father's succession to the title and his return to England, but once you are used to it, you might find it is for the better."

"He means to marry me off to be rid of me," Tansy said bluntly.

"I shall not be a party to forcing you into a marriage that is distasteful to you. I have already told him that."

Tansy looked surprised, and after a second's hesitation, she said, "You must not get into conflict with my father on my account. I can fight my own battles."

"A friend is always useful, and pray call me Claudia. Mama is too personal and Lady Belgarrick too formal, and we will be very much in each other's company. I don't see that the eight years between us will be too much of a barrier."

Tansy smiled, for the first time with real warmth. "No barrier at all. Everybody says I am very mature for my age, which is not to be wondered at because until I went to the seminary I was always in the company of older people—my mama and her parents. They were not frivolous people. I feared that you would be . . . well, just let's say you are not at all as I imagined you. When my father said he intended to marry a

165

respectable woman from the First Circles I visualized some freakish spinster at her last prayers. I forgot, of course, that in spite of his reputation he is a handsome man.''

"Has his reputation been a great burden to you?" Claudia asked.

"Yes. When I was growing up I quickly learned to appear more docile than I really am to escape lectures on my 'wild blood' and the dreadful pitfalls of being undisciplined. Very burdensome for a child! I thought you would be in the same mold and I dreaded that. I should have listened to Andrew. He told me nobody could be as bad as I was expecting, and he was right. Indeed, I like you and would very much like us to be friends.''

"Thank you," Claudia said, beginning to walk on. She would have liked to question Tansy more closely about her upbringing but this did not seem to be the right time, and instead she asked, "Andrew? Is that Sally Grantham's eldest brother?"

"No. The second eldest."

Suddenly Tansy's voice was guarded again and warning bells rang in Claudia's head. She asked carefully, "Is he also a military man?"

"No. When he came down from Oxford his father's health was precarious so he stayed at home to manage the estate. Now that Reginald has sold out and returned home, Andrew's assistance is no longer needed. As the younger son he has no expectations and must look for work, but it will be difficult. His whole heart is in the land and he has no interest in any of the suitable professions.''

A fortune-hunter? Claudia wondered, her heart sinking. Did Tansy have a *tendre* for him? There must be some reason for her guarded expression. Away from her father, she had spoken frankly enough about everything else. She must know how unequal would be a match between herself, a well-born heiress, and a squire's younger son. Certainly Giles, cynical of romance, would never countenance it.

Claudia remembered that Tansy had pleased Giles by dropping her opposition to a London Season. Had she truly bowed to the inevitable or was she merely appearing to be docile to gain her own ends? If she was, Claudia could not honestly say that she blamed her, but fathoming out what her "own ends" were would bring extra complications to an already difficult situation. They were a family of strangers, all concealing far more than was revealed, and what would be the end of it all Claudia could not begin to guess.

As soon as Tansy had been handed over to her maid and had expressed her satisfaction with the yellow bedchamber, Claudia made her way to the library. She wanted to hurry and she wanted to dawdle. She wanted to see Giles and she didn't want to see him. She wanted to think about the problems Tansy presented and shelve them until they became inevitable. She was, in fact, dithering—and that was no frame of mind in which to face her husband.

But face him she had to, and without the docility Tansy could so easily assume. It was her own heart that was thumping like a nervous schoolgirl's as she tapped on the library door and entered. Giles was sitting at the massive oak desk and he raised his eyes from the letters before him. Under his intent gaze Claudia, who had had no intention of speaking first, found herself gushing, "I thought the furniture in this room all wrong and had it put back as it was in your father's time. I hope you find it more comfortable."

"Decidedly."

That was all he said. It was better than criticism but fell far short of the compliment Claudia had hoped for.

Will he never approve of anything I do? she thought despairingly. Am I always to be despised, no matter what efforts I make?

"What do you think of Tansy?" he asked in his abrupt way.

"A fine-looking girl. She could be the belle of the Season if she wished."

"More to the point, she inherits her mother's fortune when she is twenty-one. She will not lack offers."

"She is not a commodity to be offered on the market like tea or silk or spices!"

"I am aware of it, otherwise the matter would be settled by now."

"Belgarrick, you are a most unnatural father!"

"I will give you no argument on that." He rose and came toward her and, taking a small box from his pocket, he placed it in her hand. "I have had time this past week to purchase the betrothal ring you stand in need of. The *ton* will expect to see one on your finger when we go into Society."

Claudia, taken aback, opened the box. Nestling on a bed of blue velvet was a large oval ruby, a magnificent stone that must have cost a small fortune. She could only look at it with even greater despair. It was a symbol of his wealth, nothing more. She remembered his contempt of the emerald ring Tom had bought her and again heard him say, as clearly as if he were actually saying it now, *Your rich coloring cries out for rubies— although a lover, perhaps, might be besotted enough to choose sapphires to match your eyes.*

She wanted sapphires. Oh, she wanted sapphires so much!

She could only stare numbly at the ruby, not clever enough to let her expression register pleasure or even gratitude. He must have noticed because as he turned away he said coldly, "Naturally you prefer your emerald ring, but when you become accustomed to the ruby I think you will acknowledge it is the better choice."

Claudia, too choked to speak, slid the ruby on her finger until it nestled against her wedding band, since he clearly did not intend to do so.

For some reason he did not let the matter rest there, as she had hoped, but went on, "I notice you still do not wear the emerald."

"I cannot wear it. I gave it away," she whispered.

"What?"

Claudia cleared her throat and repeated more loudly, "I gave it away."

"Why?"

She lifted her chin and stared at him defiantly. "I do not see what business it is of yours, but if you must know, I no longer felt I had the right to wear it. Tom's emerald, which it pleases you to scorn, was a symbol of love and commitment and many other things you do not understand, nor wish to. When I agreed to marry you for reasons *he* would not understand, his ring seemed to reproach me, so I gave it to two crippled beggars. They were wearing Rifleman Green, that of his old regiment. That, I think, he would have understood."

Her voice choked up again and her eyes misted. She bowed her head. Giles came back to her, took her chin between his strong fingers and forced her face up to his. He looked into her swimming eyes and said with an anger she could not comprehend, "Tears for a dead lover. Am I supposed to be touched, bearing in mind that I am the man who found myself married to his leavings?"

Claudia struck his hand away from her face. "Bearing in mind you are the man who couldn't afford to be fussy, I do not see you have cause for complaint."

169

"We shall never agree over that."

"We shall never agree over anything, not because I am unreasonable but because you are!" She swung away from him, then an overwhelming rush of fury made her swing back. "But I tell you this, Belgarrick. I will never—never!—submit again to being treated as though I am a creature too loathsome to be embraced. I may not be the unquestionable lady you contracted for, but unless you embrace me as a *woman* I will fight you until I can fight no more and you will have to rape your way to fatherhood. Violent rape, as opposed to the submissive rape I endured last time! I will be not be further humiliated and degraded because of something that happened before ever I met you. Shun me during the day if you wish, but at night come to me as a lover or do not come at all! Do I make myself clear?"

"Admirably." His anger seemed to have died in the kindling of hers. As always, she could not read his expression. He took her hand and, when she would have pulled it away, held it more tightly. Then he raised it to his lips and kissed her fingers.

"What was that for?" she asked, distrusting any and everything about him.

"Your courage," he replied, releasing her hand and turning away. "I always salute courage. Did you not know?"

## Chapter Fourteen

Did I not know? Claudia thought mutinously, on her way back to the haven of her own rooms. How could I know anything about the man when he is at such pains to conceal everything he is thinking and feeling? Always supposing he feels anything that is not rooted in anger!

The ring felt awkward and heavy on her finger. The ruby was large and she was not accustomed to it yet. She found that she was twisting it round and round, untouched by any belated pleasure at its richly glowing magnificence. Tom's ring she had stared at for hours on end, and kissed and dreamed over, and exhibited at the slightest opportunity. The ruby she felt like hiding like a guilty secret because it had nothing to do with the emotions she and Tom had shared.

She would have been pleased enough, she supposed, had it not been for Giles's careless mention of sapphires and lovers at their first meeting. Now nothing but sapphires would do for her and her heart ached because she knew she would never receive them.

Mellows noticed the ring immediately and enthused over it, even picking up the box it had come in, which Claudia had tossed on the dressing-table. Mellows also noticed something her mistress had not, the name and direction of the jeweller inscribed upon it. Raising her pale blue eyes to Claudia's, she exclaimed, "From Paris, how romantic! How surprising, too, considering we thought his lordship was in London all this time."

Claudia's nerves jumped, but she said coolly, "A man like my husband can never predict precisely where his business will take him."

"Just so, my lady." Mellows put the box back on the dressing-table and when she went into the dressing-room to lay out the clothes her mistress had chosen to wear for dinner, Claudia picked up the box herself. There was no mistaking the inscription. The ring had, indeed, come from Paris.

Claudia wanted to fling the ring back at Giles, but she could not without revealing her knowledge of his lovenest in Paris, and how she had come to know. Her frustration made her edgy, difficult to please, and she exasperated Mellows by changing her gown four times before she professed herself ready to go down to dinner. Her hair was upswept and she looked tall and graceful in a skimpy gown of red silk that accentuated the generous curves of her body. She did not think her pearl set quite went with it and so her ears and throat were bare.

Her maid was adjusting the silken shawl about her shoulders when Giles entered carrying a mahogany jewelry-box. The swift look he gave Mellows made her curtsy and leave the room. He put the box on the dressing-table, unlocked and opened it, saying curtly, "The Verylan jewels, madam. They are part of the estate, so I need not tell you they must be looked after carefully. Any jewels I might give you will, of course, be your own personal property."

Claudia could only wonder why he had seen fit to give them to her now, and not when he had first brought her home as his bride. He must have seen the question in her eyes, for after a moment he went on, "You might want to lend some pieces to Tansy when she makes her come-out, and plan her wardrobe accordingly. I know you women like to co-ordinate these things."

With his rakish history, it was unnecessary to ask him how he knew, but he had effectively destroyed any pleasure she might have felt in the glittering display of precious stones before her. He did not really want her to have them and was only giving them to her now because he felt obliged to.

He placed the key in her hand, inclined his head in what might have been a bow, and left. Mellows came in again, and when she saw the jewels she showed more appreciation than her mistress. "The family jewels, my lady? Now we can dress you as you should be dressed. I wonder his Lordship did not give them to you before."

"They were being cleaned, I expect. I did not think to ask." Claudia gave her the key, and added, "Keep the box locked and put it in a safe place."

"Surely you will wear something from it!" Mellows exclaimed, taking out a ruby necklace with a heavy ornate setting. "His lordship will be disappointed if you do not."

Claudia could not contradict her without making her suspicious, so she studied the necklace. The rubies were set in gold to form flowers and between each flower a ruby drop quivered. It was obviously of some antiquity, Elizabethan or even earlier. A fashionable lady now would break up such elaborate pieces and have them re-made in a modern style but, in this instance, she thought it would be a pity.

"If it were mine, I'd wear it all the time, underneath my dress if I could not wear it on top," Mellows said enviously. "Pray try it on, my lady. It will go magnificently with that red silk."

"Too magnificently for dining *en famille*," Claudia replied, thinking that Giles would take a great display of rubies at her throat as confirmation of his taste in choosing her a ruby betrothal ring. She had the lowering feeling that she was becoming petty, but she could not help herself.

Fortunately, Mellows thought her objection valid. She replaced the necklace in its compartment and took out a ruby pendant and fastened that round Claudia's throat. The chain was long enough for the pendant almost to disappear between her breasts, and she thought that unostentatious enough to approve. Mellows smiled, lifted out matching pendant earrings and fastened them to Claudia's ears.

"There, my lady," Mellows said, satisfied at last. "You look a picture. I'm afraid there doesn't seem to be a ruby brooch."

Claudia could only be grateful, and went down to the Blue Salon to await the summons for dinner. Giles was already there and, as she seated herself beside the fire, he fetched her a glass of sherry.

While she sipped it, he studied her intently and said, "Few women can wear rubies to advantage. I was right in supposing that you could."

If he meant it as a compliment it was an awkward one, and Claudia could think of no reason why he should be nice to her. It seemed more likely he was being smug because his taste had been proved right, and she declined to answer.

Her silence could not have pleased him, because he asked, "I take it your decision to wear rubies tonight means you are pleased with your betrothal ring?"

"A ruby was a rational choice. I scarcely expected a sapphire."

She had had no intention of letting him know she remembered the conversation they had had about jewels when first they had met, but the words were out before she could stop them. She was saved from a crushing reply by the entrance of Tansy, and the talk became more general. It was Tansy who brought Giles's attention back to Claudia by saying, "My maid tells me you have a Chinese cook. How novel! She was afraid we would be obliged to eat strange food, but was told he will cook only for my father."

"What's this?" Giles asked, swinging round to look at Claudia as he was pouring himself another sherry.

"You mentioned once how much you miss Eastern food, and I thought that could be remedied if an Indian cook could be found. I put the matter in Mr. Tigwell's hands, and he sent me a Chinese who is skilled in Indian and English cooking as well as his native dishes. Tonight he cooks a—a *biriani* I think he calls it, of rice and seafood and spices."

"You have been busier than I thought," Giles told her, his unfathomable brown eyes boring into hers.

"Is that all you can say when Claudia must have been to a great deal of trouble on your behalf?" Tansy rallied him. "If I know anything of servants, they did not accept a Chinese in their midst without a fuss."

"Was there a fuss?" Giles asked.

"Émile walked out. I promoted Mrs. Perkins, who has worked in the kitchens since she was a child, to head cook, and that was the end of the matter. Nobody has noticed any difference in the quality of the food."

Tansy smiled. "I suspect an iron fist in a velvet glove."

"Nonsense," Claudia replied lightly. "When you set up your own household you will soon discover it does not do to encourage servants to indulge in hysterics."

"I shall know who to send for if they do. I hope you

175

are as successful at keeping my father in his place. Nobody else has ever managed to."

"There is a difference between plain speaking and impertinence, Tansy," Giles told her coldly.

Claudia, embarrassed, sought to draw his wrath away but before she could think of anything to say, Tansy replied contritely, "You are right, and I beg your pardon. I lack, as you have already pointed out, town polish. I begin to think a Season in London will benefit me, after all."

Hastings came in to announce that dinner was served, and as they went in Claudia again suspected that Tansy was not as meek as she seemed. If she was right, and the girl was appeasing her father for a purpose, then it was undoubtedly her duty to find out what that purpose was and, if necessary, thwart it. Her appetite, never good since her marriage, disappeared entirely.

She waved away the dressed lobster and the goose pie and accepted a portion of chicken *à la Terragon*. As she picked at it, she had the satisfaction of seeing Giles help himself generously from the strange dishes that were set before him, and then help himself again. Strange, how it gave her pleasure to see him happy when his greatest pleasure appeared to be to make her miserable . . .

When the time came for the ladies to leave the table, Tansy said as Claudia led her to the Blue Salon, "Do you always dine in such state? I felt like a fish stranded at the middle of the table, with nobody opposite me and having to raise my voice to say anything to you at one end or my father at the other."

"It is inconvenient," Claudia admitted, "but it is the custom here."

"Change it," Tansy counseled, "while you are still a bride whose whims must be indulged."

After a swift glance, Claudia acquitted her of mockery. Tansy simply had no idea how matters stood between her father and her stepmama. The remark was made in innocence, as was the one which followed, "My father cannot be hidebound by tradition or he would not have led the life he has. Nor can you, or you wouldn't have exchanged a French cook for a Chinese one. If you mean to show me over the house tomorrow, we could look at the same time for a room more suitable for family dining. Closer to the kitchens, too, so that our food is not tepid when it reaches us."

It amused Claudia to hear so young a girl sound so housewifely, and she said, "You sound as if you cannot wait to set up your own house. Are you sure you are so against marriage?"

"I am not against marriage at all, provided my husband is of my own choosing. I do not expect to find him capering at some London ball, that is all."

Claudia said diffidently, "I fell in love in my first Season, and that was at a ball. I wouldn't say he was *capering*, but he was certainly dancing and I couldn't wait for him to ask me to dance. He did, and before the evening was out he asked me to marry him. I said Yes."

"I know what you are going to say next! It was all calf's love and by the end of the Season you discovered you had made a terrible mistake," Tansy told her with a harshness reminiscent of her father.

"By the end of the Season we loved each other more than ever," Claudia contradicted.

"Then he was unsuitable and your father parted you, and so saved you from making a terrible mistake. I have spent my life listening to such homilies from my mother and my grandparents, and more latterly from my father. There is no need for you to add your mite."

Such bitterness in one so young saddened Claudia, but she went on gently, "This is no homily, Tansy. We

177

were betrothed and were to be married on his first leave from the Peninsula. Soldiering was his profession, you see, being a younger son. In some foolish way I was convinced my love would keep him safe, but he fell in the retreat from Corunna."

Tansy's eyes filled with remorse. "I'm so sorry. I thought you were lecturing me."

Claudia smiled. "I would never make such a fatal mistake! At your age I never listened to lectures, and I'm no better now. No, I am only trying to tell you that if you should find yourself in a predicament, or in need of a confidante, you will discover I don't lack sympathy or understanding."

"You are my father's wife. It is your duty to stand by him."

"I have a duty to you as well." Thinking she had said enough for the time being, she rang for working candles and took up her embroidery. Tansy sent for her workbox, and when it arrived she began to hem a silk handkerchief with extremely neat stitches. Their conversation became desultory, each being busy with her own thoughts, although the silences when they occurred were easy ones.

This tranquillity lasted until Giles joined them some time later. Tansy looked up from her sewing, and remarked, "What an age you have been. Nothing could persuade me to stay in that state room one moment longer than I had to. It is like being at a banquet with no guests. The Verylans must have a very grand notion of their own consequence."

Giles frowned at her. "Does it amuse you to mock your own ancestors?"

"It doesn't amuse me to be a Verylan. I have no grand notions."

"And precious little civility, either."

"I beg you pardon. I did not mean to cause a dispute." Tansy's head bent once more over her sewing with the meekness Claudia was now positive was assumed.

"It appears I am the disruptive influence, but don't worry, I shall remove myself. I have some papers that need my attention." He went out, slamming the door behind him in his characteristic way.

Both ladies flinched, then Tansy whispered, "It is your pardon I must beg. I had no idea he would walk out on *you* like that. Is he always so fiery?"

Claudia bit her lip. Giles had revealed what she had been at such pains to conceal, that their marriage was already in tatters. To try to gloss over it, she replied, "He never wished to inherit the title. It has altered the course of his life. He is still coming to terms with it and allowances must be made."

Tansy accepted this mild rebuke and although her eyes were full of questions she was tactful enough not to voice them. Giles had not come back by the time the tea-tray was brought in, and shortly afterward Tansy went to bed.

Claudia sat on for a while, weary and yet wide awake, not knowing whether or not Giles would come to her that night but certain if he did so that it would not be as a lover. She would fight him, as she had promised, but now the time was approaching it seemed to her there would be more humiliation in being overpowered than in not fighting at all. What was she hoping for, that he would be humiliated enough to go away and leave her in peace? Another man might, but not, surely, one who was desperate for a son? Besides, she could not imagine Giles walking away from any kind of a fight until he had mastered his enemy.

. . . His enemy. Herself. No wonder her blood was chilling in her veins.

She had to force herself to go up to her bedchamber

179

and be disrobed and prepared for bed. It seemed that Mellows was in no doubt what her mistress could expect because she had laid out one of Claudia's most fetching nightgowns, a handful of white silk that clung to her body like a second skin.

She also left a lighted candle beside the bed and the bed-curtains undrawn on that side. Claudia, her dark hair waving across the pillow, lay and waited. She did not have to wait for long, but if it had been for hours she doubted if she would have slept. She was far too tense.

He came to her softly, with no slamming of doors to announce his arrival, and looked down at her for a moment before climbing in beside her. Claudia stared straight ahead, scorning to feign sleep but too cowardly to meet his eyes. Her defiant words of earlier seemed puny now, although she meant to stand by them. Better, perhaps, if she had stayed silent and taken him unawares.

To her horror she began to tremble, and nothing she could do had any effect on her shaking limbs. He had admired her courage earlier. Now he would know what a pitiful sham that burst of desperation had been and would despise her for it. She was a cat without claws. A hysteric who could not back up her own hysteria.

His arm went under her shoulders. Effortlessly he lifted and turned her so that she came to rest against him, her head on his shoulder. She felt the lean hard strength of him, and the warmth, and was more than ever conscious of her shameful trembling.

She tensed, belatedly preparing to fight him off when he made his next move. Nothing happened. She was bewildered. Slowly, imperceptibly, her trembling stopped. Her body, against her will, was relaxing.

As her fear left her she felt more vulnerable than ever, for she was conscious once more of the sheer animal magnetism of him. More than that, she felt that all their fighting was irrelevant when she lay in his arms like this. It wasn't, of course, but she wanted to believe that it was. For a little while, unless he said something hateful to spoil it.

Perhaps, she thought tremulously, he was under the same spell because he said nothing at all. He began to stroke her tumbled hair away from her face, then with gentle fingers he traced the line of her cheek, her neck, her shoulder.

Wonderingly she turned her face up to his and he kissed her, tenderly, searchingly. Then she understood. He had come to her as a lover, as she had asked. This must be the man Lisette knew so much better than she did, but there was no time for jealousy just then. All her restrained passion for him was flowing through her lips to his and she was certain she was receiving his in return.

She had no thought for anything after that save the joy of the moment and the exultation of knowing that while he made love to her he was hers, wholly hers. She even believed he actually loved her, although he did not say the words that matched the emotion she sensed in him.

Only when it was over did her doubts set in again, and with them came the fear of his contempt for her abandonment and the dread of another rejection.

He had thrown himself on his back but had pulled her with him so that once more she lay against his chest. She was afraid to move, afraid to do or say anything that would shatter this precious closeness and provoke him once more to anger. When she finally risked raising her head to look at him, his eyes were closed. He was sleeping.

Thankfully, she snuggled back against his chest. She tried to stay awake to prolong the marvelous feeling creeping over her that she was as much a part of him as he was of her. It was an unequal struggle against nature, as unequal as her struggle against loving him, and very soon she was sleeping with him.

Shortly before dawn Giles awoke. Claudia was lying against him, her dark hair straying across his shoulder. For a while he lay still, looking down at her, remembering the night and thinking of all the words that should have been spoken and were not. His fault, always his fault. He was set in a mold he could not break, no matter how hard he tried. His lips twisted bitterly. He eased himself away from her and got out of bed. He stood looking down at her while he put on his robe, then carefully covered up her bare shoulders. She looked so peaceful, so defenseless, so lovable. Swiftly he bent down to kiss her soft lips, and then he turned and left her.

When Claudia awoke some hours later she was alone, the place beside her cold. The joy of the night faded to the stark reality of the day. She had captured his passion. The man himself still eluded her.

## Chapter Fifteen

That night set the pattern for a curious co-existence that lasted for the remainder of their stay in Kent. During the day they led what were virtually separate lives, rarely seeing each other. At night they came together with the fervor of lovers long parted, the incompatibility that had caused their many clashes vanishing for as long as they were in each other's arms.

Giles never spoke the words of love she longed to hear, but his moods varied and sometimes he would make love to her with a gentleness that made her feel he was as truly hers as she was his. Then dawn would break and he would be gone, and she would have to endure another day of being ignored by him.

What Tansy made of the situation Claudia did not know, for the girl preserved her tactful silence in all matters relating to her father. Doubtless this close view of a marriage of convenience was hardening her resolve to avoid at all costs such an arrangement for herself.

Certainly Claudia's suspicions that she was overly fond of Andrew Grantham were reinforced when she discovered Tansy was embroidering the initials A.G. on the silk handkerchiefs she worked on so assiduously. Tansy explained this away by saying it would soon be his birthday, and she could not let the occasion pass without some small gift as he had always been so kind to her. Claudia accepted this explanation without remark but she did not miss the slight blush that accompanied it.

A squire's younger son, she thought despairingly. Giles would create merry hell if he got wind of his daughter's secret attachment. And that there was such an attachment Claudia could not doubt, because whenever Tansy spoke of her friend Sally Grantham, reminiscences of Andrew always crept in.

Sally, like Tansy, had gone to the seminary after her mother's death. This initial bond between the two girls had developed into a firm friendship. Inevitably this had widened to include Andrew who, assuming the responsibilities of the elder brother away with Wellington's army, had called frequently at the seminary to take Sally on outings and had always included her particular friend.

Sally was a weekly boarder and, when she went home at the weekends, Tansy often accompanied her so that she had matured from schoolgirl to young lady regarding Andrew with brotherly affection. It was Andrew who had lent her books on flowers, birds, domestic animals and farming—all their mutual interests. It was Andrew who walked with her, talked with her, rode with her and taught her to drive his gig.

And it was Andrew she now regarded with something far deeper than brotherly affection. It was natural enough, Claudia could see that. He must have been the first male ever to show interest in her. From what Tansy had said, her mother had had little time for her. Her grandparents had been slightly ashamed of her existence and only too happy to be rid of her when her mother died. Her father was a stranger. Small wonder the lonely girl should expand and blossom under Andrew's friendly concern.

Claudia could only hope that Tansy's entrance into the wider world would put the attachment into perspective. A beautiful heiress, she would be fêted and courted by men of rank and fashion, and it would be wonderful indeed if a squire's younger son did not fade from her mind. And if Andrew were a fortune-hunter, Tansy would certainly grow wise enough to perceive it.

In the meantime, Tansy was pleasant and welcome company, and she made a good impression on the local gentry who were now beginning to call at Belgarrick Towers. That these duty calls were continued was, in fact, due to the impression both Claudia and Tansy made.

In view of his sinister reputation, Giles was regarded with suspicion but, for all that, he was a viscount and a rich one—a personage far too important to be ignored by those of lower rank. Even so, the invitations that came in to dinners and musical evenings were inspired by the fact that his new wife and his daughter were indisputably ladies and creditable additions to anybody's social circle.

Claudia gave dinners of her own, when her experience as her father's hostess for so many years was put to good use. On these occasions Giles never let her down. He was attentive and courteous, to herself as well as her guests, and she could not help thinking wistfully how different life would be if he were the same all the time. But she knew all this was for his daughter's sake, and, once she was creditably established, would return to not caring a tinker's curse what anybody thought about him.

When they had guests, the state dining-room was utilized, but when the family was alone a smaller room was now used. This, as Claudia discovered from her housekeeper, was no innovation. There had always been a small dining-room right up to Giles's father's time. It was Gervase, who had had it turned into a sitting-room, never used, preferring to dine in state on the few occasions he was in residence.

Once more Claudia had had things put back to the way they were in Giles's youth and once more he neither objected nor complimented her on what she did. His silence could not have demonstrated more clearly that Belgarrick Towers was to be her permanent home and not his.

Then, one morning, just as suddenly as on the previous occasion, Claudia woke up to find Giles had left at dawn on another unannounced business trip. She was upset because it seemed to her that they had been particularly close the night before. How wrong she had been was proved by the fact that he could still go off without a word to her.

Once more she underwent the torments of jealousy, imagining him in Lisette's arms and unable to comprehend why he should want another woman when their own physical relationship was so perfect. She began to suspect the lure of Lisette was not sex but love, and her torment deepened.

Within a day or two she had to face another dilemma. It had been there at the back of her brain for a week, but she had shelved it while she tried to make up her mind what to do. Then Mellows mentioned it, and Claudia knew she would have to make a decision soon.

The maid was brushing her hair at bedtime when she remarked, "Your time of the month has come and gone and nothing's happened, my lady. His lordship will be overjoyed to know you are pregnant."

So, too, would Claudia have been overjoyed had she succeeded in winning Giles's love. As it was, pregnancy was something she could do without now. Certainly Giles would be pleased, but he would also stop visiting her at nights, for his purpose would have been accomplished. He would probably bring Lisette back to London and seek all his physical pleasures with her.

"Does he suspect?" Mellows continued, smiling.

"No, and if you start any rumors circulating I shall be angry with you," Claudia told her with uncharacteristic severity.

"I wouldn't spoil your surprise for him for the world!" Mellows exclaimed, sounding wounded that Claudia should suppose she might.

"It is not a matter of surprising him but of not disappointing him. You have not been with me long enough to know that I am never regular."

It was a lie, but the maid swallowed it. "I see. I beg your pardon, my lady. We must wait to see what comes then, the period or the morning sickness. Though for my part I expect the sickness. It has been noticed in the kitchens that your appetite has improved."

Why was it, Claudia thought wearily, that one lie invariably led to another, and what could she say now to allay her maid's suspicions? It was true she was eating well, but she put that down to her blissful nights with Giles, not pregnancy. She heard herself saying with shameful glibness, "A change in my way of living always affects my appetite. I believe it must take my constitution a time to adapt from town to country living, and *vice versa*. I have been resident here long enough to adjust, that is all. We shall have no more talk of babies, Mellows, until such talk is justified."

It was easy to snub Mellows, harder to fool her for any length of time. Within a week Claudia found herself having to cope in secret with the queasiness that struck her as soon as she got up. The first morning was the worst, for she had already rung for Mellows and she had to pretend nothing was amiss.

The maid, ever observant, remarked on her pallor. Claudia, contriving to yawn languidly although the effort to control her heaving stomach made her sweat slightly, replied, "I had a disturbed night. The stable cats woke me up with their caterwauling in the courtyard and it took me an age to get to sleep again. You wouldn't have heard them, I suppose, because you sleep in another wing."

"It would take more than cats to disturb me, my lady! I sleep sound and always did. Drink up your chocolate, and you'll soon feel more the thing."

Claudia's stomach heaved at the sight of the dark liquid. She would have given anything for tea, but feared her maid would take as confirmation of her condition any change in her normal habits. Then, just as suddenly as the queasiness had attacked, it went, and after a minute or two she was able to sip her chocolate, although she still craved tea.

After that, Claudia always got up before ringing for Mellows. She was never actually sick, and the nausea, acute as it was, never lasted more than a few minutes and then she felt perfectly healthy again. She supposed she was lucky although there were times when she wished she could have the relief of being actually sick, or at least the comfort of being pampered by somebody who cared. Still, she preferred to endure alone, and climbed back into bed and summoned her maid only when the attack was under control, so determined was she to have as many nights as possible with Giles before her secret was out.

This time he was away a fortnight, and although she went about her normal duties with a smiling face, inwardly she pined for him. Her love for him was a sickness that never left her, as the nausea did.

When he came back he brought her a ruby brooch—to go with the pendant set that became her so well, he said. The brooch was beautiful, a large stone with three ruby drops suspended from the gold setting. Claudia looked at it bemused, unable to imagine why he had bought it for her. A conscience gift because he had been with his mistress? Yet she was not supposed to know about that, and he did not give the impression of a man troubled by conscience.

She thanked him properly, but he must have seen the questions in her eyes because he told her brusquely, "The pendant set looks incomplete. Society thinks me a scoundrel, but it will do Tansy no good if I am thought to be a miserly one as well."

There was nothing in the explanation to please her, and she asked, "Is it to go with the family jewels?"

"I have already told you, madam, that anything I give you is your own property." He turned to Tansy and gave her a large velvet-covered box. "Your come-out gift. I understand you will not receive your mother's jewels until you come into your fortune at twenty-one. It seems a curious way to leave things, but, then, your mother was a curious woman."

Claudia had to smother a gasp at his callous reference to Tansy's mother, but the girl made no remark and merely opened the box. Inside lay a triple row of beautifully matched pearls, a pearl bracelet, a pearl brooch, dainty pearl earrings and two pearl hair decorations.

It was a superb gift, ideally suited to a débutante, but after staring at it for a while Tansy exclaimed, "I'm overwhelmed, only—only I wish you hadn't bought me anything half so magnificent. It makes me feel beholden to you."

Giles's eyebrows snapped together. "How could you possibly be beholden to me? I am your father."

"Yes, but it makes me feel as though I should marry to please you, and I have no intention of marrying anyone except to suit myself."

"We will tackle that hurdle when we come to it."

Brown eyes were locked on brown, and Tansy said militantly, "It will not be I who come a cropper."

"We are at one on that," Giles retorted grimly, and left them with their gifts.

"It's too lavish, far too lavish," Tansy murmured, closing the box. "A single strand of pearls, that would be usual, but this!"

"Now that he is a rich man, perhaps he is trying to make amends for his neglect of you in the past," Claudia suggested gently.

"He never neglected me financially. He was left an annuity by his father, a matter of only a few hundred pounds a year, but he made it over to my mother before he left her. It was not enough to support her in the style she was used to, which was why she returned to her parents' home. Still, it was all he had, and as he became rich he settled more money on her. By that time she had inherited her own fortune, of course, for she had passed her twenty-first birthday, but she chose to shun the world and remain with her parents."

Claudia was stunned, then she exclaimed, "How could she permit the world to believe Giles abandoned you both without a penny! It is infamous!"

"She lived for sympathy," Tansy answered shortly. "Without it, I think she would have shriveled up and died a great deal sooner."

"Tansy, you should not speak of your mother in such a way."

"It is the truth. She was rich and beautiful. She could have divorced my father and married again. But no, not her! She was like a spoilt child who, denied the one thing she wanted, would not reach for anything else. I

190

tell you, she *enjoyed* making a martyr of herself, but I will never understand or forgive her for making a martyr of me. I lived in the great gloomy house—oh, with every comfort!—but no joy, no friends, no pleasures. I was lectured from dawn till dusk so that I would not make the mistakes my mother did. My grandparents were obsessed with that! I could not wait to escape the place, but I had to wait until my mother died. I cannot tell you how I felt when my father gave permission for me to go to Bath. That was when my life really began."

"You poor child," Claudia breathed.

Tansy shrugged. "It's over now and I learned a lot of lessons I'll never forget. If it comes to it, my father will discover I have grown up a match for him."

"Do you hate him?" It was a question Claudia did not want to ask, but felt compelled to.

"I was taught to when I was very young. I was told he did not want me, and was a dreadful person, so that when he came back to England when I was nine or ten I would have nothing to do with him. Then I began to grow up and understand more, and what I hated him for most of all was not taking me away from that miserable house. Now I realize I gave him no encouragement to do so. It wasn't until a few months ago when his lawyer told me he was returning to England to take charge of me that I discovered he had supported me all these years. He didn't want me, but he didn't abandon me, either."

"I think it's the saddest story I've ever heard."

Tansy's lips curved in a mischievous smile. "We survive, we Verylans. We are a tough breed. My father is proof of that. My mother should have fought for him. *I* would have known that recriminations and wringing of hands was no way to keep such a man!"

"You surprise me! I have heard you speak of the Verylans with scorn."

"The spiteful reaction of one who was never admitted to their ranks." Tansy confessed freely. "Now I realize how much a Verylan I am."

"And clothe your true self with meekness?" Claudia could not resist saying.

"A woman must use what weapons she has." Tansy lowered her eyes, and when she spoke again it was on a different subject. "Why do you permit my father to call you *madam* in that awful way?"

Finding herself suddenly called to task, Claudia sought refuge in prevarication. "For a quiet life. When your father finally accepts that he is 'my lord' and there is nothing he can do about it, doubtless he will call me 'my lady.' "

"Why can't he call you Claudia?"

Claudia could think of no glib answer, but Tansy flushed and apologized, "I'm sorry. That was gauche of me. I was forgetting yours is a marriage of convenience. It is natural for you to be formal with each other."

After that, Tansy's confidences were at an end and Claudia was left with much food for thought. She saw Giles in a better light now, although she could not acquit him of being a neglectful father. Far from it. He should have made it his business to find out what sort of life his child was leading and done something about it. And what would have happened to Tansy if his inheritance had not forced him back to England? She had already been at the seminary far too long.

There was another factor, too. He should have worked longer and harder at making his marriage work instead of leaving a wife who was little more than a child-bride and, yes, a child-mother to boot. That he was very young himself did not excuse him. He, after all, was responsible for the hasty marriage in the first place.

Claudia sighed. There was no escaping what Giles was, as the world had judged him, a scoundrel—and from her own experience of him she had yet to see him show a flicker of remorse about anything. She did not know how she could love a man she could not approve of, and yet it was so. Tansy's mother must have found herself in the same incomprehensible position all those years ago, to which had been added the anguish of not being able to hold on to him. Claudia was miserably aware that she herself was faring no better.

Later, when she gave the ruby brooch to Mellows to put away, the maid held it up and admired the way the light made the stone and its attendant drops glow. Claudia saw the envy on her face, and said, "You like brooches, don't you? Was there a ruby among the ones you inherited?"

"No, my lady," Mellows replied flatly, and went to lock the brooch away with the other jewelry.

At dinner that night Claudia wore the ruby pendant set with a white gown that was cut to reveal her long neck and shapely shoulders. Dinner in the small dining-room was an intimate affair compared with the state room. They were able to converse comfortably with each other, and several times Claudia caught Giles's eyes on the pendant nestling between her breasts. Whether it was the ruby or her breasts that merited his attention she did not know, but she felt a sudden rancor that he could eye her so familiarly when he was freshly back from visiting his mistress in Paris.

It was her normal rule to avoid any provocative topic of conversation but she heard herself saying, "I wonder you do not take the Chinese cook and some of the servants with you when you go to London. It must be most uncomfortable staying at Belgarrick House with only a caretaker staff."

"I stay at Fenton's Hotel. It is not worth opening

Belgarrick House for a brief visit," Giles replied, meeting her eyes as though he had nothing to hide.

This drove Claudia to say, "I would not call a fortnight a brief visit."

"I am flattered. I didn't know you had counted the days I was away."

"I can scarcely be flattered that you did not!"

Tansy raised her eyes from the buttered crab she was eating, gave each a swift glance, then said to Giles, "I have never stayed at a hotel. It must be rather like the seminary, only without the lessons."

Claudia, aware that in trying to discompose Giles she had only embarrassed herself by sounding like a jealous shrew, was thankful that Tansy had drawn his attention away from her. She saw him smile and reply, "A hotel is not half so spartan! Not that I was much at Fenton's this time."

"Why not?" Tansy asked, but it was Claudia who most wanted to know the answer.

"I was more often at Lloyd's or the docks. I am part owner of several ships trading with India and China, and naturally part of the cargoes they carry is mine. Their sailing schedule is geared to the monsoons in the Eastern seas. They leave England between April and September and return between November and March. I was notified that a home-bound convoy had been sighted off Kent. I went up to London to meet it. The cargoes are auctioned at the dockside. I have come home a richer man than I set out."

"It must be more profitable than agriculture," Tansy mused. "Although riskier."

"There is risk in anything worth while."

"I suppose it's a respectable enough trade these days?"

"It always was. In fact, the only thing that is not respectable these days is being poor," Giles retorted with a hard edge on his voice. "Anyone who says otherwise is a hypocrite."

"Were you very poor when you first left England?"

"Damnably. I've made very sure I never will be again."

Tansy pushed away her buttered crab. "Being fabulously rich has never meant anything to me. Naturally I would not enjoy poverty, but a comfortable house, a little estate, would do me very well."

With Andrew? Claudia wondered, but Giles was saying cynically, "You are a Verylan. You would soon grow tired of that. An inferior social position wouldn't amuse you, either. You must marry well."

"I have no intention of marrying a blacksmith!"

"Just make sure you don't marry over a blacksmith's forge."

"Having tried, you know what you are talking about!" Tansy returned waspishly.

"Precisely."

Silence fell, giving Claudia the opportunity to think over her own sharp clash with him.

Had he truly been at Fenton's this past fortnight? He had certainly sounded convincing. Loving him and wanting to believe him, she gave him the benefit of the doubt.

When next she saw his eyes on her breasts she leaned forward, ostensibly to select a chestnut from a dish, but in fact to afford him a better view.

A cheap trick, perhaps, but she felt no shame. He might not love her, but he found a great deal of pleasure in her body, and there was no possible reason why she should not encourage him—provided he did not know he was being encouraged.

She dreaded the time when pregnancy would thicken her body and make his desire wane. The chill that ran over her strengthened, if possible, her determination to keep her condition secret for as long as possible.

When he came to her that night his ardor was such that she was certain he had not been to Lisette, and her joy heightened her appreciation of his love-making. She understood that, for a man, passion and love could be two different things, and yet it was hard to believe he did not care for her when he touched her like this. It was almost as though he was using his body instead of words to tell her how he felt, and if only she could trust her senses she would know she was loved.

But she had become like him, suspicious, distrustful, seeking an ulterior motive in everything. She would never now believe he loved her unless he told her directly. There was only pleasure in deceiving herself in moments like these, when she lay in his arms.

He was kissing her breasts when suddenly he raised himself and said harshly, as though the words were wrung from him, "This is what you miss when I am away, isn't it?"

She was confused, for harshness formed no part of their love-making now. Fearing she was once more about to be likened to a whore, she replied, "You are my husband. It would be unnatural if I did not miss you."

"The husband means nothing to you! It is the lover you count the days for. Do you think I don't know it?"

She could not risk his scorn by confessing she loved him. She remembered too well the contempt in his voice when he had told her: *I know the ways of women. They must always search for a heart.*

"I am a woman," she replied hesitantly. "My reactions are different from yours. For me it is difficult to separate the husband from the lover."

"You always have a clever answer." He put his hand against her face, his thumb tracing the outline of her lips. "You seem perfection . . . and yet I know you are not what you seem."

"Can't you accept me as I am?"

"Trust you, you mean?" He laughed, a scornful sound that made her wince. "No, I can't do that. Once, perhaps, but I'm no nineteen-year-old to be duped and deceived. I know that, whatever women are for, they are not to be set on pedestals."

"I don't want a pedestal! I just want . . ."

". . . this!" He kissed her savagely.

She wanted to protest, but her body responded to his demands as willfully as it always did, and there was no chance for more speech between them. Her protests drowned in a growing wave of passion, unheard and unlamented.

He was gone when she awoke. Once more she was conscious of rejection. It was always the same. The joy of the night succeeded by the doubts of the day. If ever she awoke to find him beside her, perhaps she could begin to hope she was loved as well as desired.

Her mind returned to the things he had said, and she puzzled over them. He had almost sounded tormented, as though he wished to be missed as a husband. Yet that could not be. As a husband, he avoided her as much as possible.

Baffled, she got up to do battle with her morning nausea. It was not getting any better but neither was it getting any worse, and when it was over she felt even healthier and more energetic than usual. She should, at this rate, keep her secret for some weeks to come.


February slipped into March and the servants were once more thrown into a bustle as the household prepared for the removal to London. Mellows had remarked that Claudia's time of the month had come and gone again, but had once more been silenced by being told that was nothing remarkable.

Giles had shared Claudia's bed every night since his return and, on the morning of their departure, her secret dream was realized. She awoke to find him still beside her, his tawny head against the pillow, the harsh lines of his face softened in sleep. How handsome he looked, how infinitely lovable.

She was overwhelmed by a rush of tenderness and for a while she lay unmoving, looking at him as though she could never look enough. Then she began to wonder how she herself looked. Tousled? Disheveled? Their love-making had been particularly passionate last night. Moving carefully, she touched her hair that tumbled in disarray about her shoulders. It needed brushing.

She crept out of bed and crossed naked to the dressing-table. In her anxiety to look beautiful for him she totally forgot about her morning nausea. It struck as she was brushing her hair. She could not remember such a violent attack. She doubled up, the hairbrush clattering from her hand on to the dressing-table top.

She tried to retch silently, praying that she had not woken Giles up and thankful that, with the curtains drawn along the bottom of the bed, he could not see her. To her horror the waves of nausea were increasing, not receding as usual. Her legs began to tremble. She went down on her knees, a groan escaping her.

She looked round in dismay as she heard a sound. Giles was coming round the bed, hastily throwing his dressing-gown about him. "I—I . . ." She did not know what she was trying to say. Another spasm doubled her up.

Giles took in the situation at a glance. He pulled the counterpane from the bed and wrapped it around her naked, shivering form.

"Go away," she begged, aghast that he should see her like this. "Please go away."

"Don't be missish," he told her curtly. "You are a married woman now and, by the looks of it, a pregnant one."

Claudia groaned again. He tugged the bell-pull beside the bed, grabbed a bowl from the wash-stand and held it before her. "Don't fight the sickness," he commanded. "You will feel better when it is over."

What did he know about it? she thought, resentful in her misery. Then she recollected that a pregnant wife was no novelty for him. She said with all the dignity she could muster, "I am never sick." Then she was, and she was grateful for the bowl he held for her.

When it was over, her physical misery was gone but she was twice as miserable that Giles should have seen her like this. She, who had only been trying to look beautiful for him. She could think of no way she could have disgusted him more.

He had put the bowl aside and was wiping her face with a damp cloth. Then he picked her up and carried her back to the bed. She objected fretfully, "I don't want to go to bed. I want to wash and clean my teeth."

"So you shall directly," he told her with the maddening authority an adult used to cope with a recalcitrant child. He poured a glass of water from the carafe on the bedside table, put an arm round her shoulders and lifted her so that she might drink. He held the glass against her lips and said, "You shall have something more suitable soon, but this will make you feel better just now."

She did not know how Giles, not loving her, could bear to touch her after what he had just witnessed but her head lolled gratefully against his shoulder and she sipped the water.

Claudia began to feel fully recovered. Her shivering

had stopped. She was warm again and the awful nausea had gone as though it had never been. This, she thought, would be such a joyous moment if he loved me. He would feel more than merely satisfied that his mission was accomplished, and so speedily. And she? How would she feel? Supremely happy she was carrying his child. Now, however, she faced a long term of lonely nights as well as lonely days until the time came to conceive the second child. There was no belying his promise at the beginning: *You will be bothered no more than necessary.*

She wanted to be bothered. It was the only way she could fancy that he did, indeed, in some way love her— and more than ever now she was desperate for his love.

She wished she could turn her head toward him and bury her face in his neck, but this was morning and the liberties of the night could no longer be taken. He was so tantalizingly close. His arm was still supporting her, and yet when he spoke he sounded unshaken by any of the emotions that weakened her.

"I am sorry my child should make you feel unwell. It is a condition that will pass, and you can be sure every care will be taken of you."

*Of the child,* she thought.

"Anything you want is for the asking," he went on.

*I want only what you cannot give. Your love.*

Perhaps it was her silence that made him ask, "Don't you want this child?"

"Every woman wants a child." To try to keep the issue in doubt a little longer, she added, "I am just unsure whether one bout of sickness heralds a child."

"You will see a doctor as soon as we are in London. Meanwhile I must ask you to avoid all those occupations that are unwise for pregnant women. Riding, I believe, is one of them, and excessive walking."

Claudia felt a flare of resentment against her baby.

It seemed she was to lose not only her lover but her other pleasures as well. Saba was a new mother. She had managed to produce healthy and adorable puppies without any of this fuss. Why could it not be the same with women?

Mellows came in, carrying the usual hot chocolate on a tray. She took one look at the bowl on the floor, the counterpane beside it and Giles propping up Claudia while she drank the water, and she exclaimed, "The sickness has started, then! I knew all along, my lady, you were in a delicate way for all you were saying you're too irregular to be sure." She added with a satisfaction Claudia could have throttled her for, "We can look for a baby in November by my reckoning."

It was at that point she took control and became officious where before she had been self-effacing and obliging. She put her tray on the bedside table, took the glass from Giles's hand and told him, "You may leave Lady Belgarrick to me, my lord. I know just what to do to make her comfortable. It's not the first time I've served a pregnant mistress."

Giles stood up and moved away, and Claudia, not knowing when she would ever feel him so close again, snapped, "I am—or was—perfectly comfortable, thank you."

"You will feel better when you have drunk your chocolate. Having something in your stomach before you get up helps to stop the sickness, you know."

"It is a little late for that." Claudia eyed the chocolate with loathing. "Take it away. If I have anything, it will be tea."

"Not at this hour, my lady. There are doctors who hold tea to be injurious to a delicate constitution."

"My constitution is not delicate. I will have tea or nothing!"

Giles was going to the dressing-room door, but he stopped and turned. "Bring her ladyship tea."

Mellows dropped a curtsy. "If you say so, my lord, although I will not be answerable for the consequences."

"Don't talk such rubbish! Women in the East drink tea all the time and produce God knows how many children. Be off with you, woman, and fetch her ladyship what she wants."

He went out, leaving the thunderstruck Mellows staring after him. Claudia, surprised that he had intervened on her behalf, leaned back against the pillows. It seemed she was to be pampered. Not for her own sake but for the child's. For the second time that morning she fought another silent battle. Not this time against the sickness but against an overpowering urge to burst into tears.

*Chapter Sixteen*

As the weeks passed at Balgarrick House in Grosvenor Square it seemed to Claudia that she was becoming irrational. When the fashionable doctor summoned by Giles confirmed her condition she was vexed, although she had never doubted she was pregnant. Giles expressed his pleasure that she had conceived so quickly, but she could not bask in his approval and snapped, "I only hope the child wasn't conceived that night—that night that was repugnant to both of us."

Giles's eyes hardened. "What possible difference can it make when the child was conceived? I know pregnant women are subject to strange fancies. I did not know they could be ridiculous."

"How like a man to say such a thing!"

"I am a man, dammit! I am not subject to whimsical notions. If you have it in your mind that you were raped that night, let me tell you that you were *not*. You are my wife, and I used no force."

That was unanswerable, which only heightened Claudia's resentment. After that neither risked a further confrontation by discussing the baby. It was the reason the marriage was made for, yet it was the cause of a deepening of the rift between them.

Giles became aloof, distant. He was the one now avoiding provocation. Claudia, feeling she was being treated with velvet gloves for the sake of the child, was not appreciative. She did not want to be cocooned. It was a somnambulant state that did not suit her . . . Now that the quarrels she had found so shattering were a thing of the past, she found herself recalling them with something like nostalgia. At least he had been aware of her then.

And, the real root of her discontent, she missed him dearly at night.

Her days were busy enough. There was a great deal of shopping to be done in preparing a young lady for a début, and her own wardrobe needed to be replenished. Normally more than woman enough to enjoy spending money, she still had reason for dissatisfaction.

Tansy's lack of enthusiasm effectively ruined any enjoyment Claudia might have wrung out of the proceedings. She was polite, courteous, docile, but totally uninterested in discussing the merits of this material over that, this color over that, or this hat trimming over that. Most of the time her mind seemed far away. When Claudia, exasperated, took her to task she apologized prettily and said she hated the dirt, noise and bustle of town. She did not mean to be a trial and was appreciative of all her stepmama was doing for her, but she could not help yearning for the peace, beauty and clean air of the countryside.

Pressed to choose between ermine, chinchilla and sable, Tansy said she hated the thought of some poor wild animal being killed to keep her warm, and would rabbit not do? As for ostrich and peacock feathers, she said if God had meant women to be adorned with them he surely would have given them the ability to grow their own. And when Claudia nobly sacrificed her own desire to own a particularly stylish bonnet to offer it to

Tansy, the girl begged that she would not have to be made into a figure of fun by wearing an upturned coal-bucket on her head.

Claudia, biting the bullet, began to think that her beautiful protégée would make an excellent wife for a squire's second son. In fashionable Society she would be regarded as an amiable eccentric at best, a decided oddity at worst.

The blame for this Claudia placed unhesitatingly at the unknown Andrew's door.

She had discovered, quite by accident, that Tansy was keeping up a clandestine correspondence with him. She had gone into her room one evening so that they could go down to dinner together, but Tansy had already left. One of the candles in the candelabrum on the desk was guttering. Claudia took the candle-snuffers from the mantelpiece, and while she was extinguishing the candle her eye fell on a letter Tansy was writing and she read the first few lines involuntarily:

My dearest Andrew,

Pray come to me quickly. I cannot keep up this charade unless you are close to me. Just to know you are near would make so much difference. To see you . . . to hear your voice. Claudia is kindness itself and my father civil and generous, and I can feel no gratitude. None at all. It makes me feel such a wretch. But I am lost without you, my darling. Every second is an hour, every hour a day . . .

With a mammoth effort of will, Claudia averted her gaze. It was her duty as Tansy's chaperon to read every line of the letter so that she could know what her charge was up to. Read it and then destroy it, and make sure no more were sent.

She could not do it. She understood too well the lone-liness and anguish that lay behind every word. She had written many letters in a similar vein to Tom, and had been a year younger than Tansy then. She could understand Giles's determination to present his daughter to the *ton*, that was only proper, but she could not identify with his wish that she marry for financial and social considerations. In that, all her sympathies were with Tansy—provided that her Andrew did not turn out to be a fortune-hunting rogue. It was all too easy for such a man to take advantage of a young girl who had grown up lonely and unloved.

Toward the end of March she had the opportunity to judge him for herself. One afternoon she was in her apartment when there was a knock on her door. Mellows answered it, and Claudia heard a footman say, "Mr. Andrew Grantham has called to pay his respects to Lady Belgarrick."

"I have never heard of him," Mellows replied. "Tell him her ladyship cannot be disturbed. She is resting, as the doctor ordered."

Claudia, who loathed lying around during the day, was off the day-bed in a flash. She hurried to the door and told the footman, "Show Mr. Grantham into the Yellow Salon. I will be down directly. Oh, and inform Miss Verylan that he has called."

"She was in the hall when he arrived, my lady, and has already taken him into the salon," the footman replied apprehensively.

So, Tansy was alone with her lover. It was naughty of her, but in her position Claudia knew she would have done the same. For the servants' sake, she said, "That is natural enough. She and Mr. Grantham are—were—childhood friends."

The footman looked relieved and went away. Mellows closed the door and said disapprovingly, "A full hour's rest the doctor said you were to have every afternoon. My lord will be displeased if he discovers you are risking the child."

Claudia counted ten before she answered. It was unfair to snap at a servant who could not snap back, but the truth was that Mellows was beginning to irritate her intensely. She seemed positively to glory in the disadvantages carrying a child brought to her mistress. Claudia could not acquit her of being sorry when the morning-sickness phase had passed, her disappointment that the child had not yet begun to alter her mistress's figure was evident when she had suggested that Claudia was not eating enough. She had been snubbed then, and only when she had reached ten was Claudia sufficiently in control of her irritation to refrain from snubbing her again.

Instead she said evenly, "I am risking nothing save losing my temper with you. You must understand, Mellows, that my pregnancy has turned me into neither an invalid nor an idiot. Kindly do not presume to make my decisions for me in future. The Granthams were exceedingly kind to Miss Tansy while her father was abroad. I would not have one of them turned away from my door for anything."

Mellows took this stricture without comment, merely holding up a green round grown as her mistress discarded her robe.

Claudia decided to be difficult, not to annoy Mellows but to allow Tansy and Andrew as much time as possible alone. After several weeks apart they would have much to say to each other. Better they got it over with now than at some risky clandestine meeting. She wrinkled her nose at the gown Mellows held. "I am not in the mood for green."

"If you are feeling bilious . . ." Mellows began.

Again irritation struck Claudia, and she interrupted,

"I never felt better in my life. Fetch me the lavender cambric with the chenille lace."

"The flounce needs a stitch or two."

"I can wait."

"I don't think his lordship would want Miss Tansy left alone with Mr. Grantham any longer than possible."

"When my husband wants you to think for him I'm sure he'll advise me of the fact," Claudia replied with deceptive sweetness. "Mr. Grantham is a gentleman, and you cannot mean to imply that Miss Tansy would be guilty of unseemly behavior."

"No, my lady, of course not." Mellows fetched the lavender cambric and set hasty stitches in the offending flounce.

Claudia pulled on her robe, sat down and waited, observing her maid thoughtfully. Mellows had become more opinionated and assertive since the pregnancy had been confirmed, and sometimes Claudia had the peculiar feeling that she was gloating. Quite why was a mystery there was no fathoming. It was almost as if she were expecting, and waiting, for her mistress to go into a decline. What benefit she could possibly reap from that, unless she enjoyed nursing and fussing, Claudia could not imagine. But the maid had changed, no doubt about that—unless she herself was once more being irrational.

It was a full twenty minutes before she made her way downstairs. The butler, after ushering the young couple into the Yellow Salon, had decorously left the door ajar. She pushed it further open, and the scene that met her eyes revealed that Tansy was behaving very unseemly indeed.

She was locked in the arms of a tall, fair-haired young man. Claudia was unable to see her face, which was pressed against his shoulder. Andrew's head was lying against her tawny curls and his expression Claudia could see. His eyes were closed and he looked as though he were holding in his arms everything that was most precious to him.

Claudia's romantic heart contracted. *Not* a fortune-hunter, she thought. Just a young man foolish enough to love a girl immensely above him in wealth and breeding.

She retreated quietly, walked back along the passage and as she turned to approach once more, she coughed. When she entered the room for the second time Andrew was standing by the fire and Tansy was seated demurely several feet away. Both were a trifle flushed and both turned apprehensive eyes toward her.

Am I so formidable? Claudia thought with a pang. It does not seem so very long ago when this might have been Tom and me.

Then she found herself wishing that Giles had just once held her as though he could not bear to let her go. That would have been something. Enough, perhaps, to make up for all the rest.

Becoming aware that her scrutiny was increasing the young couple's apprehension, she pulled herself together and walked toward Andrew with a welcoming smile. Tansy stood up and said hastily, "Claudia, may I present Andy—I mean, Mr. Andrew Grantham to you. Andrew, Lady Belgarrick."

They shook hands and Claudia studied him carefully. He was a well-built young man correctly dressed for visiting in a long-tailed coat of bottle-green, fawn pantaloons, starched cravat, waistcoat and Hessian boots, but she could easily believe he would be more comfortable in less formal wear, striding about the fields with a dog at his heels and his carefully brushed hair tousled by wind and rain. Indeed, although his face was boyish his complexion was so weather-beaten

209

it was obvious he spent more time out of doors than in. He was not handsome in the strictest sense, but his features were pleasant, easy to look at, and his smile was warm.

Claudia, ever sensitive, realized he was ill at ease and thought that, in his own surroundings, he would be merry and good fun. At the moment he reminded her of nothing so much as an overgrown puppy anxious to please but afraid that he had not. She liked him, and was not at all surprised that Tansy loved him, but whether the attraction would survive after she had met men of greater polish and address remained to be seen.

"I know that to visit unexpectedly in the afternoon like this is not at all the thing, but I arrived in town too late to call this morning, and—and I did not wish to appear backward in paying my respects," he said.

"You are very welcome," Claudia assured him, thinking: You have come poste-haste in response to Tansy's letter. What lover could resist such a plea? Aloud, she went on, "Pray sit down and tell me how your family does. I hope to meet them all one day. You have all been so very kind to Tansy."

Under her gentle questioning Andrew lost his restraint and became very much more natural. He stayed, very correctly, no more than twenty minutes after Claudia had joined them, and during this time she was able to come to further conclusions about him. She was certain he was honest and that his affection for Tansy was free of avarice.

When he rose to go, she said, "I am giving a dinner the week after next. Would you like to come?"

Andrew's face flushed with pleasure and he bowed. "I would be delighted, Lady Belgarrick."

She smiled. "Leave your direction with the butler and I will send you an invitation. It will be good for

Tansy to have someone she knows. Most of the other guests are strangers to her."

After he had gone, she remarked to Tansy, "A charming young man."

"He is everything that is amiable." Tansy made a creditable attempt to sound nonchalant.

"A paragon?" Claudia asked, aware that this was no laughing matter but unable to resist the temptation to tease.

"No, not that, but he is a *brick*, Claudia. He would never let me—that is, anyone—down."

"He cannot be much above twenty."

"He is almost twenty-three."

"Poor Andrew. Almost in his dotage, and I never suspected it!"

Tansy grinned. "You are mocking me but, indeed, when I was a schoolgirl he always seemed so very much older than me. It was only lately that—that . . ."

"You caught up with him?"

"Yes," Tansy agreed gratefully. "I cannot say quite how or when I—I . . ."

"Fell in love with him?"

Tansy stared at her. "Am I so transparent?"

"To me you are." Claudia hesitated, then went on, "You know, of course, that your father will never permit such a match? A squire's younger son with no money, no profession . . ."

"I know," Tansy whispered. "But you—you will stand my friend as you promised? You will not try to separate us?"

"No." Claudia could think of no action more likely to precipitate an elopement. "I cannot, however, encourage you further. It wouldn't be fair and it wouldn't be right. You must remember that your father has entrusted you to my care. I will not lightly break that trust."

*"Further?"* Tansy repeated. "Then . . . Then the length of time we were left alone was not accidental? We wondered about that. How could you have know before ever you saw us together?"

"Whenever you spoke of Sally Grantham your conversation was soon dominated by Andrew. It was not hard to deduce that he was always on your mind. Then one evening I went to your room. You were not there, and my eyes fell on a letter you were writing. I had taken in the first few lines before I was aware of it. They were enough."

"Oh!"

She looked more annoyed at her own negligence than contrite, and after surveying her for a moment, Claudia could not resist saying, "Tansy, you wretch. You have been writing frequently to Andrew and addressing the letters to Sally. She was only your go-between but as if that were not enough, you have been getting your father to frank the letters for you!"

"I was desperate. If I could not have remained in contact with Andy I do not know what I would have done. It was he who talked me into having this London Season. He said I must meet lots of other men and be positive of my feelings for him before we—we decided what next was to be done. Otherwise he said he would be castigated as a fortune-hunter who snatched an heiress from the cradle, as my father did."

"Had your father been interested only in your mother's money, he would scarcely have left her before she inherited it."

"I know. That's what makes the business so strange. Still, all that is ancient history now. Why didn't you stop me writing to Andy, Claudia?"

"Perhaps because I am no always as wise as I should be. Perhaps because I remember too well writing similar letters myself, although I did not have to be furtive about it."

"I would die if I lost Andy," Tansy said with utter conviction.

"I thought I would if I lost Thomas, but I didn't." Claudia gave herself a little shake. "We are back to ancient history again, and that won't help you and Andrew."

Tansy, who had been plucking disconsolately at a bow on her dress, raised suddenly hopeful eyes. "Does that mean . . . ? But you said you wouldn't encourage us!"

"I won't. However, if you change your attitude to your début and genuinely do your best to widen your circle of friends and your interests, your father will at least know that you have co-operated with his wishes. It's the sensible way. Sulking will only harden his attitude."

Claudia saw Tansy open her mouth to protest, and went on determinedly, "You said yourself that a woman has to use what weapons she has to gain what she wants. Docility is not enough to impress your father. He is not a fool. You say you love Andrew. Very well, put the feeling to the test by giving more suitable partners a fair chance. If you can do that, and if by the end of the Season your love has stood the test, then I will give you and Andrew whatever support I can."

Tansy dropped to her knees beside Claudia and buried her head in her lap. "Oh, thank you!" she breathed, her voice muffled and wobbly with tears. "We have been at our wits' end. Andrew's father, although he has always been kind to me, dislikes the match as much as my father. He is very strait-laced, and thinks the Verylans a ramshackle lot."

Claudia sighed and stroked her stepdaughter's glossy curls. "So does the rest of the world. We must hope

213

your début alters all that. Now dry your tears and run away to wash your face. The dressmaker will be here shortly to stick more pins in you."

Tansy got to her feet, then swooped to hug Claudia swiftly. "You are not near old enough, of course, but I do wish you had been my mother."

Then she was gone, leaving Claudia to reflect grimly that she would be lucky, if, by the time the Season was over, she did not feel old enough to be Methuselah's mother.

## Chapter Seventeen

In fact, Claudia did not look much older than her step-daughter when she stood at the top of the stairs welcoming her guests to dinner a fortnight later. She was wearing a white crepe gown open down the front over a white satin slip, and round her throat was the ornate Elizabethan ruby necklace. She looked magnificent and a perfect partner for Giles, who stood beside her looking devastatingly handsome in a tailed coat, white waistcoat and neckcloth, knee-breches and silk stockings. On her other side stood Tansy, stunning in rose muslin with pearls gleaming at her throat, ears, wrist and in her hair. That she also looked radiant was not because this was her big night but because Andrew had been the very first arrival.

Claudia had thought long and deeply about the best way to present Tansy to the *ton*. She had come to the conclusion that she dare not risk a ball for fear it might, because of Giles's reputation, be thinly attended. A dinner with friends she could count upon, whatever they might think of her choice of husband, seemed the answer, and she was right.

The wealth and handsomeness of the family standing at the top of the stairs, the excellence of the dinner and

Claudia's outstanding qualities as a hostess worked their magic. Giles played his part nobly. He was charming to the ladies, courteous to the gentleman and generally gave the impression of a rake whose reformation made him wish for no more than making his peace with the world. Tansy, the débutante, was judged unaffected and unpretentious. These advantages, combined with her beauty and wealth, balanced the scales against her father's scandalous past.

She did not, to Claudia's relief, betray her partiality for Andrew, and he was similarly restrained. As the evening wore on, Claudia had the satisfaction of seeing that her dinner was a success, and by the time the evening ended she knew it to be a triumph.

She had invited two of the patronesses of Almack's, that holy of holies for all aspiring débutantes. One had come out of friendship, the other out of curiosity. Before they left, they promised that vouchers would be issued to Tansy. This was the crowning achievement for Claudia. It did not matter now what other doors might remain closed to Giles's daughter. The most important one had been breached.

When Giles had done his duty by the more important ladies among their guests, he waltzed with Claudia. For appearances' sake, she told herself, but that scarcely marred the joy of being in his arms. Those were bitter-sweet minutes, and once, when she stole a glance at him, he was looking down at her with an expression she could not, as usual, fathom.

She raised her eyebrows enquiringly, and he said, as though the words had been torn from him, "You do me credit."

Claudia, a perfect dancer, almost missed her step. A glow that had nothing to do with the champagne she had drunk spread through her. From Giles, those few words meant more than the most fulsome compliment from any other man. His arm tightened round her to steady her, and she replied a little breathlessly, "Thank you. I thought something had displeased you. You were frowning so."

"You have not been off your feet for hours. I was wondering if all this dancing was tiring you."

She smiled, the radiant smile that had been missing from her lovely face for so long. "Oh, I never tire of dancing. I love it so, and always have. If we could persuade our guests to stay until dawn, I would be dancing still."

"Is that wise?"

"While one has partners, it is irresistible!" She put her head a little on one side and looked up at him through her thick dark lashes, daring to flirt with him because everything was going so well.

"Your popularity is evident. What is not, is your condition. That is why I ask whether it is wise."

She felt as though he had thrown cold water into her smiling face. For several hours she had forgotten her condition and the joy it had taken from her life. To be reminded of it in such a way robbed her of the glow that warmed her beauty to radiance. She stiffened in his arms. The bitter-sweet moments were over. Her hostility now matched his, and she snapped, "Planning this evening has been a great deal of hard work. I did not know I was to be denied pleasure in its success."

"You resent the child, don't you?"

"I resent being reminded of it every minute of every day."

"That is the grossest exaggeration!"

"It does not seem so to me."

"Before, you never quarreled with me unless you had reason," he told her harshly. "Now you quarrel over nothing."

"You should have advertised for a perfect lady as

well as an unquestionable one! I am neither, and we both know it, don't we? What baffles me is why you feel justified in criticizing me at every turn. Whatever I am, you are a hundred times worse!"

"Thank you," he said bitterly.

"Think nothing of it. I tell you one thing, Belgarrick! If, after it is born, this wretched baby frowns at me as much as you do I shall certainly resent it."

"Wretched baby, is it now? I knew you didn't want it. What is it that you fear, madam? That you won't find so many men to flirt with—if nothing worse!"

Claudia was speechless, and she had to remain so because the waltz had ended. Giles led her off the floor and she was immediately surrounded by her admirers, all begging the honor of the next dance. There was nothing wrong in that, and Giles knew it. Every lady, married or otherwise, was expected to hold her own court; and in the smart world any wife who sat in her husband's pocket was not only a rarity but an oddity.

Unable to find any legitimate cause for complaint, Giles was picking on her for no reason at all. The triumph of the evening was tarnished for Claudia and she did her best to ensure it was also tarnished for her impossible husband. She danced the rest of the night away, careful to keep a smile on her face, for she was aware how closely he was watching her.

It was only the next day that she remembered the first thing he had said to her: *You do me credit.* Why praise her if he was only biding his time to attack her? It did not make sense. It just proved that Giles, her darling and her demon, remained as he had begun, an enigma.

Her duties as a chaperon did not allow her much time to brood. The invitations flooded in. Breakfasts, al fresco parties, balls, routs and, every Wednesday evening, Almack's. April and May sped by, and with the coming of June, the more determined of Tansy's suitors began to declare themselves. She rejected them all, even those whose ardor had not overcome the correctness of applying first to her father for permission to lay their hands, hearts, titles and wealth at her beautifully-shod feet.

All of them were worthy suitors, for Claudia had diligently weeded out the fortune-hunters, but Tansy's fears that she would be pressured into accepting one of them had not yet been realized. She did not know that Giles had bigger game in his sights. In the meantime, she met Andrew at many of the functions she attended, and Claudia, against her better judgment, often invited him to accompany them when they drove out into the country.

Tansy, in spite of all the frivolity and all the fuss that was made over her, had not altered one iota. She was amiable, but the way she smiled at the extravagant compliments paid to her suggested that she regarded them as no more than part of a game she was obliged to play. No matter how extravagant a party or how grand a ball, it was tedious for her if Andrew was not there. Strolling through Hyde Park at the fashionable hour, showing off an elegant new toilette, bored her beyond words; she would much rather be striding through the countryside in sturdy shoes and wearing clothes which were not ruined by rain or the claws of a dog jumping up at her.

On the surface she was very much *à la mode*. Underneath, she remained a bumpkin. Claudia knew it, just as she knew that the only thing that made town life tolerable for Tansy was Andrew's company. That had to be rationed. It would never do to make Giles suspicious. But suspicious he was, as Claudia discovered when he walked into the drawing-room one morning with a frown on his face.

"Has young Grantham taken up residence here?" he demanded. "I seem to be forever bumping into him whenever I enter or leave this house."

"You exaggerate, surely?" Claudia replied lightly. "It is natural he should call. He and Tansy have been friends for a long time, and I have developed a great liking for him myself."

"Have you, indeed? Well, I take leave to tell you I see nothing natural in Grantham being in London while the rest of his family are in Bath for his sister's début."

"A young man doesn't care to hang about his sister," Claudia pointed out reasonably.

"I don't like him hanging about my daughter. Discourage him, madam."

He went out, leaving Claudia with the unenviable task of relating the incident to Tansy. "So you see, my dear, it would be better if Andrew did not call here again. The Season is very nearly over, in any case. Next month everybody will be going to Brighton for the sea air."

"It's beginning, isn't it?" Tansy said bitterly. "The parting of Andrew and myself. I won't let it happen, Claudia. I won't!"

"You must abide by your father's wishes, and also your promise to complete the Season."

Tansy walked restlessly about the room. "Will we go to Brighton?"

"No."

"Why ever not? Andy could go there too, and we could see each other sometimes. By chance, of course. If we go back to Belgarrick Towers, he will go home to Somerset. We might just as well be in different countries." Tansy sat on the sofa beside Claudia and took her hands. "Please, Claudia! Persuade my father to go to Brighton."

"We have already discussed it. He thinks it ineligible because of my condition."

"The baby! I forgot. That's not difficult because you are always so healthy and energetic, and it doesn't *show*."

"That's not a situation that can continue much longer," Claudia replied with a hint of bitterness in her own voice. Only this morning Mellows had observed with unnecessary glee that the much-wanted heir was putting a noticeable curve on my lady's stomach. It was time, she had said, to put away the skimpy gowns and wear the fuller ones.

"There are some ladies who do not retire from Society until they are six months' or more."

"I know. Your father, however, is adamant that we retire to Kent." Claudia, realizing that her own depression was hardly likely to cheer up Tansy, went on, "At least Charles Reveson will be there. He was my father's steward, you know, and now Belgarrick has taken him on. It will be good to have an old friend there."

Tansy looked at her curiously. "I know you are well used to the fashionable life, but sometimes it has seemed to me that you are not much happier than I am. Are—Are you *sad*, Claudia?"

"Sad? Good heavens, no! Sometimes I miss Saba and my horse, that is all." This seemed inadequate and she tried again, "Being pregnant means I cannot ride and I used to do that every day whether I was in town or country."

"Lonely, then?"

"With you for company and a dozen different engagements every day! How could I be?"

"There is such a thing as loneliness of the heart."

"You feel it because you are eighteen. I am six-and-

221

twenty, a married lady with a child on the way. I am past such things," Claudia lied.

Tansy did not look utterly convinced, but she returned to her own troubles. "What am I to do? If my father forbids me ever to see Andy again I don't know what will happen."

"It hasn't come to that pass yet. Your father cannot know how deep the attachment is between you. When he spoke of Andrew always being here it was with irritation, not alarm. Besides, there's no possible way he can part you for any length of time . . ."

Tansy thought this over, then agreed, "You're right. If Andy and I stay true there's not much anybody can do, is there? Discouraging him, after all, is not the same as banning him. How good it is to have someone to talk things over with. All it is, really, is a setback—and I am used to those. There is, as Andy told me when I first learned I was to be brought to London, no need to panic. One way or another we shall overcome every obstacle that is put in our way."

Tansy would not have been half so sanguine had she known the forces that were being marshaled against her. One of them came in the personable form of Farley Sharless, a young man with the blood of half the English aristocracy running through his veins, and a fair sprinkling of the Scottish.

He was twenty-five and, unlike many of his contemporaries, he had no inclination to fritter away his inherited wealth at the gaming tables. More important, he was heir to an earldom, being the oldest nephew of the childless Lord Briddlesham. It was Lord Briddlesham who had been groomsman to Giles on his wedding day. They had been friends since Eton, and the friendship had survived all the pressures Giles's scandalous life had placed upon it.

Between them they agreed that nothing could be

more suitable than a match between Tansy and Farley. Farley was no problem. A few words dropped in his ear by his uncle the earl, and he was only too willing to become more particular in his attentions to the beautiful heiress.

Giles waited for nature to take its course, but as the Season drew to its close and Tansy showed no signs of being smitten by the handsome and charming heir, he looked round for the cause and quite correctly deduced it was Andrew Grantham. It was then that he told Claudia that Andrew must be discouraged. Shortly afterward Andrew's father arrived, bent on driving a further wedge between the young couple.

"For," he told Giles in the privacy of the library at Belgarrick House, "I've no wish to see my son make a cake of himself by dangling for an heiress far above his touch. People will be calling him a gazetted fortune-hunter next, and we've never had one of those in my family." Suddenly realizing he was speaking to one who had been accused of the same crime in his time, he went on rapidly, "Besides, you must dislike the match as I do."

Giles, handing his worried guest a glass of sherry, replied drily, "I do."

"Then why the deuce have you done nothing about it?"

"My dear sir, the days of locking one's daughters up in towers have long since passed. I thought the opposite course more advisable—to expose her to the attentions of a great many young men. However, it hasn't answered. Not yet, at any rate. I don't care to precipitate an elopement by becoming too heavy-handed. Don't look so alarmed. Lady Belgarrick is aware of the danger, and we can depend on her to scotch any such endeavor."

"I'm relieved to hear it!" Mr. Grantham swallowed

Giles's excellent sherry in one mouthful as though it were an indifferent ale, and went on, "What's to be done, then?"

Giles savored his own sherry, then said, "I gather from my daughter that the ostensible reason for Andrew's presence in town is to find some form of respectable employment. Has he been successful?"

"No. Estate management is all he knows and I'm not in a position to set him up on his own land. He's no taste for the church, or for the army now that the war is over. I did think of diplomacy, but I've no influence there, or in any government circles."

"I, however, have a great deal of influence with the East India Company, always supposing he has a taste for travel and craves an opportunity to make his fortune."

"Good God!" Mr. Grantham's harassed face lit up. "If you would speak for him, it would be the very thing."

"Look upon it as settled." Giles held out his hand.

It was gripped firmly. "I'm obliged to you, my lord."

"My obligation is the greater. You were very kind to Tansy at a time when she needed kindness."

"Pshaw! A pretty, taking lass. I always liked her, quite apart from the way she helped my Sally get over the loss of her mother. But there's not getting round the fact that Tansy is aristocracy and Andrew is gentility, and I never knew any good come yet of mixing up the classes." Mr. Grantham paused, then added more practically, "The sooner they are parted the better. Andrew will know he'll never get a better offer to set himself up than with John Company. It's one he can't refuse, that's the beauty of it. Can it be arranged quickly?"

"You can depend on me, sir, not to drag my feet," Giles assured him.

In a very few days a beaming Mr. Grantham was able to inform his son that he intended to take him back to Somerset to take leave of his family.

"Take leave of my family, sir?" Andrew asked, mystified. "Why should I do that?"

"You're off to Calcutta, my boy, to make your fortune as many a young clerk with the Company has done already. Apply yourself, and in a few years you'll be able to come home with enough money to buy that estate you've always dreamed of."

While Andrew was reeling from this shock, Tansy was reeling from another. Farley, for once in his life allowing ardor to overcome propriety, was so smitten by the sight of Tansy in a rose gauze gown over a pink underslip that he proposed to her without first seeking Belgarrick's leave to do so.

It was not Farley's passion that alarmed Tansy, but the fact that he told her he already knew Belgarrick approved of his suit. Tansy flew straight to Andrew, and when they heard each other's news, they knew they could no longer buy time by trying to appease their respective fathers. Unless they acted immediately, time, for them, would run out.

## Chapter Eighteen

Giles was out when Tansy got home and, balked of her prey, she poured out her bitterness to Claudia. "Was I supposed to be so stupid that I could not detect my Father's hand in this?" she stormed. "Andy to be sent to India, myself to be married to Farley Sharless. Good God, I didn't think even Belgarrick could be so gothic!"

Clumsy was the word that occurred to Claudia, not gothic. Had Giles, normally so astute, really been so duped by Tansy's assumed docility that he believed she would bend to his bidding? Certainly the match with Farley would be a brilliant one, but this was not the way to bring it about.

She let Tansy storm on without interruption until she was calmer, then said quietly, "I cannot stop him parting you and Andrew, but I vowed I would not be a party to your being married against your will—and I meant it. We will see him together when he comes in."

"What good will that do? He will not listen to you anymore than he will listen to me. I would have to be deaf, dumb and blind not to know how things are between you. He holds you in subjection, just as he means to hold me—only with me he will not get away with it!"

Claudia flushed. "Not subjection . . ."

"No? What would you call it then?" Tansy challenged. "He is a tyrant. He is civil enough, provided we do just as we are told; but if we do not, we are crushed. We are allowed no thoughts or feelings of our own—not if they run contrary to his. You married into this state but I will marry *out* of it. I swear I will!"

"You do not know how things stand between Belgarrick and myself. You only think you do."

"I know enough to want no part of a marriage of convenience for myself—even if I did not love Andrew. I will *not* spend my life being bullied and ground down until I have no will or mind of my own left!"

She caught sight of Claudia's stricken face and was instantly on her knees beside her, full of remorse. "Listen to me railing against my father's bullying ways and behaving no better myself! I fear there is more of him in me than I want or ever suspected. Most truly do I beg your pardon. You have troubles enough. I am a wretch to burden you with mine!"

Claudia pulled herself together and managed a smile. "I would be upset if you did not do so. It's what I'm here for."

"And who, pray, do you tell your troubles to? Not my father, I'm sure. There I go again, saying things I know you wish I would not." She got back to her feet. "I will take myself off until I can discuss this business without upsetting you as much as I am myself."

Claudia caught her hand as she moved away. "Tansy, promise me you will not do anything foolish."

Tansy looked down at her a moment, that enigmatic look Claudia so associated with her father upon her face. Then she said, "I promise."

Claudia had to be satisfied with that. For the time being, at least. She released her hand. There was no point in detaining Tansy any longer. Both of them would benefit from time alone to reflect before they faced Belgarrick together.

She was dressing for dinner when a note was brought to her in his strong scrawl. He had been detained by business in the City and would not be home for dinner. Claudia could have screamed with vexation. This matter would be better brought into the open tonight, not left smoldering until tomorrow. But there was no address on the note, no clue at all where an urgent plea to come home might reach him. She could only hope that he would return after dinner, by which time she and Tansy would have had the opportunity to talk more rationally.

In the event, she dined alone, Tansy pleading she was still no fit company for anybody just then. Claudia, understanding the turmoil that must be going on in her heart, did not press her. After dinner, she sat and waited for Giles until she was forced to the conclusion that he must have gone to his club and might not return until the early hours.

She went to bed. Her body was weary but her mind was wide awake. Somewhere a clock chimed twelve, and shortly afterward she heard Giles come up to bed. In the quiet of the house she caught the murmur of his and his valet's voices, then all was silent. She toyed with the idea of going alone to see him, then decided against it. All that was said would have to be repeated in Tansy's presence in the morning, and Giles was not a patient man at the best of times.

She tried to settle herself to sleep, and failed. After much turning this way and that, she got up to draw back the blinds and open a window. Moonlight flooded in and, with it, a welcome breath of fresh air to relieve the oppressive high-summer stuffiness of the room. She sat by the window, trying to think of some way out of

Tansy's predicament that would cause neither a scandal nor a series of dreadful scenes.

She could think of no such way unless Giles could be talked out of his attempt to part the lovers, and that did not seem likely. She began to wonder if Tansy was wakeful, too, and plotting some dreadful course that would lead to her social ruin. She was spirited enough to try anything, but she had given her word to do nothing foolish. She was safe enough for tonight.

Safe but unhappy. If she was indeed awake, perhaps she would welcome somebody to talk to by now. Claudia knew that she would herself. Lighting a candle from the branch beside her bed, she stole softly out of her room, along the passage, and crept just as softly into Tansy's room. She had no wish to waken her if she had managed to fall asleep.

The room was in darkness, but to be positive she went up to the bed and held her candle aloft. No tawny head rested on the lacy pillows. The bed was empty. Shock held Claudia motionless for a second then she stripped aside the covers, a purely reflex action since it was obvious that nobody was there. A note slipped down from the pillow to the sheet.

Claudia picked it up with fingers that were not quite steady. She put her candle on the bedside table, opened the note and held it close to the flame, knowing already what it contained. Nor was she surprised as she read:

Dear Claudia,
You are dear to me, although you will not believe it after you have heard what I have done. Andrew and I have eloped. He wanted me to have this Season so that I could meet other men and be certain of my feelings, but I would never have consented had he not given me his vow that he would not permit us to be parted. He will be

blamed, but it is I who made him keep the vow. We shall be married at Gretna and go to India together. It's not what either of us wanted, but it is the only way. Pray don't think I've broken my vow to you. The height of foolishness to me would be to allow my father to part me from the man I truly love. You will understand that, although my father will not. My only regret is leaving you to face my father's wrath. Pray forgive me, and believe we will return as soon as we are married to share the burden with you.

Fondest love, Tansy

The distant clock chimed one. Claudia hurried over to the dressing-table and touched the lamp. It was still warm. She had not been gone long. She must have waited until Giles was safely abed before she fled. There was still time to stop her.

She ran to the door, wrenched it open, then stopped. She stood there, thinking deeply, then quietly she stepped back and closed it.

She went to the bed, straightened the covers, picked up her candle and went out into the passage. She hesitated only once more, and that was outside Giles's room. Roused now, his powerful team would overtake hired hacks long before the first posting-stage was reached on the road north. The elopement would be foiled, the scandal squashed. The family could retire quietly to Kent with nobody any the wiser.

It was what a dutiful wife would do. Claudia walked on. Tansy and Andrew would have their chance of happiness. She only wished she and Tom had had as much resolution when her father had said they must wait a year until they were married. She had allowed Tom to go off to Portugal without her, foolishly certain her love would keep him safe. She had never seen him again, did not even know where he was buried. Tansy was taking no such chances, and Claudia could not find it in her heart to blame her.

Giles was not a restrained man. All hell would break loose tomorrow. Claudia knew it, but she climbed back into bed with an easier mind than she had climbed out of it. She had learned from her mistake with Tom. When she had seen a chance of happiness with Giles, she had grabbed at it. It had eluded her, but in her bones she felt Tansy would be luckier.

Those bones were very weary now. With a little sigh she snuggled deeper into her pillow, and slept at last.

She did not wake until eleven o'clock. The fact that she had been left undisturbed told her that Tansy's flight had not been discovered yet. The flight over the border into Scotland to Gretna Green would take, what, two days? Even so, they had a ten-hour start. Pursuit would be useless now.

She made a leisurely toilette, instructing Mellows to put out a blue morning gown that she knew particularly became her. When the maid slipped it over her head and the long loose folds fell to her feet, Claudia looked around. "Where is the sash?"

"I didn't put it out, my lady. I didn't think it wise, not now the baby is beginning to show."

"Good heavens, I am not gross! If you can see the child, it is because you will stare so, and I wish you would not!"

"You cannot fight the inevitable, my lady," Mellows replied, patting Claudia's stomach with evident satisfaction.

Claudia struck her hand away with something close to loathing. "I have no intention of fighting anything save your impertinence. You had best change your ways or you will find yourself looking for another mistress."

The maid looked jolted and dropped an instant

curtsy. "I beg your pardon. I had no wish to offend. Your ladyship used not to be so cross."

"You did not give me reason to be. Now fetch the sash instantly."

The maid reverted to her former inoffensive, helpful self, but the damage was done. Claudia's confidence was shaken, and though she went downstairs defiantly wearing the sash, she was not as pleased with her appearance as she might have been. It was all for nothing, anyway. Hard as she tried every day to make herself beautiful for Giles, he never noticed. Or never cared.

By the time she had finished her usual conference with Mrs. Binns, her nerves were jumping. Occasionally Tansy, worn down by the frantic pace of the Season, would sleep the morning away, but it was now past midday. At any moment her maid would tire of waiting for her summons and go to see for herself that all was well with her mistress. Then the cat would be out of the bag.

Before she left the housekeeper, she asked, she hoped casually, "Is my lord at home?"

Mrs. Binns glanced at the circular clock on the wall of the housekeeper's room. "He should be back, my lady. He said he would be home for luncheon, and Hastings will be setting it out now."

The housekeeper was right. Giles was already seated at the table when she joined him, carving thick slices of cold sirloin. He was wearing the clothes she thought suited him best, riding breeches, long-tailed blue coat and top-boots. He looked so strong and virile that she could only wonder where she found the nerve to cross him. She had well and truly crossed him now, and it could not be much longer before she was called to account for it.

She was as much on edge as if there had been a fuse-bomb ticking away on the table between them. She meant to play the innocent when the news broke, and she hoped she had learned enough about play-acting since her marriage to be convincing.

Hastings fetched the hot toast and potted shrimps she had developed a craving for, poured her a glass of lemonade, bowed and left.

"Where's Tansy?" Giles asked abruptly.

"Still abed. It was a very sultry night. I had trouble sleeping myself."

"Are you sure she is not sulking?"

Claudia did not trust herself to answer and when she merely raised her eyebrows, he went on, "I shouldn't think young Grantham wasted any time in telling her he is to go to India. I expected to have her at my throat before the day was this old. I credited her with more spirit than she is showing, not that anything she might say would be to the point. Grantham needs to make his fortune, and he'll never get a better opportunity."

"You are deliberately separating her from the man she loves."

"She'll soon outgrow that nonsense!"

"Tansy is neither immature nor fickle. If you think so, you know as little about her as you know about me."

Claudia knew she had to remain calm, but in spite of herself she felt her temper rising. He was always so sure of himself, so arrogantly convinced he was right, and nothing goaded her more. She sought for a way to strike back, and found it. "If you knew half as much about women as you think you do, you would never have been so crass as to encourage Sharless to propose to her on the same day she learned she is to be separated from Andrew. That was the height of stupidity."

"*What?* Sharless has proposed? I did not give him leave." Giles's face darkened with anger and his fist

233

crashed down on the table, making the crockery rattle. "The idiot! He might have ruined everything."

"You favored his suit. He told Tansy so."

"Of course I did, but he was not supposed to declare himself until Tansy had had a few months to forget Grantham."

"A few months? To forget the man she loves? You are ridiculous!"

"And you, madam, are . . ." Giles broke off, swore, then stared fixedly at Claudia. "Are you sure Tansy is in bed?"

She hesitated. It was only fractional, but enough to harden his suspicion into certainty. He grasped her wrist so painfully that she cried out, but he was too angry to pay any heed. He stood up, pulling her up with him, and shook her, saying, "She's run off! And you've helped her, haven't you? *Haven't you?*"

Claudia thought her wrist would surely break. She gritted her teeth against the pain and said between them, "Somebody had to help her against you. The poor child! You ignore her when she is growing up and needs you. You come back, not to make amends but to part her from the man she truly loves and force her into a marriage that is odious to her. You are monstrous, Belgarrick. Monstrous!"

"Fustian! She fancies herself in love with Grantham. Parted from him, she could just as soon have fancied herself in love with somebody else. It is the way of women."

"It is not!" Claudia denied furiously. The pain he was inflicting on her wrist brought a sheen of perspiration to her face, but she would not cry for mercy. "You told me you had no heart. You omitted to tell me your mind is twisted. I'm glad Tansy has escaped you! She and Andrew are free now to find the love Tom and I were denied."

She had said too much. His eyes blazed with new anger. "Am I to understand you have been filling my daughter's head with your own sickly sentimentality? You have! I see it in your face. The devil take you. How dare you use her to fulfil your mawkish fantasies! Your illicit affair ended abruptly, so you've lived it again through her to bring it to a more satisfactory conclusion. And you say *my* mind is twisted. Good God, to think I trusted my daughter to you!"

Claudia was too aghast to deny his ravings, nor was she given the opportunity. With a contemptuous gesture he flung her from him. Her feet caught in the loose folds of her gown, and she fell. He stared down at her as though he could not believe what he had done, then he was on his knees beside her.

She struck away his reaching arms. "Don't touch me! Don't dare touch me ever again!"

She scrambled to her feet, backing away from him. He, too, stood up. She had sustained the fall, but he was the one who looked dazed. He also sounded it as he said, "I didn't mean ... I would never ... Oh, God, I shall call a doctor."

"No!" She reached out for an armchair she knew to be behind her, found it and sat down. "I am all right."

"You can't know that. The child ..."

"... is well enough. It has to be." The child, that was all he cared about. Not she or Tansy nor anyone else. She pulled up her sleeve and revealed her wrist, turning it so he could see the heavy bruising on it. "A doctor would never believe I did this in a fall, and I have no wish to be pitied. When we have decided what must be done, I shall go and rest. A doctor would recommend no more."

He looked about him in a helpless way, seeing her reticule on the floor and restoring it to her with the air of one who was unsure of what he was doing, or why.

I have checkmated him, she thought with savage satisfaction. He cannot drag me screaming to a doctor, and he knows it!

"Is the shouting over?" she asked, surprised that her voice could sound as cold as his. "Can we be rational now?"

He moved toward her, stopped as she recoiled, and moved away. Then he said, as though the words were forced to him. "I am willing to listen to anything that will get you to your bed."

"You need to do more than listen, Belgarrick. You need to co-operate. I think we can rehabilitate Tansy with Society if we handle this the right way."

"They will say: like father, like daughter. The tattlemongers will have a field-day."

"Not if their guns are spiked. We shall say we agreed to the marriage, but they felt they could not wait the year we specified, and so eloped. When they return, we shall give them our blessing and arrange a church wedding. We shall make no attempt to hush the matter up. Quite the reverse, we shall be open about everything. We shall appear as caring and indulgent parents, and Society, robbed of any real spice, will soon turn to something more titillating. The elopement will not be forgotten, but I believe it will soon be forgiven, and that is what really matters."

She paused. When he said nothing, she continued, "Andrew's heart is not in commerce, it is in farming, and so is Tansy's. India is out of the question now, anyway, for people would say we were packing them off to get rid of them. Buy them an estate as a bride gift. It might not be the way you meant to fulfil your duty as a father, but it is the way Tansy will appreciate most."

"Very well."

Just like that! Claudia could not believe it. She had

236

expected to have to fight him, point by point, to gain only half of what she wanted.

He went on, "Will you now go to bed?"

Of course . . . He was willing to concede anything to ensure the safety of his child. She wondered how she would have fared had she not been pregnant. She was rising to her feet when a tap sounded on the door and she sat down again.

"Dammit, what now?" Giles exclaimed.

Mrs. Binns came in with a shrinking maid in tow. "My lord, my lady, I do not quite know how to tell you this, but—but Miss Tansy's maid says her bed has not been slept in."

"Thank you, we know. We have just been discussing what must be done."

The maid repeated, "You know? Then you must have the note. I knew there had to be one."

"What note?" Giles asked.

The maid, apprehensive again, shrank back. "My mistress said if she was gone one morning, she would leave a note and I was to take it to Lady Belgarrick."

"I have it," Claudia confirmed, then turned to Mrs. Binns. "If you will keep this quiet for the moment, Lord Belgarrick will give you his orders in a little while."

"Certainly, my lady." Mrs. Binns curtsied and withdrew with the maid.

Giles was frowning. "Why should she leave you a note if you knew she was eloping. To dupe me into believing you were not involved?"

"I wasn't involved."

"Then why the deuce did you let me believe you were?"

"I could have stopped it. I went to her room just after she had fled. I found the note and did nothing. I deserved your anger."

"You are the strangest woman . . ." he began, then stopped. When he spoke again it was to ask, "May I see the note?"

A request, not an order. How different he was in this conciliatory mood, but it could not last. Not with Belgarrick! She must not let her defenses down so that he could pounce again and find her all unprepared. She reached into her reticule and passed him the note without a word.

He read it through twice, and said, "It seems she found a better friend in you than she did in me."

"You will not let anybody be your friend, Belgarrick."

The glitter came back into his eyes and he crushed the note between his powerful fingers. "Monsters don't have friends. Didn't I tell you once that you and Tansy would find you had a lot in common? A common enemy, in fact. The little fool!" he broke out suddenly. "If she had talked to me, none of this would have happened."

"She did, many times. You never listened. You hear only your own voice, and that never *talks*, only gives commands." She stood up. His mood was turning. It was time to get away.

His lips twisted. "A pretty picture you paint of me."

She looked at him and thought of that other picture of him, the portrait at Belgarrick Towers where he smiled at her without bitterness or mockery. She had met him too late but; oh, how desperately she still wanted to believe the man she loved was not frozen for ever in time and lived still behind Giles's forbidding exterior. She had glimpsed him sometimes, she knew it. He must still be there.

Frantically she tried to check her thoughts. They softened her, changed her all too quickly into a willing victim. To her dismay, she found she was still shocked from her fall. She felt vulnerable and tearful, and her legs were trembling. She held on to the back of the armchair for support.

Giles came hastily to her. "I shall carry you up."

"No!" She warded him off wildly. If she felt his arms around her, there was a danger she would cling to him and very likely blurt out her love. Better to die where she stood than let such a thing happen. To her relief, her strength came back. Her legs steadied, and she moved away from the chair. "I am perfectly all right now."

"You are not," he told her harshly. "I shall accompany you to make sure you reach your room safely. Do not fear. There's no danger I shall forget a second time that you have forbidden me ever to touch you again."

*Chapter Nineteen*

Two months had passed since the elopement. Claudia reclined in a chair in the rose arbor at Belgarrick Towers and allowed the late August sun to kiss her cheeks. She was already as brown as a milkmaid, but she did not care. Her pleasures these days were all rustic: the warmth of the sun, the smell of the roses, the rich abundant beauty of the Kentish countryside in high bloom.

A bee buzzed lazily around her and she just as lazily brushed it away. Saba, lying in the shade with the two female puppies Claudia had decided to keep, raised her head to see what had disturbed her mistress. Finding nothing amiss, she flopped back into sleep once more.

Claudia smiled and eased herself into a more comfortable position. She was six months pregnant and no longer quarreled with Mellows over whether or not she could wear a sash. She couldn't. That did not vex her, either.

Some weeks ago, when the baby had made its first positive stirrings in her womb, her feelings toward it had undergone a dramatic change. She had felt wonder that there was a separate life within her, a fierce instinct to protect it, and her resentment was washed away on a flood of maternal love. How *could* she have blamed the child for her estrangement from Giles? It was her own fault that she had failed to make him love her.

She saw him so rarely. She never knew where he was, although she suspected Paris. Lisette would be enjoying his passion now. It was not jealousy that told her that, but reason. Giles could not live like a monk. His whole past was evidence of that. He had not touched her since their last quarrel, not even to take her arm when they went into the dining-room together on his brief visits home.

Claudia closed her eyes. She did not want to think of him. He had wrapped her in luxury, given her everything she could possibly need, and yet every time he went away he took her heart with him. Indeed, she had come to resent his gifts, knowing them to be the expensive trifles a rich man showered on his neglected wife to keep her contented while she bore his child. He never came home empty-handed. Her jewelry-case was overflowing and she had more fans, shawls and furs that she knew what to do with.

Only one of his gifts had genuinely pleased her, and she was reminded of it as a peacock and six attendant peahens strutted through the arbour on their way to the park. Giles had sent them down to her after she had expressed, during one of his visits, her admiration for the peacocks she had seen on a neighboring estate. The gift had seemed more personal, somehow, as though he had genuinely wanted to please her.

Saba, ever watchful, raised her head again to watch the peacocks' progress, but she was used to them and soon lost interest. Her puppies, too young to know that everything that approached their mistress had to be inspected and, if strange, challenged, slept on.

Claudia could feel the urge to sleep overtaking her, too. Lying down on her bed at nights seemed to be the signal for her baby to move vigorously, and it kept her wakeful. It was stirring now, but languorously. She would have to wait for it to settle before she composed herself for sleep. Her thoughts drifted back over the past two months, to Tansy's radiant return from Scotland and the second wedding at St. George's, where Giles and Claudia had exchanged their vows. Only close family had attended, Claudia declining to put her friends in the embarrassing position of refusing an invitation or accepting it, and thus condoning anything as disgraceful as an elopement.

Her tactics appeared to have worked. Certainly there had been a scandal, but it had been a five days' wonder. When the young couple had retired to Kent with Claudia and Giles, it was generally thought that if any such affair could be well handled, this one had.

Giles, of course, had not remained above two days, but Claudia had had the warmth and pleasure of the young couple until the week before, when they had moved to the estate Giles had purchased for them. It was in Sussex, roughly midway between the Granthams' family home in Somerset and the Verylans' principal seat in Kent, and thus, as Tansy enthused, ideally situated.

"For I will be able to visit you often, Claudia, and by the time you have had the baby we will have everything fit for you to visit us." She had hugged Claudia warmly, her love for Andrew overflowing in all directions. "I shall never know how you managed to talk my father into such a *reasonable* state of mind, but Andrew and I will thank you for it until our dying day."

"You need not. Your father soon saw the advantages in making the best of a bad job," Claudia had replied.

"So you say, but I can imagine . . . No, I won't bore you with my thanks all over again." Her face had changed and she had gone on to say, with difficulty, "If you should ever need a—a refuge, promise you will come to me."

Claudia had tried to bluster. "A refuge? Whatever can you mean? Your father is spoiling me to death." She touched the new pearl earrings she was wearing to make her point.

Tansy was not deceived. "Promise."

Brown eyes met blue, and it was the blue that wavered. "I promise," Claudia had said.

Satisfied, Tansy had departed with her Andrew. Claudia still missed them both, but as she reflected now on that episode, she felt a warmth that had nothing to do with the sun. She had her blessings, and they were better things to count than her miseries. She had the affection of Tansy and Andrew, the companionship of her dogs, a respectful staff, a beautiful home, her father's former steward to sort out any thorny problems that arose, and her baby to look forward to.

It was only Giles, the provider of these blessings, who bedeviled her. Contemplating this paradox, she fell asleep.

A little later something, she wasn't sure what, disturbed her. She drifted up through layers of sleep, reluctant to awake yet. In her drowsy state she thought it must be the child moving again, and she put her hand on her stomach in the vain hope of quietening it. She touched not the soft muslin of her yellow gown but another hand.

Her eyes flew open, and she gasped. Her shock was hardly less than Giles's as he snatched his hand from her stomach and stepped back. "I beg your pardon," he said. "I did not mean to disturb you."

She did not know what to say. She had never seen

Giles look embarrassed. She did not know he could! In her own confusion she thought her thin dress must have moved with the stirring of the child. He must have been curious and reached out to touch it, not her.

She looked down at herself and was smitten with an embarrassment as bad as his. How ungainly she looked, stretched out like this. She sat up hastily and rearranged the folds of her gown so that her bulging stomach was not so obvious. "You did not disturb me," she replied at last. "The baby kicked."

"I saw it. That was why I . . ." He broke off, and when he spoke again he sounded more himself. "Are you well?"

"Perfectly, thank you."

"The doctor is satisfied everything is proceeding normally?"

"Yes."

The same stilted questions, the same stilted answers they exchanged whenever he came home. Who would believe they had been married for seven months and had shared such passionate nights? There had been less constraint between them on the day they had contracted to marry than there was now. Then they had had plenty to say to each other. Yet here they were, having difficulty stringing a few civil sentences together.

The silence must be as uncomfortable for him as it was for her. Any moment now he would escape to his beloved library. His sanctuary, the one place he could be sure of not encountering her. She avoided it while he was at home.

But still he lingered, looking about him at the roses. Her love of flowers was evident. She filled the house with them, not always with the approval of Phipps, the head gardener. "The roses are making a fine display this year," he said.

She looked at him with astonishment. Giles was not one for small talk. He met her gaze then looked away, continuing, "I have fetched you down some dahlias. They are in full bloom, but they are potted and can be planted out for a few weeks."

"Dahlias?" Her brows puckered. "I have never heard of them."

"They have not long been introduced into the country. I think you will like them. The tubers—the roots—have to be lifted up before the first frost and stored in ashes through the winter. I have spoken to Phipps about them. He is waiting for you to instruct him where you would like them situated. I understand they like plenty of sun."

"How kind of you. I will see him now." She made a move to get up, forgetting in her interest in the new flowers that her body was not as supple and graceful as it used to be. Before she could make an extra effort to reach her feet, he said, "No, have your tea first. I can see Hastings bringing the tray now. I shall see you at dinner." He walked a pace or two away, then swung back. "The ships that have been keeping me busy have sailed for the East. There is little for me to do in London just now. I mean to remain in Kent for some weeks. You need not fear that I shall disturb you. I have a great deal of business concerning this estate and the others to catch up on."

He inclined his head in what might have been meant for a bow, and walked toward the house as Hastings arrived with the tray, followed by a footman who carried a bowl of water for the dogs.

They understood her well now, the servants, and since Giles had followed up his gift of peacocks with flowers she wondered whether he, too, was getting a notion of what pleased her. The trouble was that she was also beginning to follow his line of thinking.

As she sipped her tea, she did not flatter herself that Giles meant to spend several weeks with her because his interest in Lisette was waning. No, he never lost sight of his main objective, and that objective was an heir. It was because of the baby that he had made no fuss when Tansy and Andrew had returned from Gretna. He had feared to upset not Tansy but herself. Her doctor's favorite maxim, which he repeated often enough so there was no chance of her or Giles forgetting it, was that a happy mother meant a healthy child. That was why her every whim was being granted and he was putting more thought into his gifts. She was not the magnet that had drawn him home to stay. It was the baby. He meant to watch her himself during the last months before the birth to be sure she did nothing stupid to threaten its safe arrival. As if she would!

And watch her Giles did as August gave way to the slow decay of September, when the first leaves fell to be trodden underfoot by Claudia as she roamed the park and gardens, her dogs at her heels. His observation was never open, but she was always aware of it. Even in the safety of the dining-room or the drawing-room, where nothing could possibly happen to her, she often surprised him staring at her before he looked hastily away.

Not that she need fear his scrutiny. Her waistline might be gone, but her breasts had never looked more tempting in the low-cut gowns she wore to display them to full advantage. Mellows might cluck, and say it was a time for modesty, but Claudia never listened to her. What assets she had she meant to show. Her pregnancy had made her more of a woman, not less of one. The richness of her body seemed to endow her hair and complexion with extra richness, too.

So Giles could stare, and Mellows could snipe, as much as they wished. The Right Honorable the Viscountess Belgarrick, at peace with her burgeoning body, was wrapped in a serenity of her own. If her heart still ached for love, it was an ache she had learned to live with. Forced by circumstance to become absorbed with herself, she was at one with Giles in wanting nothing to disturb the tranquility of the home she had come to love as much as Tallon Manor.

The nursery wing where Giles and his brothers, and all the infant Verylans before them, had spent their early years had been refurbished. Claudia wandered there on rainy days when she could not exercise outside as often as she wandered to the portrait gallery to stare at the painting of her husband as a young man. They were dual needs and dual pleasures, though of the two she did not doubt it was healthier to haunt the nursery. Therein lay the future. Nothing had happened to make her suppose the Giles of the past would reappear to make her impossible dreams a reality.

She and Mrs. Binns discussed wet-nurses and nursery-maids, but the all-important position of Nurse to preside over the nursery had still to be decided. Claudia had interviewed several sent down to her by Mr. Tigwell, and had found them wanting. She was seeking another Miss Laleham, her own old nurse, and could not find a likely substitute.

Lally, as Claudia had always called her, had stayed on when Claudia's mother had died to fill the necessary role of chaperon when Claudia had become her father's hostess. After her father's death she had remained as companion until pensioned off by the new and jealous Lady Tallon. Lally had gone to live with her three older and retired sisters in a cottage in Lincolnshire, and Claudia longed to recall her. But Lally was well into her fifties now and, from her letters, she appeared happy. It seemed to Claudia to be selfish and unkind to ask her to take charge of her own child. No, she must put Lally's best interests first and persevere in finding a substitute for her.

She wrote to Mr. Tigwell, specifying her requirements in greater detail. There must, somewhere, be another nurse like Lally. It was during this time she was seized by a powerful urge to turn everything upside down. She moved into a guest-room, and had the carpets in her own rooms taken up and beaten, the bed and window curtains washed and the loose cushions recovered.

No sooner was this done and she was back in her own apartment than she went through all her clothes, discarding items she had no wish to wear again. "Whatever is the matter with me?" she asked Mellows. "I can't seem to keep still or leave anything in peace."

"You're getting your nest ready," Mellows replied, her eyes gleaming as she surveyed the pile of clothes Claudia had given her to wear or to dispose of as she wished. It was one of the perks of her profession and, since they were very fine clothes, most of them she aimed to keep. The ones she sold would bring in some very useful pounds.

"I'm doing what?" Claudia exclaimed, throwing an ostrich fan on to the heap of discards.

"Getting your nest ready before the baby's born. It's a phase women go through—the energetic ones, at least." That said, Mellows did not counsel her to rest, but held up a paisley shawl. "What about this one?"

"I'll keep it. It's one of my favorites."

Mellows looked disappointed as she folded and packed it away again.

When the wardrobe was pruned to Claudia's satisfaction, she sat down and put her feet up, weary but content. She raised her eyebrows when Mellows brought a jewel-case to her, her personal one, not the large box containing the Verylan jewels.

"I was thinking you might want to go through this while you're about it," Mellows explained, opening the case. "There are some items here you never wear. This pearl and turquoise brooch, for instance. If you do not think me too bold, it would go beautifully with the blue twill gown you have given me."

"You are too bold, too bold by half," Claudia told her frigidly, taking the brooch and putting it back in the case. "I may not wear it but I shall never part with it. I inherited it from my mother, and perhaps I shall have a daughter to pass it on to one day. Even if that were not so, I cannot discard my jewels as I do my gowns, and you must know it."

Mellows apologized, but Claudia scarcely heeded her, snapping the case shut and telling her to put it away. She was within an ace of dismissing her but held back, still fearing that her growing animosity toward the maid was nothing but the over-sensitive reaction of a pregnant woman.

Claudia's burst of energy showed no signs of exhausting itself, although she spent the last day of September languorously. It was her birthday and, to complete the pendant set, Giles had given her a delicate ruby tiara.

She told Mellows, "I shall wear it tonight with the ivory silk and the rest of the rubies."

"Oh, no, my lady. That will be too grand. You have no guests tonight."

"Dining tête-à-tête with one's husband is the time to look grand," Claudia told her coolly. "I shall have my hair fixed at the side with one—no, two!—ringlets brought forward over my shoulder."

"Don't you think," Mellows suggested with irritating delicacy, "that style might be a little young for you?"

"I am seven-and-twenty, not seventy! My mother

dressed her hair that way for grand occasions when she was far older than I."

"Old-fashioned, then."

Claudia gritted her teeth. "Tonight it will be the rubies, the ivory silk and shoulder ringlets, and pray stop your quibbling."

She felt vindicated in sticking by her own decisions, for when she later went down to dinner, her own eyes told her she had never been in better looks.

Giles stared at her as she entered the Blue Salon, a vision in flowing ivory silk and rich rubies. She smiled her special smile. She could not help herself. It was her birthday, she looked beautiful, and surely that was approval gleaming in his eyes?

It was more than that. Giles felt as though his breath had been taken away. She had never looked more radiant, more lovable. His heart lurched, as it so often did when he looked at her, but once again he suffered an instant and unavoidable reaction. He froze. He could neither say nor do the things he wanted to. He could only turn away and cover his confusion by saying curtly, "The tiara suits you. I chose well."

He had hurt her again. He knew it. Something within him pleaded with her to understand, but how could she? She did not know how helpless she made him feel, how quickly he defended, shut himself off. Tonight he had hoped it would be different, but he was still trapped, still driving away the one woman he wanted to take into his arms and hold and never let go.

Claudia's smile faded. She had dared to come out of her shell and smile at him in an inviting way, and he wanted none of it. The compliment she yearned for he had paid to himself: *I chose well.*

She felt a surge of hatred toward him. It was her birthday. She wanted to be courted and fêted and spoiled, not by jewels, but by his attention and approval. But nothing had changed. He could give freely of his money but he could not give anything of himself. Neither, then, would she. She had exposed herself to one snub. She would not expose herself to another.

During dinner she made no polite attempts at conversation. When the last course was removed, she rose immediately and left him. She did not go into the drawing-room to bear him company when it pleased him to leave his port and brandy, but went straight up to her rooms. She had never done so before. Tonight, however, she was beyond playing the dutiful wife.

It was not in her power to shatter him the way he could shatter her, but she hoped he felt snubbed. It might make him think twice in future before heaping on himself the praise his wife was so desperate to hear.

She was relieved to find her rooms empty. Mellows, not expecting her mistress back for another couple of hours, would be having her own meal. Claudia was thankful for it. After her proud boast that dining tête-à-tête with one's husband was the time to look grand, she did not relish meeting her maid's all-too-knowing eyes. She took off the tiara, stripped off the rest of her jewels and threw them on the dressing-table. It took her longer to remove her gown with its awkward back fastening, but when it finally fluttered to her feet she stepped out of it and kicked it away. It was beautiful, but it had worked no magic for her.

She washed in cold water, donned a nightshift, pulled the pins from her hair and got into bed. She wanted to pull the curtains round it for further privacy, although she resisted the impulse. It had been a humid day and she felt she could not bear the stuffiness of being entirely closed in.

She lay tense and sleepless, fighting the urge to shed tears of self-pity by trying to transform her love for Giles into strengthening and more satisfying hate. Love

251

was a weakening emotion. Giles was invulnerable because he couldn't feel it. She didn't want to feel it, either. She wanted to be invulnerable like him.

She wanted . . . Oh, the devil take it! She wanted what she had always wanted. She wanted Giles. Hard as she tried, she could not sustain hate for any length of time—except against herself for wanting him so.

After an hour or so she heard the door open, soft footfalls and the rustle of long skirts. Mellows. She, too, must have had a taste for grandness tonight because it sounded as though she was wearing one of the silk gowns recently given to her. Claudia heard the maid stop and exclaim, presumably when she saw the ivory silk on the floor.

Claudia feigned sleep, knowing that the maid would come to bed next. The room was filled with moonlight, but her closed eyelids registered the extra light of a branch of candles held aloft. After a few seconds the light was removed and she heard the opening and closing of drawers as, from habit, the maid tidied up. Presently she went away and all was still again.

Another hour, perhaps two, passed and Claudia was still wakeful when someone else came to stare down at her. She was too weary and too fretful to feign sleep this time. She saw it was Giles who had come to her, but her heart did not leap for joy. He had a glass in one hand and a decanter in the other, and he was very drunk.

## Chapter Twenty

Giles swayed above her, a dark and menacing figure in the moonlight. He put the glass and decanter on the bedside cabinet, knocking over a silver candelabrum as he did so. He grabbed at it, missed and swayed forward, only stopping himself from falling by holding on to the cabinet. The decanter and glass swayed but stayed upright.

"For heavens sake, Belgarrick, what are you about?" Claudia had never seen him drunk before, nor anywhere near it, and she was too revolted to be frightened.

He stood upright carefully, swayed, then said with slow slurred speech, "You—ran away. Fetched you—a birthday drink."

"I don't want it."

"Yes, you do. Brandy. For—For fortifying."

"I don't want it!"

This seemed to confound him. He thought a long while before repeating, "Don't want it? What—What ails you, then?"

"Nothing save yourself. Go away."

He thought about this a long while, too, then said,

253

"I ail you. Thought so. I—shall—relieve you of my—my unwanted presence."

He swept her a bow, nearly fell, recovered himself and, grasping the decanter swayed toward the dressing-room door. Claudia never thought he would get that far but he did, and, after some fumbling with the handle, managed to open and go through it.

He crashed into something. Claudia flung back the covers, but before she could get out of bed Mellows came in through the other door and hurried toward her. "Don't you disturb yourself, my lady. His valet will see to my lord."

As she spoke, they heard the valet's voice encouraging his master toward his own bedroom. "There, what did I say!" Mellows put down her candlestick and tucked up Claudia again. She saw the glass beside the bed and said, "What's this? Brandy? Just what you need, my lady."

"I do not want it."

"It's what you need. A shock like this at this time of night! If you will not drink it for yourself, pray drink it for the baby. You must have your sleep."

The glass was against Claudia's lips and she was still too taken aback by the episode to demur. She sipped it and, as a glow spread through her, sipped again. "What are you doing here?" she asked.

Mellows was in a dressing-gown with long fair hair escaping from her nightcap. "I was not quite easy about you, my lady. I came to see all was well before I went to bed."

"Thank you. It was thoughtful of you. I am all right now. You may go to bed."

"As soon as you've finished the brandy," Mellows coaxed.

Claudia drank the last of it to be rid of her. She did appreciate her concern but she wished the maid had not witnessed Giles's loathsome condition. She settled back against the pillows and, satisfied, her maid picked up her candle and went quietly away.

The brandy had been neat and more than Claudia had ever drunk at one time before. She found her own head whirling, and closed her eyes. Presently she would think over what had happened. Not just now. She had not quite got over the shock of it yet . . .

When Claudia opened her eyes again she thought the moonlight brighter than ever, but as she came more fully awake she realized it was dawn bathing her room with pearly gray light.

The events of the night came back with a rush and, if not, the dryness of her throat would have reminded her of them. The brandy, of course. She got out of bed to get herself a glass of water, and trod on something which made her cry out. She sat on the edge of the bed and rubbed her foot, no easy task with the size of her stomach. As the pain abated, she looked about for what had caused it and saw a small jeweler's box on the carpet.

She stooped to pick it up, and pushing her tumbled hair back from her face, opened it. It was a ring. A glowing sapphire the color of her eyes, surrounded by smaller but equally bright sapphires.

Her sleep-flushed skin prickled with gooseflesh as Giles's voice came out of the past to her: " . . . a lover might be besotted enough to choose sapphires to match your eyes."

And he had bought her sapphires. For some time she could not believe it. Who could believe a dream come true? Especially long after all hope was gone.

She smiled dazedly at the ring, she wept a little over it, and eventually she frowned at it. Why had he not given it to her? Why had she found it on her bedroom floor?

Why, oh why, did everything about Giles have to be such a puzzle? She took the ring out of the box and stared at it, and, as she stared, she thought she knew the answer. He had meant to give her this before dinner last night but she, misunderstanding his awkwardness, had taken offense and given him no opportunity.

He needed help to say the words that were so alien to him, and she had snubbed him. He had turned to brandy to get up his courage to come to her here, where they had known such passion, and she had repulsed him again. The ring must have fallen from his pocket, or perhaps his hand, when he himself had nearly fallen.

Claudia was tempted to put the ring on her finger but, no, after all this time of dreaming of such a moment she would not deny herself the happiness of seeing Giles do it himself. It would be enough. She would spare him the embarrassment of finding the right words to go with the act by saying them herself.

She could wait to find out just when the miracle had happened and he had fallen in love with her. She had become very good at waiting . . .

It was at this point that Claudia felt a little quiver of panic. He was a proud man who never displayed weakness. He would despise himself for the condition he had come to her in last night. If she was not careful, he might slip away to London, as he had so often infuriated her by doing in the past.

She threw a robe over her shoulders, shut the jeweler's box, and clutching it tightly hurried through the adjoining dressing-rooms to his bedroom. The air was heavy with stale brandy, but this morning she did not care.

His valet had drawn the curtains round the great four-poster after seeing his master to bed, and, smiling to herself, she parted the crimson velvet. Her happiness was so great that she was whispering, "Giles, oh, Giles, my love . . ." over and over to herself.

The words died on her lips at the scene that met her eyes. The little jeweler's box slipped from her nerveless fingers and she clutched the curtain for support. Two half-naked figures lay there.

Her beloved Giles, his russet hair curling wildly across his forehead, golden stubble on his chin.

And Mellows, her maid. Her prim nightcap gone, her long fair hair stretching lankly across the pillows to Giles. The silk and lace nightdress ruched up about her thighs was one of Claudia's own. The smell of brandy was overpowering within the curtains. The decanter was empty and the glasses on either side of the bed half full. To complete the scene of debauchery, the covers had slipped from the bed so that nothing was hidden from Claudia's disbelieving eyes.

Her maid, her gaunt unattractive maid, and *Giles!* She would never have believed it had she not seen it with her own eyes, could scarcely believe it now.

Sickened, and her sickness was far more than merely physical, she could only cling to the curtain and retch.

Giles opened his eyes. He stared at her without comprehension for a moment, then murmured, "Claudia . . ." With an abrupt movement, he sat up. His hand touched Mellows, and he turned to stare at her as uncomprehendingly as he had stared at Claudia.

His touch had disturbed the maid. Her eyes opened sleepily and she said thickly, "Again, my lord? Aren't you the naughty one!"

Giles recoiled and looked again at Claudia, his eyes as despairing as hers were disgusted. Mellows peered past his shoulder and saw her mistress. She did not recoil or look the least apprehensive. Instead, a wide satisfied smile spread across her face, and she said, "Well, well, now the fat is in the fire!"

Claudia knew then what true humiliation was. She released the curtain and stood upright. What a figure of fun she must look, she thought vaguely. A heavily pregnant wife innocently discovering her husband's infidelity. Revulsion iced her voice with loathing as she said, "You appear to have some kind of vermin in your bed, Belgarrick. Get rid of it."

Then she turned and walked back to her own room. She sat down at her dressing-table, scarcely recognizing the ashen face that stared back at her. She was all ice now, and she began to shudder, long violent shudders that racked her shocked body. She even found herself whimpering, and clenched her teeth in self-disgust to smother the sound. But it was the sound of heartbreak, and there was no smothering it. So Claudia whimpered and shuddered and hated herself for it. This was the time to rant and rave and drag Giles through a scene to end all scenes, yet here she was, all to pieces and hiding herself away as though she were the guilty one.

She was the one who felt besmirched. Dirty. She was the one who felt shame. This was no fashionable affair with the mistress kept tidily out of the husband's domestic life. This was her own maid, under her own roof, and she had discovered it herself.

It was the ultimate betrayal.

For some time Claudia could not think beyond that. Then slowly the painful shudders and the degrading whimpers faded away. Her mind began to question what, thus far, it had accepted. How long had the affair been going on?

Then all Mellows's carping remarks these past weeks began to make sense. She had had her sights set on Giles from the beginning. She had done her best to undermine Claudia's confidence in her appearance, at the same time counseling celibacy for the baby's sake. She had been plotting for the day when Giles looked elsewhere for an outlet for his passion, and when that day had come she had been ready. Last night when she had been tidying up she had sneaked out a silken nightgown in which to seduce him. No wonder she had insisted that Claudia drink up that brandy.

Mrs. Hewitt, her former employer, had not been lying when she had said Mellows had seduced her husband, and Claudia had been too incredulous to believe her. All those brooches the maid was so proud of—they had not come from an inheritance but from husbands who had needed to buy her silence!

Claudia's mind jumped to the sapphire ring. It could never have been meant for her. A man did not give his wife a token of love and then bed her maid. It must have been intended for Mellows.

Giles was generous to his women. Rubies for his wife, diamonds for his mistress—and sapphires for the maid who substituted for both of them. No wonder Mellows had looked so pleased with herself! She had every reason to be. She was finished here now, but she would be leaving her post richer than she had begun it—and gloating, no doubt, that she had smashed the marriage Claudia had been trying so hard to hold together. She was depraved, loathsome. And Giles was no better.

The worst of it was that Claudia, too, felt contaminated. Mellows's success with Giles was only a measure of her own failure. Suddenly she could not bear to be under the same roof with either of them. She had to get away until both had gone. Then, perhaps, she could begin to feel clean again.

She washed and dressed quickly, choosing clothes that did not need a maid's helping hand. She was pinning up her hair when something made her swing round. Giles was standing at the dressing-room door, silently watching her. He was washed and shaved, and dressed in riding clothes.

"Get out," she said.

He took a step toward her, then stopped. "You have a right to despise me," he told her quietly. "I despise myself. There is no excuse for my behavior, but there are circumstances . . ."

"I am not interested in them," she interrupted. "Just looking at you makes me feel sick."

He flinched, and it was a moment before he continued in the same quiet tone, "I shall not distress you with my presence any longer than necessary, but there are some things you must know. For appearances' sake I shall ride out as usual this morning . . ."

"I just want you and that harlot out of here. I am not worried about appearances!"

"Then I must worry for you. I shall call at the receiving office myself for the mail. Among it will be a letter summoning Mellows to Liverpool to nurse a sick aunt. She will leave immediately. She has been well paid to keep her mouth shut."

With the ring I believed was mine, Claudia thought bitterly. The only person besotted in this household is myself, to imagine such a thing possible.

"There will also be a letter summoning me to London on a business matter. I shall leave this afternoon so that the two departures cannot be linked, although that is unlikely. I shall not return unless you send for me, so that you can be certain your peace here will not be further disturbed."

He fell silent. Claudia stared stonily at him. He met her gaze and, for once, she did not attempt to interpret the expression in his eyes. It was bound to be deceitful.

When he spoke again, it was with an awkwardness that had nothing to do with the Belgarrick she knew. "I beg you will take better care of yourself than I have."

*Better care of the child*, he meant. She scorned to answer.

He took another step toward her. "Claudia, I am so sorry . . ."

"Get out!"

He checked abruptly, then stepped back. Whatever else he meant to say, he thought better of it. He bowed and turned and left her.

Claudia felt very calm. Curiously so. Before, she had been feeling too much. Now she was feeling nothing at all. She put a light pelisse over her gown, went downstairs to collect her dogs and then left the house. They frolicked about her as she walked through her beloved rose arbor to the park. It was the first of October. A bright morning, although there was not enough heat in the sun yet to dry the dew from the grass.

She realized with surprise that the day had scarcely begun. How curious that was, too, because she felt as if her life were over.

She walked for several hours, her mind, like her emotions, a blank. She was not aware she had turned for home until she heard the sound of hoofbeats approaching fast. She looked about her, realized she was on one of the more secluded paths in the home wood, and stood to one side to allow the rider to pass.

It was Charles Reveson. He reined in, dismounted, and exclaimed, "Thank goodness! You have been gone so long we feared you had been taken ill. My lord, the grooms, we have all been out searching for you." He fended off the dogs as they jumped to greet him, and, turning his horse, began to walk beside her.

"I'm sorry to cause a stir, but there's nought amiss. I have merely been walking up an appetite for breakfast."

"Breakfast? It is time for luncheon!"

"Oh!" Had she really been gone so long? It didn't

seem like it. "Well, you of all people should know how I love to walk. Pray go and call off the search."

"I shall see you safely home first. I'm afraid we've had something of an upset, which you could do without at this time. Mellows received news this morning that her aunt is gravely ill and she must go to nurse her. She will be gone several weeks, perhaps months. I shall write to Tigwell immediately for another dresser. No lady likes strangers about her when her child is due."

They came out of the wood, and there before them were the gray towers of home. She did not feel the usual surge of pleasure at the sight, nor did it appear as welcoming as it normally did. It was almost as if a veil separated her from every normal reaction. She could see and hear, but she could not feel.

"I don't want another dresser." Her voice sounded too harsh, too petulant. She softened it, and explained, "There is no need for one while I am living in such seclusion. One of the maids can do all I require. Ask Mrs. Binns to see to it."

"If you're sure . . ." Charles hesitated, then asked, "Are you positive you're quite well, my lady?"

"A little weary, perhaps. I'll have a luncheon tray sent up to my room, and rest."

This was done, and the search called off. If Giles was angry with her for over-exerting herself he kept his anger to himself. She heard his carriage leave about an hour later, and was thankful for it. She had no further need to feel threatened. She could relax.

So she thought, but relaxing proved impossible. She was edgy, prone to wander about the house with no fixed objective in mind. Finally it came to her what she wanted. She wanted Lally with her. Dear, gentle Lally, who always made her feel safe, and to whom she had written such deceitfully reassuring letters about her marriage.

There was nothing deceitful about the terse note she sat down and wrote to her then:

Dearest Lally,

I have need of you. Can you come to me straight away?

Claudia

She sealed the note and took it to Charles Reveson. She asked as she gave it to him, "Which carriage did my lord take to London?"

"He drove his curricle, my lady."

"Then pray send the traveling carriage to bring Lally to me. I want her here, Charles, as soon as possible."

There was no need to explain about Lally to Charles. They had both known Claudia since she was a baby. "It will be done immediately. Forgive me, but are you *sure* you're quite well?"

The strange, disconnected person she had become smiled and rallied him, "Shame on you Charles! Must I be ill because I want to see my old nurse?"

"The haste . . ." he began.

"The whim of a pregnant woman. You must have heard about those!"

She smiled again and left him, but it seemed she wanted more than Lally, because she still could not settle. She found herself in the nursery, sitting in the chair beside the cradle Giles had once slept in, rocking it to and fro, to and fro.

When she realized what she was doing, she felt bewildered. What was she looking for? Comfort? There was none here. The room was ready but lifeless. That was how she herself felt. It was a horrid state. She went in search of Mrs. Binns and ordered a fire to be lighted in the nursery. "To keep the damp away," she explained.

Mrs. Binns turned to look at the sunlight outside the window. Certainly it was autumn, but the weather was still mild. She opened her mouth to say something, then closed it again. In any case, Claudia was wandering away again, in search of something she could not find.

She would not go down to dinner. She did not want to be reminded of last night, her birthday, when she had been splendid in rubies and ivory silk and Giles had had the sapphire ring in his pocket for Mellows.

She had another tray sent up and made a good meal without being aware of eating so much as a morsel. Richards, the rosy-cheeked parlor-maid promoted to the giddy heights of my lady's maid, prepared her for bed, so anxious to please that Claudia could not help but smile at her. Somebody in this great house was happy. Why could it never be herself?

Real sleep eluded her. She dozed fitfully and when dawn came she lay looking at the window. It was going to be another fine dry day. Another good day for trying to walk away her wretchedness, and yet she did not feel the slightest inclination to move. She lay there, heavy and listless, listening to the sound of maids busy with pans and brushes, and watching the room grow ever brighter. The pains, when they began, were scarcely pains at all. Just little niggles that were gone by the time she had moved to a more comfortable position.

Mild though they were, they were persistent, and she began to feel uncomfortable. She rang for Richards, and when her tea was brought she asked for a potion for indigestion. It was not a potion that was brought but Mrs. Binns, who dropped a curtsy and asked, "Where are these pains, my lady?"

"Why, here," Claudia replied, placing her hands on her stomach. It was only then that realization dawned. "Oh, no! It is too soon. It can't be!"

"So we must hope, but we can take no chances. I'll send for Dr. Hudson directly."

Claudia shook her head, not wanting to accept the possibility. "It is indigestion, I tell you! I'll get up. I shall feel better then."

Mrs. Binns pressed her gently back on to the pillows. "You stay right where you are. I wondered yesterday. Your restlessness, sending for your own nurse, having a fire lit in the nursery. A woman always knows, even if she doesn't know," she ended somewhat obscurely.

The housekeeper hurried away and a groom was despatched to fetch the doctor. Then she consulted with Charles Reveson, and between them they decided to send a courier up to London without waiting for the doctor's diagnosis. My lord, they agreed, would rather be brought back for a false alarm than not be alerted at all.

In the event, the alarm was not a false one. The doctor confirmed that my lady was in labor.

"Can't you stop it?" Claudia asked desperately. "I am only seven months gone. What chance will the baby have?"

But the doctor only patted her hand and returned soothing, non-committal answers. As the hours passed and the pains increased, Claudia fought them, stubbornly waging her own battle against having her baby too soon. Midway through the afternoon, her will and her resistance weakened, and she wanted nothing more than to be rid of the physical torture that had blotted out her mental and emotional sufferings.

Yet no sooner was the baby born than she was propping herself up and demanding, "Does he live? Tell me, does he live?"

A weak cry answered her, and thankfully she fell back against the pillows, closing her eyes in exhaustion. He lived. Her baby lived!

She lay passively while Richards washed her, changed her shift and brushed her tangled hair. When it was done she was very tired, but she felt refreshed. She held out her arms. "I will have my baby now."

Richards looked from her to the doctor, who came to her and said gently, "You must sleep now, my lady, and not be bothering your head about anything else."

"I will not sleep until I have seen my baby."

The doctor went to the other side of the room and came back with a glass in his hand. "A composer for you, my lady. It will help you to sleep."

Claudia frowned at him and then she thought she understood. "It is a girl, is it? That doesn't matter, not to me. Girl or boy, I want my baby."

Dr. Hudson said quietly, kindly, "It is a boy, but you must understand that a seven-month child has little chance of survival."

"No! You've taken him away to die, haven't you? I won't have it!" She knocked the glass out of the doctor's hand and flung back her covers. "If you won't bring him to me, I will go to him."

The doctor tried to restrain her, but desperation gave her the strength to fight him. Richards, after an agony of indecision, helped him, causing Claudia to struggle more wildly than ever. "Let me go!" she shouted. "I want my baby!"

"What in God's name is going on here?"

The harsh voice had its effect. The doctor and Richards straightened up and stared at the doorway. Giles stood there, a towering, dominating figure still swathed in his many-caped driving-coat, his hair disheveled from the mad dash back to Kent.

"My lord," Dr. Hudson exclaimed, "thank heaven you are here! My lady is distraught . . ."

"Giles!" In her panic for her child, Claudia saw him

266

not as her oppressor but as her savior. She sat up and held out her arms to him. "Oh, Giles!"

He strode rapidly toward the bed and sat beside her. Claudia threw herself into his arms and clung to him. "Stop them, Giles, stop them! They have taken our baby away to die. They won't let me have him."

She felt his arms tighten round her, then he was stroking her hair and saying soothingly, "Nobody will do anything you dislike. You must not distress yourself."

Claudia buried her face in the rough cloth of his driving-coat and burst into tears. Over her head, Giles looked questioningly at the doctor.

"I made a composer for my lady, but she knocked it out of my hand," the doctor said. "I am trying to spare her distress, not cause it. The baby is perfectly formed but weak and tiny, as one must expect a seven-month child to be. His chances of survival are very slender. In my opinion, it is better for my lady never to see him than to come to love him and then lose him."

Claudia raised her head and turned to glare at him. "What do you know of how I feel? I do not have to see my baby to love him. I have loved him for months! I won't let you talk of losing him. He won't die if he is brought to me. He won't!"

Dr. Hudson appealed to Giles. "My lord, you must understand that newly-delivered mothers are often irrational. I fear for her future mental health if her whim is indulged now."

"Whim?" Claudia repeated. She turned back to Giles and put her hand against his face to try to transmit her urgency, her belief, to him. "He is weak now, Giles, but we made him and our strength must be in him. If he is with me, he will know he is loved and that will make him fight for life. It *must*, because love is the most powerful force in life. That is not irrational, it is right." She leaned her face against his and pleaded, "Bring me my baby. Please."

For once his brown eyes were not impassive. Her anguish must have penetrated the barrier he kept up against her because she thought she saw understanding in him. Yesterday she would have died rather than beg anything from him. Today she did not care. "Please," she repeated. "I want my baby."

"You shall have him." Gently he released her clutching fingers and laid her back on the pillows. Then he stood up and went toward the door.

"My lord . . ." the doctor began.

"Dr. Hudson, there is something you must understand." Giles's voice was clipped, flat, final. "I am not concerned with my wife's well-being in the next hour, the next day or the next month. I am concerned with it now. She must, and will, have what she wants."

"I cannot advise . . ."

"Under my roof you can certainly advise, and I thank you for it. I know your intentions are the best. But what you cannot do is to order. That is my prerogative—and my responsibility."

Dr. Hudson relaxed. "So long as you understand that."

"I do." Giles went swiftly to the nursery. The nurse the doctor had summoned from the village to help him was sitting by the cradle. She rose and curtsied. "My lord, a sad day this. The child came too soon, much too soon. I fear he is not long for this world."

Giles, looking into the cradle, could believe her. The baby was tiny, mere skin over bone, lost in the cotton that swaddled him. He hesitated, knowing a moment's doubt, then he picked him up. It was like holding nothing. Again he hesitated, then he strode out of the room.

"My lord, whatever are you doing?" The nurse ran

after him, protesting all the way, but when they entered Claudia's bedchamber she fell silent at a signal from the doctor. Claudia, her eyes straining toward the door, held out her arms. He placed the baby in them.

Her face was transformed. The anxiety, the anguish, was lost in a glow he could only wonder at. She did not seem to see the baby's fragility nor comprehend how tenuous was his hold on life. She settled the baby between her breasts and said, "I shall need somebody sitting by me all the time to see he doesn't slip or that I don't turn in my sleep and smother him."

Giles, watching her with troubled eyes, promised, "It shall be done."

"And he won't be taken from me?"

"While he lives, he shall remain with you."

"He is safe, then. You'll see." She closed her eyes, and slept.

The doctor went to the far side of the room and began to pack his bag. Giles went over to him and shook his hand. "Thank you for all you have done. My wife is safe?"

"Physically, yes. I only wish I could say the same for the baby. Alas . . ."

"The baby is of secondary importance," Giles interrupted brusquely.

Dr. Hudson looked at him a long time, then nodded. "That's how it should be, but I thought . . . Damme, man, your need for an heir is well known. I thought . . ."

"A great many people think a great many things, and they are nearly always wrong." Giles turned abruptly and went back to Claudia's bedside, looking down at her in a manner the doctor could not comprehend.

"My lord," the Reverend should be summoned to receive the child into the Church. With a child so pre-

mature, one can never tell. There may not be much
time."

"No. My wife sees life where we can see only death.
For my part, I mean—for once!—to share her faith."

# Chapter Twenty-One

Claudia awoke several hours later to a dimly-lighted room. The baby still lay between her breasts. She touched his face. Warm, living flesh. Her instinct had been right, then. Dr. Hudson might know more about other people's babies, but she knew best about her own.

A movement in the chair beside her bed made her turn her head. It was Giles. He stood up. "I shall send Richards in. You cannot want me here."

"There's no need to go on my account. He's your baby as well as mine."

"I thought, after yesterday . . ."

"I don't want to discuss yesterday." She didn't, either. It seemed irrelevant somehow.

"But it's my fault the baby was premature."

"Now is not the time for recriminations. We must be forward-looking until—until the baby is strong enough for us to consider other things."

Claudia lifted the baby into her arms and studied him for the first time. He was little more than skin wrinkled on tiny bones. She was neither appalled nor frightened. Indeed, she smiled fondly. "There's plenty of room for improvement. He will be handsome yet."

Giles's face looked sombre in the candlelight. "You mustn't pin your hopes too high."

"Or too low. We never discussed names for him. Have you one in mind?"

"Piers, if you like it. It was my father's name." Giles hesitated, then added, "He was a good man."

"Piers . . ." She savored the name, and nodded. "Very well, Piers it is. And Justin after my own father."

The Honorable Piers Justin Verylan survived his first night, and the next day Claudia, dispensing with the wet-nurse Dr. Hudson brought with him, put the baby to her own breast. It was an anxious moment because if he couldn't suck he couldn't survive, but, like herself, there were some things he did not need to be taught. She scarcely had to tease his lips with her nipple before he seized it and instinctively sucked.

Claudia smiled triumphantly, but Dr. Hudson cautioned, "It's early days yet."

Toward evening, Lally arrived. Closer to sixty than fifty, her small form rounder than ever, she was still the bundle of energy Claudia remembered so well. She had been sent for as a confidante, but within five minutes of stepping into Belgarrick Towers and discovering what the situation was, she had taken charge.

The dreadful knot of anxiety underlying Claudia's determination that Piers should live eased a little. There was another pair of arms besides Giles's and her own she could trust the baby to. And, if her own instinct failed, she could also trust Lally to know what to do.

When Tansy and Andrew, posting up from Sussex, arrived the following day, they found a household not gloomy with foreboding but buoyant with hope. It was a hope they could not share when they saw the tiny child, although they kept their misgivings to themselves. They stood godparents to him in a simple ceremony held in Claudia's bedroom and stayed a fortnight, after which time Claudia packed them off home.

"You have your own lives to lead," she told them, "and there's no need for you too look so gloomy. Even Dr. Hudson is swinging round to my belief that Piers will live. It's only a question now of keeping him free from colds and suchlike until he is stronger."

Tansy smiled, and said, "I shall know who to send for if ever I find myself in a similar fix."

"Indeed you will, but you will find, as I did, how much you already *know* without ever being told."

"Are you sure you don't want me to stay longer?"

"I'm positive. Go home and enjoy being a bride. Come back to us for Christmas and you will see how bonny Piers is then."

So Tansy permitted Andrew to take her home, not because of this conversation but because she had seen how Pier's premature arrival had drawn her father and Claudia together. She did not know they were rigidly observing a truce while their son's life was still in question.

Piers was gaining weight slowly, although he was three weeks old before there was any noticeable improvement in him. Then, almost overnight it seemed, the wrinkled skin began to flesh out and from then on he appeared to gain daily. After six weeks, Giles, watching the vigorous movements of his arms and legs as he was changed, said almost disbelievingly, "He is going to live."

Claudia smiled. "I never doubted it."

"You were the only one who didn't!"

She began to relax her vigil. She had recovered her health and strength quickly after Pier's birth but instinct had kept her tied to him. Now she began to pick up the threads of her normal life, going downstairs for her meals, exercising her dogs and, as December approached, riding her mare. She was slender again and began to think once more as a woman as well as a mother. The past, with all its smoldering resentments and hurts, began to intrude on her maternal serenity. The truce between herself and Giles could not last much longer.

She was right. It broke down when Piers was two months old. This was when Claudia decided he was strong enough to be moved to the nursery wing and treated like any other normal healthy baby. She had never poured out her heart to Lally, as she had intended, because the situation had changed so utterly between summoning her and her arrival, and she had needed Lally as a nurse too much. She was reluctant to release her to return to her normal life, but she had been selfish for far too long.

Lally reacted to her dismissal indignantly. "If you think I am going to turn over Master Piers to another nurse who very likely won't know one end of him from the other, then you don't know *me*, my lady! And after all these years, too."

"I don't want you to go, but it isn't fair to keep you. You were happy in your retirement. All your letters said so."

"I didn't want you to worry about me. A house full of spinsters, even if they are my sisters, is what I can't abide. It frets me to flinders. I'm not happy unless I'm busy, so you just leave Master Piers to me."

Thankfully, Claudia let her have her way. She need have no fears for Piers with Lally in charge of the nursery. But the ultimate result of the removal of the baby to the nursery was that Giles no longer had reason to spend most of his time in Claudia's rooms. He did not look for one, either. The rift between them was exposed. They resumed their separate lives under the same roof.

Claudia was not surprised. As far as she was concerned, he had shared her vigil over Piers as some kind of self-inflicted penance for precipitating his birth. She had not questioned his motives because she had needed his support. She began to question them now, because daily she expected to awaken to find he had gone away again. It was months since he had seen Lisette. Mellows had provided a temporary substitute but, since then, as far as Claudia knew, he had been celibate. An unnatural state for him. Why, then, was he remaining? The only conclusion she could come to was that he was still tied to Belgarrick Towers by guilt. He must be waiting—hoping!—for her to precipitate a quarrel that would drive him away with an easy conscience. He had gone soon enough last time when she had told him to get out.

Claudia did not want to quarrel. She did not want all those violent emotions released again, nor did she want to reveal her humiliation and her hurt. There must be a safer, a more civilized, way of freeing him. How far, she thought sadly, she had strayed from the bride who had been willing to keep him by her side at any cost. Now she would rather concede than fight—anything to spare herself further humiliation.

After dinner that night, when she was folding away her embroidery before going to bed, she said, "It will be Christmas in two weeks' time. If you have any business in London, you'd best attend to it."

Usually they avoided looking directly at each other, but their gaze met now. His face was as inscrutable as ever, his thoughts and feelings as carefully hidden from her as they had always been. So much has happened, she thought, and so little has changed.

"Do you want me back for Christmas?" he asked abruptly.

She was taken aback, and that nettled her. "Tansy and Andrew are coming. It will be awkward if you are not here."

"Surely it will be more awkward if I am?"

Claudia closed the lid of her workbox and stood up. She was *not* going to be provoked into a quarrel. "If there is somewhere else you would rather be, then that is up to you. You must do what you think best. Perhaps you will let me know tomorrow what you have decided."

She left him then and went up to her room. She had achieved her object and avoided a quarrel. Strangely, she did not feel satisfied. She felt cheated.

She puzzled over this while Richards prepared her for bed. For once in her life she had taken the easy way out and it had done her no more good than a blazing row would have done. What else was left to her? Counting her blessings again? She had a healthy child to add to them now, but there was still something vital missing.

Giles, of course. Yet if the opportunity to lie in his arms occurred again, she would deny him. She might not be cured, but she had learned her lesson. Even so, she found herself glancing covertly at her body while Richards removed her clothes. She had recovered her shape; her walking and riding were firming up her muscles. She looked little different now from the bride she had been almost as year ago. She wondered if Giles had noticed, and the thought made her angry.

Richards was fastening her into a cotton nightdress, and a housemaid was running a warming-pan over the sheets when Giles walked into the room. He looked as he always did. Handsome, powerful, purposeful. The maids exchanged smiling glances, then looked at Claudia for instruction. She said automatically, "Thank you. That will be all."

When they had gone, she said, "If you have been drinking brandy . . ."

"I am not likely to make that mistake again!" His voice was harsh, but his eyes were not.

She said warily, "What do you want?"

He came up to her and took her hand. She snatched it back. "Don't touch me. I don't want you to touch me."

"I know it." All the same, he took her hand again. Into it he pressed the sapphire ring she thought he had given to Mellows.

Her eyes glowed more brightly than the blue stones, but it was the glow of ice not fire. "What is this for?"

"You. To tell you everything I cannot. I have been trying to give it to you for months." He hesitated, then asked, "Does it mean anything to you?"

"Once it might have. Now it does not," she replied stonily.

He released her hand and stepped back. "Then I am bothering you to no purpose. I shall go up to London tomorrow and take passage on the first available ship to India. You will not be bothered by me again."

"Then take that with you!" Claudia slapped the sapphire ring back into his hand as all the fury and pain she had suppressed for so long spilled over. "It might mean more to you than it does to me. It might mean the wife you have called a whore and humiliated and betrayed. It might mean the son who exists merely to perpetuate your name. It will certainly mean your main objective in coming to England has been achieved, no matter what suffering you happened to cause along the way."

"Claudia . . ."

"Don't Claudia me! Must I remind you that I am the

277

woman who isn't worth the dignity of a name? I am madam—or madam wife, if you can bear it. *I* have had to!"

She turned from him and began to stalk about the room, hugging her arms to her as though trying to contain the deep well of resentment within her. It was no use. She swung back to him as it burst forth once more.

"So you are going away. What's new about that? I have been expecting it this age. The only thing that surprises me is that it is to India. Are you sure India is far enough away from this most *inconvenient* marriage with this far from *unquestionable* lady? Why not make it China to be on the safe side? Or do you mean to return when it is time to make me pregnant again? I haven't yet fully honored my contract, have I? Another son was definitely called for. I mustn't expect to escape from giving full value for my title, my home and my trinkets. But wear your damned sapphires I will not! Give the ring to your mistress, or the next maid who takes your fancy, or any woman who will sit up and beg for you. I am done with it. Now get out! You shouldn't find it difficult. Nobody is more experienced at being thrown out of your own home than you are. I just pray to God that this time you stay out!"

She was quivering with fury that was still far from spent. She felt frustrated, as though she had not exacted full justice from him because there was no way such justice could be given, short of murdering him. She felt the impulse strongly, and it showed in her clenched fists and blazing eyes. "Get out," she repeated through clenched teeth, "or I swear I will not be responsible for what I do next. Get out of this house and my life."

He did not go, but seized her in his arms and crushed her to him. "That is just what I cannot do," he breathed against her hair. "I can't get out of your life or get you out of mine. I love you so—damnably."

She went rigid in his arms. "How dare you speak of love! You don't know what it means."

"Yes, I do. You have taught me only too well, my darling."

He picked her up, and she began to struggle. "If you mean you are going to *make* love to me, then you had best not fall asleep afterward—or ever. I will kill you when you do. I swear it."

"Would you believe I would rather be murdered by you than be living with any other woman?" He looked down into her stormy eyes and continued, "No, I see you wouldn't. I shall have to find some other way of convincing you."

He carried her not to the bed but to one of the armchairs by the fire, and sat down with her still in his arms. "I shall not bore you with the entire story of my life, only the parts which affected my attitude to women, and thus to you."

Claudia did not want to be in his arms and she did not want to listen. She remained rigid, making sure he understood she was being held only under duress. He took her hand and went to slide the sapphire ring on it. "No!" she exclaimed, clenching her hand into a fist.

"Yes." Gently he straightened her fingers, took off the ruby betrothal ring, threw it down and slid the sapphire in its place. "I bought it for you the day after we were married. After I had called you whore and all those other things I never believed even as I said them. I loved you even then, you see, but I didn't know how to say it. And I was out of my mind with jealousy over your precious Tom—a man I couldn't even get at because he was dead. The worst part, though, was that I couldn't trust the love I felt for you, far less the love I sensed you had for me. It made me vulnerable, afraid of you. So I tried to drive you away, but all the time I was doing it I was terrified of succeeding. The sapphire ring was to let you know the truth, but I lost my nerve and couldn't give it to you, so I bought the ruby instead. That was safe. I wanted to be safe. I still had to learn there was nothing safe about loving. I've tried so many times since to give you the sapphires, and I always ended up giving you something else instead. Now that I've succeeded, wear it, because you'll never find a lover more besotted than I am, Claudia."

She looked wonderingly form the ring to his face. She was afraid of what she saw there, and looked away. It was she who couldn't trust now. "I—I still don't understand. Sometimes I thought you were two people in one, but now I don't know. You have always been an enigma to me."

"These past months I have been an enigma to myself. More out of my mind than in it. If you are ever to understand, I must tell you first that Tansy is not my daughter."

"Giles!" Claudia snapped upright. "How can you deny her? She is every inch a Verylan."

"True, but she is Gervase's daughter, not mine."

"Good God!" she breathed.

"There was no good in any of it," he retorted with a touch of his old bitterness. "Letitia, Tansy's mother, had one of those restricted puritanical upbringings which often proves so disastrous when the reins are finally loosened. During her first Season she fancied herself in love with Gervase, and they had an affair. He was already married with a child on the way. He was the eldest son—the important one!—and my father was dying. My father was of the old school. Family honor was everything. A scandal concerning his heir would have broken his heart, particularly as Gervase could not do the honorable thing and marry Letitia. So the family honor had to be retrieved by my next brother George or myself. George refused, saying an elopement would wreck his military career. That left me."

Claudia thought of the portraits of the three brothers hanging side by side in the gallery. Now she understood what had eluded her for so long. It was all there in their expressions. Giles was the one she would have picked from those other self-satisfied faces to do the gallant and honorable thing. "You were only nineteen . . ." she recalled.

"Young enough to be idealistic. And trusting. Also painfully romantic." His face twisted into a self-mocking smile. "I was up at Oxford at the time and loved to distraction a girl called Barbara, daughter of one of the dons. I couldn't explain the circumstances of my marriage to her, but I believed there would come another time for us. Letitia and I had agreed, you see, that the marriage was to be in name only. Once Gervase's child was born, we would separate and petition for divorce."

Claudia, without realizing it, had relaxed against Giles's shoulder. "Why didn't you? Why did you act in a way that made the world believe you were a rogue?"

"Having fancied herself in love with Gervase, Letitia then fancied herself in love with me. I think the truth of it was that she never loved anybody but herself. She wouldn't let me go. I never touched her, and she hated me for it. More often than not she was hysterical. She even persuaded herself I married her for her money. I endured it because I wanted a divorce. Then I heard that Barbara had married Lord Barlowe. After that, I didn't care about anything. I went to India."

"Then—Then Barbara was your baroness?"

"Yes."

"Was she the reason you came back to England?"

"No. My father had died shortly after my marriage. Not, I hope, by the shock of my elopement, but I don't know. All I can be certain of is that it would have been a greater shock had he known the truth. While he lived, he would not permit me to enter this house. Gervase and George were of the same mind. I had become a skeleton they preferred to be thrust into any cupboard save their own. No, I came back to see Tansy. She wanted as little to do with me by then as her mother. I met Barbara. She persuaded me that her heart had been breaking for me all those years, so I ran off with her. One scandal more or less meant nothing to me by then."

His flippancy jarred on Claudia, and she told him, "It should have. You ruined her."

"If it hadn't been me it would have been someone else. Barlowe didn't shoot himself because he lost her. He did it because he'd bankrupted himself trying to keep up with her, and keep her out of other men's arms. An impossible task, as I soon discovered. My fair Barbara had an insatiable lust for men and for spending money. I sent her to Europe with enough money to finance a half-dozen affairs and counted myself lucky to be rid of her. But it hurt. She had been my first love, and whatever romantic dreams I'd salvaged from my reprehensible life were wrapped up in her."

Giles fell silent. Claudia found herself twisting the sapphire ring on her finger. There were still many things she needed to know before she could feel it belonged there.

"Does Tansy know?" she asked.

"No. Her grandparents do, but they will never tell."

"Is it because she isn't your daughter that you were so harsh with her?"

"I didn't mean to be harsh. I genuinely believed a

282

good marriage would be best for her. I feared she would turn out like her mother—or her father. I wronged her. She escaped the taint from both sides." He began, idly she thought, to play with her hair.

"Why have you never told her the truth?"

"Either way she would have had a rogue for a father, and I didn't think it would help if she knew her true father never acknowledged her. It isn't comfortable to be an embarrassment to the people who should care for you most."

Claudia took some minutes to think over all this, then observed, "I'm glad she's happy now. She deserved it."

"Yes. I don't deserve it but I mean to, if you will make me happy, Claudia."

Her eyes rose to his, then fell. She began twisting the ring again. "What about your mistress? The one with the dreadful perfume?"

His hand strayed from her hair and began to trace the line of her cheek. "She's not important."

She pushed his hand away. "She is to me."

"Very well. She was a young woman married to an elderly merchant in India. She loathed the place and him. When he died, we took passage home on the same ship and continued a liaison I must confess had been going on for some time. I can only repeat that she wasn't important. She obliged, and I paid. She liked to call herself Lisette, although she was Irish. I set her up in Paris because I thought I would need relief from a fright of a wife. But I found myself with a beautiful wife, and I loved her so much that I dispensed with my mistress. There has been none since."

Claudia greeted this with frigid silence.

Giles said in an altered tone, "You are thinking of Mellows, of course. The one person I can't excuse or expect you to forgive." His arms tightened round her and he crushed her to him. "I can only beg you to try to understand. I had hidden my love from you for so long because experience had taught me to expect another betrayal. Every time I hurt you, or loved you *unbearably*, I went away because I couldn't face you or myself. But you always drew me back, and I could do nothing but stare at you and want you. That night I came to you so drunk it was because I had used brandy to find the courage to give you the sapphire ring. If I could do that, I thought you would understand everything I could never bring myself to say. Even then I failed. I thought you despised me. When I found Mellows in my bed, I didn't even know who she was. I only knew that I wanted you, and—and there was somebody there. I've done a lot of things in my life I'm not proud of, but I've never loathed myself so much as I did then. I know I humiliated you, but the true humiliation is, and must always be, mine."

He loosened his grip slightly and raised her hand to kiss the ring on her betrothal finger. "You can trust the sapphires. I love you, and I always shall. If you don't believe me, I mean to spend the rest of my life convincing you. I'm not going away again. I can't. Not now. Not ever."

Claudia looked into the brown eyes that had mystified her for so long. They hid nothing from her now. It was all there for her to see. His love, his hope, his uncertainty.

This was the lost man she had been searching for, the man she had almost come to believe did not exist outside the portrait in the gallery and her own dreams.

"I'll put you to bed," he said. "You'll want time to think over all I've said. I don't want to risk distressing you again."

The dreadful hurt within Claudia was gone. In its place was a radiance that glowed in her eyes and warmed her smile. She spoke from the heart because there were no barriers left to make her wary, "Then you had best come to bed with me. I think I'd be very distressed if you didn't."

"Claudia!" He stood up with her in his arms. "I can't believe . . ."

"Neither can I, so pray make haste convincing me. And afterward," she added as he carried her to the bed, "I shall finish telling you precisely what I think of you, my lord Belgarrick."

He stopped and looked down at her. "Tell me now. This time, I want not recriminations afterward, no partings, no damned despair."

She pulled his head down and kissed him. "That is most of it. The rest is that I love you and I always have. It was never a marriage of convenience to me."

He looked dazed. "Then I never had any reason to be jealous of Tom?"

She shook her head.

"I wish you had told me so at the beginning."

"I couldn't. You had forbidden me to. Besides, as I said, I was married to an enigma. It's take me all this time to find the man."

"Just try to lose him now . . ." Giles said, and carried her the rest of the way to the bed.

# HEARTFIRE ROMANCES

**SWEET TEXAS NIGHTS**                    (2610, $3.75)
by Vivian Vaughan

Meg Britton grew up on the railroads, working proudly at her father's side. Nothing was going to stop them from setting the rails clear to Silver Creek, Texas—certainly not some crazy prospector. As Meg set out to confront the old coot, she planned her strategy with cool precision. But soon she was speechless with shock. For instead of a harmless geezer, she found a boldly handsome stranger whose determination matched her own.

**CAPTIVE DESIRE**                    (2612, $3.75)
by Jane Archer

Victoria Malone fancied herself a great adventuress, but being kidnapped was too much excitement for even Victoria! Especially when her arrogant kidnapper thought she was part of Red Duke's outlaw gang. Trying to convince the overbearing, handsome stranger that she had been an innocent bystander when the stagecoach was robbed, proved futile. But when he thought he could maker her confess by crushing her to his warm, broad chest, by caressing her with his strong, capable hands, Victoria was willing to admit to anything. . . .

**LAWLESS ECSTASY**                    (2613, $3.75)
by Susan Sackett

Abra Beaumont could spot a thief a mile away. After all, her father was once one of the best. But he'd been on the right side of the law for years now, and she wasn't about to let a man like Dash Thorne lead him astray with some wild plan for stealing the Tear of Allah, the world's most fabulous ruby. Dash was just the sort of man she most distrusted—sophisticated, handsome, and altogether too sure of his considerable charm. Abra shivered at the devilish gleam in his blue eyes and swore he would need more than smooth kisses and skilled caresses to rob her of her virtue . . . and much more than sweet promises to steal her heart!

*Available wherever paperbacks are sold, or order direct from the Publisher. Send cover price plus 50¢ per copy for mailing and handling to Zebra Books, Dept. 3151, 475 Park Avenue South, New York, N.Y. 10016. Residents of New York, New Jersey and Pennsylvania must include sales tax. DO NOT SEND CASH.*